Advance Praise for EMET

"The news of today meets the magic of the ancients in a thriller that's as fast and furious as it is thoughtful and smart. After a long wait, it's great to have a new Roger Simon novel to race through."

— Andrew Klavan, *New York Times* bestselling novelist

"In *EMET*, literary legend Roger L. Simon drops the Golem myth in today's world, crafting a novel that's equal parts thriller, spiritual quest, and geopolitical drama. *EMET* is a tour de force full of Simon's wit and wisdom and positivity amid peril."

— Kurt Schlichter, novelist, senior columnist, Townhall.com

"Master storyteller Roger L. Simon combines today's conflicts with 500-year-old legends to produce a thrilling page-turner with a satisfying ending. Highly recommended."

— Glenn Reynolds, American legal scholar, Instapundit

"Far more than just a riveting thriller, Roger L. Simon's *EMET* addresses the biggest mystery of all—who governs the universe."

— Wayne Allyn Root, author, television and radio host

"Roger Simon's creativity, historical and religious knowledge, and political and cultural insight combine to make *EMET* a fascinating thriller, which doubles as a political and religious commentary, making it even more captivating and enlightening. This book screams for sequels and an equally riveting television streaming series."

— David Limbaugh, *New York Times* bestselling author and political commentator

BOOK 1 OF THE TRUTH CYCLE

ROGER L. SIMON

Green Hills Books – Nashville, TN

Book design by Logotecture.

First American edition published by Green Hills Books

FIRST AMERICAN EDITION

ISBN: 979-8-9941093-0-4 (ebook)

ISBN: 979-8-9941093-1-1 (paperback)

ISBN: 979-8-9941093-2-8 (hardcover)

Also by Roger L. Simon

BOOKS

Heir

The Mama Tass Manifesto

The Big Fix

Wild Turkey

Peking Duck

California Roll

The Straight Man

Raising the Dead

The Lost Coast

Director's Cut

Turning Right at Hollywood & Vine

I Know Best

The GOAT

SCREENPLAYS

The Big Fix

Bustin' Loose (story by Richard Pryor)

Enemies, A Love Story (with Paul Mazursky)

Scenes from a Mall (with Paul Mazursky)

Prague Duet (with Sheryl Longin)

A Better Life (story)

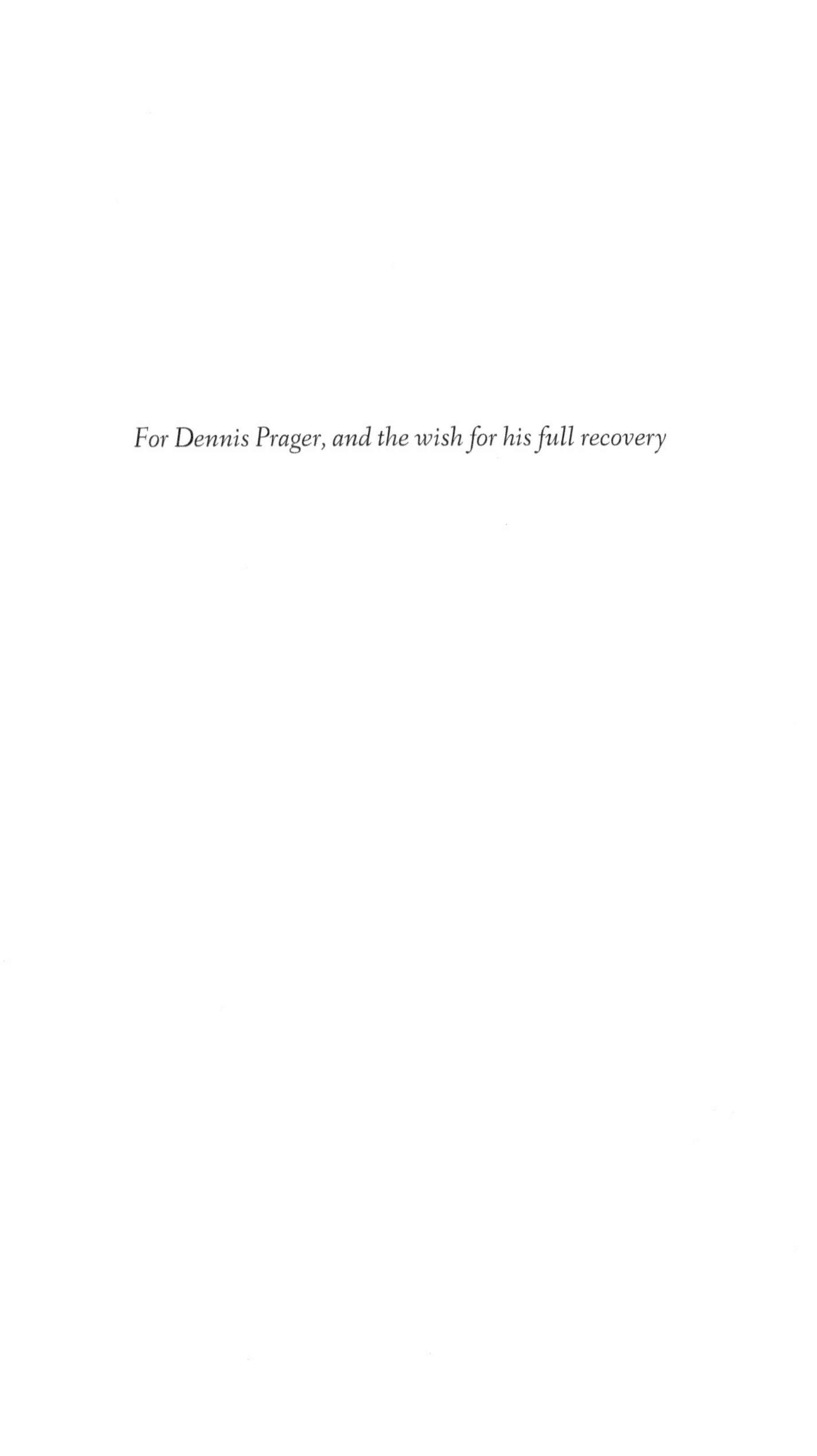

For Dennis Prager, and the wish for his full recovery

Everything that G-d created in His world, He created only for His glory, as it is stated, "All that is attributed to My name, for My glory I created it, formed it, and made it."

— ISAIAH 43:7

STATE OF ISRAEL

The Institute for Intelligence and Special Operations (Mossad)

TOP SECRET – EYES ONLY

Document ID: 4519-ALPHA-ME/25

Date: 2025-06-22

Classification: TS/SCI -Compartmentalized

Distribution: DG-MOSSAD/OpsDir/Sigint/Field Station Daled

OPERATIONAL BRIEFING MEMO

The attached manuscript was offered as a "courtesy" pre-publication by its author [REDACTED], a United States citizen currently residing in [REDACTED].

Commentary and recommendations at end.

APPROVED BY:

[REDACTED]
Director of Operations
Mossad HQ, Glilot

WARNING

This document contains sensitive national security information. Unauthorized disclosure is a criminal offense under Israeli law.

I

I am writing this not just because the extraordinary events of the recent past are still fresh in my mind—too fresh, actually-- but because I realize that I am likely to be criminally liable for, at a minimum, aiding and abetting. To be honest, I am not as familiar as I should be with the niceties of the so-called clergy privilege. I declined to take that particular course. But the laws vary from state to state anyway, and these incidents, if you could call them that, only began in Tennessee. I was trained in God's law, and even there I admit to considerable weakness.

I am a rabbi but did not always believe in His existence. Lately, I have had reason to be less skeptical.

I also realize that this document may ultimately be subpoenaed by a court of law or a congressional investigation for multiple reasons that I can only guess at now. Indeed, I could be under attack, legal and otherwise, from many sides. We live in a time when a large part of the population is suspicious of the government, while others adhere to it almost as a religion;

therefore, it is impossible to predict where the problems will arise.

Nevertheless, readers will have to indulge me if I occasionally engage in a little inappropriate levity about grisly happenings concerning which some may feel a seemingly frivolous attitude does not apply. Such remarks just emerge spontaneously, as if part of my DNA or as a coping mechanism.

The other thing you should know is that some of this will be conjecture, what I have put together second hand, as hearsay, if you will, and some from direct observation or personal involvement. It should be obvious which is which, but to tell a believable and coherent story, difficult as it is under these circumstances, I felt I had to, shall we say, fill in the blanks. In order to do that, some chapters I will write from the point of view of other participants in this narrative, imagining, as best I can, what they are seeing and feeling.

Lastly, at the outset, you should know something about me, your narrator and sometime participant, although you will learn more (I will probably learn more) as this unfolds.

My name is Benjamin Golub, though most call me "Rabbi Ben" or just "Ben." I am sixty-eight years old, the youngest of three children, and come from the Chicago area, Wilmette to be exact. My parents were upper-middle-class Jews, my father an import-export man and my mother a housewife. They were not particularly religious, more the bagels-and-lox on Sunday types, members of a Jewish country club because my father was a devoted golfer and, at one point, club champion. They wanted me to be a doctor, but I did not perform well in what are now called STEM subjects. Not quite Ivy League material, I attended Union College and briefly aspired to be a writer, but realizing I had to make a living, I sort of drifted into rabbinical school. Part of me was rather gregarious, superficially anyway, a people person, and I thought I would like it. I chose Hebrew Union College in Cincinnati because it was reform, the others being a bit too intimidating. Truth to tell, I wasn't always comfortable as a rabbi and spent about a dozen years teaching high school English in Maine. I came back to the rabbinate when I was offered a position at an initially conservative synagogue that was turning reform in the comfortable suburban Green Hills neighborhood of Nashville. Their current rabbi, an old school friend with whom I had attended Chicago Bulls games and who had been offered a bigger and clearly better-paying appointment in West Los Angeles himself, had prevailed on his board to reach out to me. I have been there ever since, fourteen years now.

I should also make clear that though I was once something of a conventional undergraduate leftie who showed up at the usual demonstrations, I am now, to my personal astonishment, rather more conservative, leaning towards libertarian. I may have gone the route of that old saying, attributed to Churchill and others, if you are not liberal at 20, you have no heart, and if not conservative at 40, you have no brain. Or perhaps the times have just changed and what was once considered left is now right, as some suggest.

Nevertheless, I do my best to hide my opinions for two reasons. The obvious one is that the occupation of rabbi, whatever else it is, is a business like any other and you don't want to alienate potential customers. Also, as life has gone on, I have become more risk-averse, almost to a fault, less interested in making waves. I already have a brother-in-law back in Chicago who thinks I'm the second coming of Attila the Hun.

Still, whatever efforts I make to seem apolitical, the truth eventually leaks out. In these wildly divisive times, everyone has become his or her own Sherlock Holmes, sniffing out every nuance of the other person's views lest they make the fatal mistake of consorting with their ideological enemy or become tarnished through guilt by association.

So most people know my leanings despite those efforts, and this has, for the most part, been reflected in the makeup of the congregants in my temple who are either neutral or take approaches similar to mine, although some old guard members of the board, including its chairman, have become suspicious of me. I often wonder if they wish to remove me. But whatever tension, largely unstated, exists, the congregation has been growing due to the horrific rise in antisemitism that is all around us, of which I will have more to say as this story evolves.

One last thing you should want to know. I've been married. Twice. The second time took, although my wife, Maya Golub, née Feingold, as with many in her generation, sometimes chafed at being pigeonholed as a "rebbetzin," the dutiful helpmate of the rabbi. A former dance major at Oberlin, after our children grew up, she started working part-time as a physical therapist while continuing to function, when necessary, as what you might call a "closet rebbetzin." We had two children and now have three grandchildren, including Menahem "Max" Golub, age 11, currently in residence with his grandparents for reasons I explain later.

But that's enough about my life for now. At this point, you need to hear about Ed and Tamara, what happened to them, and what is still happening. I would never have been writing this had I not known them, and I would like to state now, for the record, that despite my profession, I never initially believed that what emerged from our contact was actually real. I assumed it was folklore taken to an extreme, basically a game. It seems I was wrong.

I also realize any reputable lawyer would be urging me not to write a word of this. In fact, I am considering destroying it when I finish, if not before. I realize this will not be easy because digital files can almost always be recovered with forensic tools. So I have taken the precaution of typing this on an old, outmoded laptop, disconnected from the internet, that I can easily drop in Watauga Lake, the deepest in Tennessee, or in the Florida Gulf, as the case may be. It's heavier than the modern ones and should sink rapidly, never to be seen again.

But back to Ed and Tamara. I first laid eyes on them in the course of my daily life without paying undue attention. Ed is an artist who owns what became three coffee shops in the Nashville area, the first, in the 12 South neighborhood, called "The Orphanage" and the others "Orphan Two" and "Orphan Three" as he expanded from some popularity. This playful naming contained an element of truth since Ed was Ed Ristic, by birth an orphan from Serbia, rescued from that war-torn nation at the age of two after his parents died in a bombing.

He worked on his art, largely sculpture, at a studio in the back of the original "The Orphanage." Some of it sold, but the artistic results, to be kind, were what one might call of "local interest." Ed was a better businessman, a rather good one in fact, than he was a sculptor. He was meticulous about managing his shops, and it showed. Their success was due to his making certain that he always had the freshest pastries available and coffee as good as was served at the finest hotels, let alone coffee bars. He tried to replicate the brew he had tasted at the Four Seasons Hualalai on a trip to Hawaii when he still lived in California by importing his beans from the Big Island Coffee Roasters. Ed was one of the many migrants from California to Tennessee, having arrived eight years ago before the onslaught that occurred during COVID.

He was equally attentive to his customers, befriending many and remembering the names of more. An athlete in his youth and once a competitive skier, he was also a dedicated sports fan, just like many of those customers in a sports-obsessed state. He had signage for the Nashville Predators and Tennessee Titans all over the walls of the three coffee shops and attended many of their games. In homage to his country of birth, Ed had a portrait he painted himself of Novak Djokovic serving in a prominent spot in the first shop. As it happened, he shared the same surname as the Serbian tennis star's wife, Jelena Ristic, though they were not, as far as he knew, related. Below what he called "the original Novak" was a magazine rack with a carefully curated, ecumenical selection of magazines and newspapers for his patrons, including the New York Times and the Wall Street Journal. Ed, the businessman, had, as I tried to do, avoided proselytizing in favor of commerce and harmony.

But my first interactions with him—I dropped into the coffee shop, not far from my synagogue residence, from time to time for a cappuccino—were about the art that was clearly his first love. It was easy to get him talking about his admiration for famous sculptors like Henry Moore or Auguste Rodin as if being like them was the great unattainable dream he had reconciled himself to never achieving.

With all I had the sense Ed considered himself a bit of a failure, not just because he was no Rodin and never would be. He had also been a failure in marriage, if you could call it that, or at least been betrayed by it. After I had been coming in and out of the coffee shop for several months, I heard him confiding in one of the regulars, a man who once coached the Vanderbilt baseball team and had had a short, big league career himself, about his ex-wife, who evidently left him for another woman, one of the couple's best friends. Ed hadn't realized what was going on until it was too late, not that he could, he admitted to the former ballplayer, have probably done much about it.

This was a common enough modern story, alas. It had happened a couple of times among my congregants in the last ten or so years, yet it was still a painful occurrence. I wasn't certain, but I was pretty sure Ed wanted me to overhear it, though I don't think he was looking for pity, mainly, I thought, since I too was becoming a regular, so I would know who he was. Also, as a presumed man of faith, people tended to confide in me, directly or indirectly. That surprised, even unnerved, me at first, but by then I was used to it.

Tamara was also a patron of "The Orphanage." I remember seeing her sitting at a table, coffee and a Danish in front of her, sometimes huddled with someone in deep conversation, sometimes talking on her cellphone. She seemed lively and had what we call an infectious laugh. I didn't know then that she was a publicist, originally from New York, where she worked in the classical music field. She had been a Manhattanite, living on the Upper West Side, what I heard her describe, half-jokingly, as "the belly of the beast." As had many, she had become tired of dealing with the often-dangerous daily life in that declining city as well as with being surrounded by people whose heads were too far in the sand to do anything about it. So this native New Yorker had some five years before, and to the astonishment of her family, for whom ever abandoning the Big Apple was an unheard of, almost inconceivable, act, nervously accepted a job with the Nashville Philharmonic. Until then, she had barely been to the South, unless you counted Miami. But she fit right in more quickly than she expected. Given her new location, she soon found herself representing country musicians as well as what are deemed serious ones, discovering, to her surprise, they were more to her liking than the often-moody classicists, not that the country singers were necessarily angels and could be as much egomaniacs as the most renowned soprano at Lincoln Center.

Still, at moments, she later told me, she missed New York,

just as I at moments missed Chicago. Those instances of nostalgia, however, were brief.

I learned most of that after the catastrophe occurred that eventually brought me closer together with the two near fifty-year-olds, and they, even more, with each other. No one could have imagined at that point any of this would result in the emergence of what was first called "*monstruo*," the Spanish cognate for monster.

It all began when Tamara invited her niece, Allison, down to Nashville to get over a breakup. Allison Carter, aged 21 and the product of a mixed marriage, lapsed Catholic with lapsed Jew, was about to start business school at NYU when she broke up with a boyfriend she had had since the tenth grade and had expected to marry. The breakup was supposedly mutual, but the young woman was despondent.

Although such things are hardly surprising, Tamara was sympathetic because she, like Ed Ristic, had been unlucky in marriage. Later, I came to think they would come together in part because of this. But that was far too simple, I soon realized. They were, to some degree, as they say in Yiddish, a language at which I wish I were more proficient, but my parents only knew a few words, *bashert* or preordained. Tamara Klein—she had taken back her maiden name -- had discovered her husband of eleven years, Dr. Emanuel Lieberman, a distinguished psychoanalyst and graduate of the revered William Alanson White Institute of Psychiatry, had been having serial affairs, mostly with his patients. He was far from the first of his profession to do this, but Tamara was badly shaken by her own blindness. Having prided herself on the skills at judging people she thought she had honed through her profession, she was propelled into a dark period in her life that continued for several years. For obvious reasons, she had become suspicious of psychotherapy in general, so, despite often feeling as if she needed it, she elected to stay away, trying to heal herself. Eventually, she felt better, and this was part of the motivation, she told me later, for the move from New York to Nashville. A new life was called for and she got one and more.

It was Tamara's invitation to her niece that set in motion the series of events that brought forth this narrative and that are still unfolding. Those who are religious are told everything happens for a reason. Whether I believe that depends on the day, but I do know this is where the pendulum of our lives began to swing, actually gyrate.

Tamara's was prompted by her having met the boyfriend a couple of times and concluding Allison was well rid of the young man. Although technically a grown-up or near, he was one of those who spent most of his days and nights playing computer games or talking about them. She wanted to help her niece avoid the mistake of reconciliation that she thought could well happen out of that most common human weakness—in fact, she sensed in her niece's tone- the fear of being alone. So she urged Allison to come live with her for a bit. It would be summer vacation anyway, and although it would be hot and muggy, Tamara had a membership in a club that had a swimming pool with cabanas. They could hang out there, drink frozen cocktails, and be chums, even if the latter presented its own difficulties. In Tamara's view, the new generation spent so much of their lives staring at devices that they had trouble relating on a personal level. Most of her friends agreed, having had similar disappointments with younger relatives, so Tamara had a certain trepidation she tried not to show her niece. Instead, she emphasized excitement and fun, country music concerts under the stars with hunky guys on guitar.

Her urgings worked, and Allison did come for a visit. At first it was surprisingly pleasant with her niece proving less a victim of modern technology than Tamara had surmised.

Already an attractive and fit young woman, she redoubled her efforts post-breakup, rising at six to go jogging before it became oppressively hot. Sometimes, Tamara would go with her, but other times her older bones just said no. Eventually, they developed into a pattern with Tamara going every other day. On those days, they would stop at "The Orphanage," but as it happens, I was never there at the same time and never saw Allison in the flesh, only later, in the newspapers and on television.

The pendulum began its fateful swing one relatively cool July morning when Tamara shook her head and rolled over for more sleep, even though it was one of those days she normally joined Allison on her run along the Cumberland River. Tamara's excuse, which she was barely able to mumble, was that she had been up the previous night to the small hours with a client who desperately wanted her to promote a new whiskey that would be branded with his name. The client, Cody Brent, a singer songwriter, had just had his first semi-hit, a song that had been number eleven on the country charts for all of a week, and Tamara was trying to explain to him, tactfully, that perhaps he was being premature, that such glamourous emoluments were in his future and the wise man—he was only 20, still a year shy of the legal drinking age—bided his time.

So Tamara rolled over while her niece went out for her run. When she woke up two hours later, Allison had not returned. Tamara didn't think much of it at first. Perhaps she had gone further without an older woman holding her back. There were some beautiful, wooded areas further north on the Cumberland that she had said she wanted to explore.

Tamara made a pot of coffee and sat down to read whatever global disaster had occurred in the last twelve hours on her iPad and to answer the usually unending stream of text messages. Another forty-five minutes went by uneventfully before one of those messages brought her up short more than she had ever been.

"Absolutely horrible what happened to your niece. If there is anything at all I can do, please let me know!" It came from Ed Ristic, who had never texted her before that she could recall.

Tamara was instantly filled with dread as she fumbled for the remote and switched on Channel 5, which was usually first with local news. What came up immediately was an ambulance among a cluster of four or five cop cars with their lights flashing. Somebody—was it Allison?—was being loaded into the ambulance on a gurney. Reporters were already on the scene. In the coming hours and days, she learned details of what was being called one of the most horrific crimes in recent Nashville history. And Nashville had had its fill, including the child murders at a religious school that were still tearing the community apart.

On July 9, police estimated between 6:35 and 6:45 AM. Allison Carter, 21, visiting from New York City, had been raped and murdered, several body parts literally dismembered, in a wooded area on the banks of the Cumberland River. It almost had aspects of a rage killing. As much as a month later, remnants of her blood-spattered clothing and the lid from her handheld water bottle were still being discovered as far as five miles away, but a perpetrator, alleged or otherwise, had not been found.

It was natural that Allison would have a Jewish funeral. Her mother was the Jewish side of her family, and our religion is matrilineal, mostly anyway, except for some deviations by the reform community for mixed marriages when the father was Jewish. A date was set three days away, although Jewish funerals were traditionally to be held within twenty-four hours. That was difficult these days, and in this case, the remains needed to be shipped to New York, and arrangements were made that would take at least that long. Tamara was involved in all that, I knew, although I didn't get to speak with her. I didn't want to intrude, realizing how stressed she must have been, and communicated via text, very tentatively offering the services of my trade. She did not reply.

I did go to the funeral, however, which was held at the Frank Campbell home on Madison Avenue. Maya canceled some physical therapy appointments and stayed home to manage things at the synagogue while I was away, and taught one of my classes, for which she was highly competent. Ed was also at the funeral, but I didn't recognize anyone else from Nashville. Several of Tamara's New York friends were there, as well as friends of the deceased. The occasion was grim in the extreme—how could it have been otherwise—and I felt great compassion for Allison's family, but, as a complete stranger, I barely spoke to any of them besides offering the condolences one does at these events.

The normally voluble and upbeat Tamara stood off to the side, head slightly bowed for the most part except when someone addressed her. Then she would try to smile and connect, but the strain was visible. It wasn't hard to imagine how she was feeling, having been the cause of Allison's leaving the city in the first place and then having slept through the opportunity to accompany her on her last run. Everything might have been different, or, if not, two women, not one, would have met their maker at the hands of whoever this mad person was. It was hard to say which was the better result. She also stood some feet off as Allison's coffin was later laid into the ground at a family plot at Mt. Zion Cemetery in Queens, male relatives covering the hardwood with the ritual shovels of earth. As it piled higher, someone handed a shovel to Ed, who dug into the ground dutifully and, strong man that he was, pitched a large mound onto the coffin, covering it more thoroughly than any had done before. As he did so, I noticed Tamara had turned away. Tears were streaming down her face.

The next day I took the early flight back to Nashville. As I pulled up to the entrance of the synagogue compound, I waved to the guard on duty, Jorge Estevez, a barrel-chested former member of the El Salvador special forces who had once worked for their president in his battles with that country's gangs. He recognized me immediately and opened the motorized gate, simultaneously lowering into the ground the half dozen steel pipes that stood like sentinels in front of the driveway that we had, given the state of the world, recently installed for extra security.

I was about to get out of my car when something compelled me to repeat the prayer one is supposed to recite on rising—*Modeh Ani*—that I had already done, too quickly I felt, in my haste to make my flight. I told myself I needed centering, as did everyone entwined in this tragedy. So I sat there for a couple of minutes and did so. "I give thanks to You, Adonai, that, in mercy, You have restored my soul within me. Endless is Your compassion, great is Your faithfulness." But I wondered, where were His compassion and faithfulness for Tamara, or her niece?

I did not hear from Tamara for several weeks, although I sent her some traditional words of consolation I had been taught were common to our faith. "Blessed is the true judge. May you be comforted from Heaven." It was pro forma, and I wished I could have done more. It was one of those times that I felt fake.

She did not appear at The Orphanage either, although Ed kept a place for her at the table where she usually sat. He put a fresh red rose there every day in a clear glass vase and stopped anyone who wanted to sit there. Soon enough, the other regulars understood he was saving it for Tamara and automatically complied, leaving the table empty even on days when the coffee shop was jammed with customers.

Then one morning she walked in and sat right down at her table. Ed came straight over. "Cappuccino with oat milk?" he said, knowing her favorite.

"With a couple of extra shots. I was up until three, dealing with crazy Cody. Kid thinks he's the next Morgan Wallen and knocked up two girls in the last month. Thank God they were 18... Hello, Rabbi." I was sitting two tables away.

"Hello, Tamara," I replied. "Great to see you."

"I've been reading your website. By any chance do you have room in your Wednesday night class?"

That was a surprise. "Absolutely," I said. "We'd be delighted to have you, if you'd like to come."

"I will be there this Wednesday. Looking forward to it."

She was referring to a seminar I gave called "Welcome Home" that was meant to be an introduction to Judaism for Jews who had been secular most of their lives and, for various reasons, had taken a new interest in their heritage. I wasn't keen on the title, but it had been chosen by the board chairman's wife, who wrote the newsletter, and I didn't change it for diplomatic reasons. Nevertheless, I was fairly well-suited to teach the class because, in some ways, it described me. I thought of it as my self-hypnosis class that I gave to convince myself I had after all picked the right profession. I was relatively successful at it precisely because I wasn't that far ahead of the students and could relate to their struggles. The class had grown over the years, and sometimes there was a waiting list. Having Tamara suddenly join would have its awkward side, as the other students were clearly aware of the recent tragedy. It had been brought up and discussed, with compassion, weeks before. But I had to admit I was flattered she had chosen my class to help ease her pain, even if, on another level, I felt slightly unworthy and unsure if I could help. Still, I knew this was a step forward for her.

Shortly thereafter, I noticed Ed was sitting opposite her, talking quietly. Her head was bowed again to hide the visible tears that had returned. This wouldn't be simple.

Indeed she was on an emotional roller coaster for the next several weeks and likely beyond. Sometimes she participated actively in the class, which I ran as a discussion after my initial lecture out of respect for the often widely varied background of the group and frankly because it was easier for me. It took less preparation. Other times she was silent, sitting in the most distant corner of the long seminar table with the proverbial faraway look in her eyes. She would often rouse herself to dispute the class liberals, the Nussbaums, both retired personal injury lawyers, that she knew I sometimes coddled to keep some semblance of balance.

Ours was, as I have mentioned, titularly a Conservative synagogue that, over the years, seemed to have drifted to Reform. I had some responsibility in that, initiating studies in Jewish writers from Kafka to Norman Mailer, but downplaying the overtly religious texts. I dubbed the program the Philip Roth Society, in honor of the recently deceased author, and most congregants liked it; those traditional religious texts were less relevant to them and heavy going, even more so in Hebrew. Several years ago, I almost got fired for taking it too far, assigning Freud's "Moses and Monotheism" as one of the readings, a work in which the father of psychoanalysis posits that Moses wasn't Jewish but an Egyptian adherent of the monotheistic pharaoh Akhenaten. When Akhenaten got thrown out by the traditional polytheists, Freud's Egyptian Moses, feeling rejected, led the Jews out of slavery while inculcating them with his beloved pharaoh's ideas that became the basis for Judaism as we know it. Taking this even slightly seriously was a bit much for the synagogue board, and I had to do some fancy verbal dancing, as well as make some promises, to maintain my position. At the same time, Maya and I had been sponsoring sing-alongs with not always Jewish musical choices, like Lennon's "Imagine" or "Don't Stop Thinking About Tomorrow," to which Maya would often dance or later, as she aged, choreograph for others. It was all very Clinton/Gore, but somewhat past its time and soon waned.

Meanwhile, in private, and without fully realizing it, I gradually sensed myself drifting back toward a kind of Jewish musical orthodoxy, abjuring the pop rock and humming to myself "Adon Olam": "Eternal master who reigned supreme before any creation was created." This went on for some time as if I were being morphed by the music as much as anything else. I was less interested in the Roth and Bellow novels, posthumous though they were. I failed to gobble them up as I usually did. I moved on to religious texts, like parts of the Tanya, I am embarrassed to say I had never read before or in some cases even known about, not that I fully understood them.

To my surprise and totally unplanned, I automatically began to write the word G-d without the middle vowel as the more devout do since it is considered too holy to spell out the name of the Lord in the Hebrew language or in English. Was it superstition or an attempt to expiate past sins? Sometimes I think this was no more than my taking a chance ion Pascal's famous wager. According to the French philosopher, betting that G-d existed and living accordingly was smarter than risking the opposite, which could bring eternal damnation if wrong, just for some short-term pleasures in the present. Other times, I feel I am being sincere. Or is it just because I am approaching seventy and sooner or later will have to come to a decision one way or the other? Happily, none of this caused a rift with Maya because, in her own manner, she was finding her way through a similar transition.

But I am getting ahead of myself. More importantly, our story — and our futures, in this life anyway —took another, yet more fateful, if that were possible, turn in the midst of one of the Wednesday arguments between Tamara and the Nussbaums. These started to become more frequent when the two lawyers, to their evident irritation, discovered the apparently conservative public relations woman was friendly with several prominent country artists who were her clients. It wasn't supposed to be that way. Liberals controlled the arts because they deserved to. They were the sensitive ones who understood the human condition.

On one particular Wednesday, some weeks after Tamara joined us, we were discussing the order of importance of the Jewish holidays with the Sabbath, the Jewish New Year, the Day of Atonement, and Passover taking their traditional roles in the lead. I mentioned Simchat Torah, when we dance with the scroll in our arms to celebrate its new annual reading. An argument broke out over Hanukkah when Tamara pointed out, drawing from her childhood, that the holiday was not considered of great magnitude in New York until the late-lamented Gimbels department store publicized it heavily to give Jewish children some excitement (and toys, available, needless to say, at the huge department in that very store) to compete with what their gentile peers were getting over Christmas. Although it appeared Tamara was half-kidding, the Nussbaums took umbrage and an argument escalated, seemingly out of nothing.

Another time, also out of nowhere, Mr. Nussbaum started singing the praises of our then Secretary of State, Jeremy Bogen, who happens to be Jewish and went to Oxford and some fancy school in France, saying we should all be proud such an exceptional diplomat and scholar was a "member of the tribe." Tamara then muttered under her breath that he was a sellout to Iran's mullahs and would get us all killed, at which point Mrs. Nussbaum hissed that Tamara was a "rightwing nut." Within seconds they were screaming across the table.

Obviously, both sides were sick of each other. Trying to regain some calm, I mentioned that arguments won't kill us; disputation is historically part of the Jewish tradition, even Moses—not the Freudian one, but the real one — had argued with God. That didn't particularly work, and I was still searching for a way to cool things off when several of the fifteen or so people around that table began getting the same beeping alerts on their smartphones that overrode whatever "Do Not Disturb" functions they might have applied for class.

It wasn't, however, one of those yellow alerts warning of a child abduction.

It was a tornado.

And it was close to us. Very close.

So much for arguments.

II

If you live in Tennessee as long as I have, you take such warnings seriously. I had been through several of these events, including a large one recently in East Nashville in which two of our congregants were severely injured and another lost her house, but none thus far had affected the synagogue, my family or me directly.

Nevertheless, I had ensured, some years ago, that our safe room was modernized with working radio equipment, retrofitted walls, and even its own generator. I was glad of this that night as the weather map visible on my phone showed our part of Nashville a direct target of two tornadoes coming straight at us from the west and north. We were the apex of what looked like a tornado pincer. We had little time, less than five minutes, in fact, and I urged everyone to follow Maya — who had grandson, Max, visiting from Indianapolis, in tow —down the stairs into the safe room at the back of the subterranean garage. Some of the class were reluctant, thinking they could still make it home in their own cars, but I insisted there wasn't time. Photos were already popping up on our phones of houses in neighboring Spring Hill with their roofs blown off. They had better use the safe room. There was room for all of us—more or less.

So we crammed into the windowless room, all eighteen of us by my count. Fortunately, Maya had stocked it with a copious supply of deodorant, if we had to stay there for a while, plus a battery-driven dehumidifier, several boxes of protein bars and water bottles. But none of that could prevent what came next, first an ominous rattle that sounded like bolts coming out of beams and then a cacophonous roar beyond anything I had ever experienced. It felt as if the earth was shaking from sound alone as the rattling noise kept growing. This was followed by a volcano-like gush I suspected was coming from the hill behind us from which mud often flowed, even from a light rain, so much so that the yard area behind the synagogue turned into an ugly brown lake that often didn't go away for weeks. This was accompanied by repeated giant thunderclaps that sounded like a thousand bombs exploding directly over our heads with a downpour that wouldn't let up, then severe cracking sounds that could only have been trees splitting, some of the several giant oaks sprinkled across our grounds, their huge branches alone capable of crashing through the ceiling and obliterating anything or anyone in their paths.

I clutched Maya in one hand and Max in the other and glanced over at Tamara. She had a calm expression as if this were nothing compared to what she had experienced in her heart. Nothing could harm her now. The Nussbaums, despite their longtime Nashville residency, had the open-mouthed look we associate with terrified extras in a horror movie.

A clock fell from the wall, its plastic rim cracking, and the lights went out. The wall shimmied—I was sure they were about to collapse. And then, praise G-d, it stopped, more suddenly than it had begun. It was as if the tornado or tornadoes, if there were two, were like a pair of whirling dervish dancers who, after having driven us to the brink of insanity for a few minutes, threatened our lives even, winked and sashayed off into the horizon, never to be seen again. I said the Shema quietly to myself and others started to join when someone's phone rang. It was Tamara's. "Yes, Ed, I'm fine," she said, looking around the room. "All of us are fine."

Well, mostly. The group in the room was fine, but there were injuries to some dozen people, though fortunately no fatalities, it was later reported, in the path of the tornado. Several edifices in the area were damaged, most of them in the vicinity of our synagogue. Since it was hours after sunset, I wasn't in the mood or, frankly, emotionally prepared, to have a thorough look. That would wait for morning.

When I did go out slightly after 6 AM that next morning, I found Ed there, shovel in hand, already clearing mud from the back wall of the synagogue that had reached the sill of our communal kitchen. The pile he was making was already shoulder high on one end. He must have gotten there an hour or two before dawn. "Figured you'd need a hand," he said. "I had to cut some of your barbed wire to get in. Don't worry. I'll put it back. Tamara says she'll be here in a while to help," he added before I could express my gratitude. "She needs more rest than I do, especially now."

It seemed their relationship was progressing more rapidly than I had expected. It was nice to see. Shortly, Maya came out with a coffee thermos and three of us took shovels in hand and started back on the heavy mud, though it must be said the much stronger Ed was doing the bulk of the work. Soon, Max joined us, clutching his iPad. Precocious, my son, an engineer, had taught him to program at age six, if he hadn't taught himself. Already. I wouldn't have been surprised. He had been up much of the night plotting the tornado's potential path on an app that employed some new version of AI I had little hope of understanding. My son and daughter-in-law had sent him down to us because he had been suspended from his tony private school. He had responded to a teacher asking what his pronouns were with "I identify as a donkey. He/haw." Some of his classmates laughed, but the teacher didn't think it was funny, and things went south from there. He later told me the joke wasn't his original idea. He had seen it on a website. His parents had shipped him off to us with the hope we would teach him to be more tactful, but somehow Maya and I never got around to it. Maybe we were the wrong people.

Max made some perfunctory attempts to help us with our digging but kept going back to the iPad, on the trail of something fascinating to him but indecipherable to the other three of us. But by the time Tamara arrived, a significant percentage of the clearing work, at least the part nearest the synagogue and our residence wing, had been done. Still, the yard behind was a mess, filled with broken tree limbs and some not insubstantial boulders not more than thirty feet away. We had dodged a serious rockslide.

Again the hard work had been mainly done by Ed, who had fashioned his portion into a surprisingly well-formed and seemingly unnecessarily meticulously shaped rotund mound of mud.

"Nice work," said Tamara, walking around the mound to inspect it as if she were in his studio. "Is that supposed to be a Moore or a Rodin?"

"It's no Giacometti," said Ed, playfully alluding to the Italian whose sculptures frequently resembled anorexics. "Actually, it *is* rather like a Moore," he continued. "If I do say so myself. Just needs some rounding of the shoulders and butt." He started using the shovel as if to complete it. "If I could only get it to stand without falling apart, I'd have something....

Unless I call it 'ten-foot man lying on back' and try to sell it to the Whitney."

"We've already seen a sculpture of a ten-foot man lying on his back a while ago," said Maya. She was looking straight at me with a knowing expression, but I was drawing a blank. "Where did we go on our twentieth, my love?"

"Prague," I said. She meant our twentieth anniversary. I hadn't disgraced myself by forgetting, as husbands do legendarily. "You're talking about the Golem." I turned to Ed and Tamara. "Prague's famous for it. Their Rabbi Loew made one, around 1600, I think. They have a museum.... Sort of looks like one," I added, gazing down in amusement at what seemed increasingly to be a supine man, but without mouth, ears, or eyes.

"What's a Golem?" said Max. There was something he didn't know? Ed and Tamara didn't seem to either. I was about to explain when Mr. Busy Fingers got there first, reading from his iPad: "A Golem is a creature formed out of a lifeless substance like dust or earth, usually brought into life by a rabbi writing Hebrew letters on his forehead. The Golem then becomes the rescuer of an imperiled Jewish community... Hey, you're a rabbi, grandpa. Go for it!"

"It's folklore, boychik." He looked disappointed.

"What do they write on the forehead?" Tamara asked.

"There are many versions, some even predate Judaism, from primitive times," I replied, sounding more academic than I wanted. "But the famous one... the one with Rabbi Loew... the word '*emet*,' meaning truth, if I remember correctly. Spelling out G-d's name was forbidden, so he wrote '*emet*' I guess symbolically."

"C'mon, grandpa. Try it," Max insisted.

Somehow, I didn't feel like getting involved with this. It was a tale from the Middle Ages and too hocus-pocus for me, a mythical monster to fight the pogroms.

Ed sensed my hesitation. "If you show me the Hebrew letters," he said. "I'd be glad to do the inscribing. I've done it on my own sculptures." He reached for a nearby stick.

"You're not a rabbi," said Max, before turning to me. "Can he do it?"

Maya frowned as I shrugged.

"Does it matter?" Ed interjected. "Everybody knows there's an imperiled Jewish community these days, to say the least. Every bit helps... So *'emet'*. E... M... E... T.... How is that in Hebrew?" He stood there, stick in hand, waiting, I suppose, for me to give the word.

"I think," said Maya, pausing to get everyone's attention, "it's time for lunch. I smell brisket somebody made." She winked. "Golems can wait. Since Rabbi Loew made his around 1600, we have time... But please," she added, acknowledging the dirt covering all of us, "wash up first."

As we walked inside, Tamara nodded behind her and said, only half-jokingly, "What if it's real?"

At that moment, I had mixed feelings about her joining my class. I wondered if she was too vulnerable to the Kabbalistic mysticism talk I didn't always believe myself and could veer to the cultish. I had seen that happen, especially to artsy types. They were particularly susceptible.

"It is real," I said. "Real mud." She laughed. But later at the lunch table, she had that distant expression again. I could see the roller coaster wasn't over. Why would it be?

That night Maya went off to do PT at a local assisted living place where she volunteered, so I sat with Max watching a football game and eating leftover brisket. I was developing a deep affection for the boy and could see, despite or maybe because of his obviously high IQ, that he was struggling. I wanted to help him in some way and probed a bit about what happened in school. Apparently, he did more than mock the pronoun foolishness. He had gone on to explain in front of the class that the human body contained approximately thirty trillion cells, all of which had either xx or xy chromosomes, which assigned the person's sex and dictated how their body would grow and function. There were minute exceptions, but to pretend people could choose their own gender was scientifically "irresponsible" —I think that's what he said-- and anyone who thought that had been propagandized. He used the word "brainwashed." The teacher told him to step outside. In the corridor, she asked him if he was okay. When he said he was fine, she ignored him and said she was recommending special therapy sessions with the school nurse. He shouldn't be alarmed. It would be good for him in the end and there would be things to consider, including, if it were determined to be beneficial, even transitioning. Two of his classmates were doing so and were already "feeling better about themselves". He might too. She started to tell him about their hormone treatments when he told her to go to f- herself in French. She didn't speak French, which he knew, but she got the gist, and he ended up being suspended. By the way, he added, he thought the teacher was trans herself, but he wasn't sure.

"What'd your parents think of all this?" I asked.

"I never really told them the whole story," he said. "They'd pull me out of the school." They would, I thought, knowing my son and daughter-in-law, when he continued. "It's supposed to be the best in Indianapolis. It's the feeder for Harvard."

"You don't want to go there, do you?"

"That place?" He made a face. "Anyway, I'm not sure I want to go to college. Everybody's crazy there. Maybe there are better places to learn."

I shrugged. He had a point.

"But if they do, I want to go to CalTech or the Technion in Israel, and major in math."

"You're only eleven. That could change."

"The schools, sure. But not the math. It's the basis of everything. That's probably why the Maharal studied it?"

"The Maharal? That's what they called Rabbi Loew."

"Yes, he was also a mathematician. And an astronomer. He worked with Tycho Brahe, one of the first astronomers to map the stars. Don't you know that?"

"Well, yes, sort of. But not the details."

"Study up, grandpa. Anyway, I think maybe I should tell my parents what happened."

"I think maybe you should."

Not long thereafter, I put the eleven-year-old to bed, reassuring him I was looking for a good homeschool teacher for him. Maya was too. She had put out the word through her physical therapy connections that often were wider than a rabbi's, since it seemed practically everyone over forty was working through some bodily issue. Max wanted a scientist, if possible, and I assured him, kissing him goodnight on his forehead, that I would try, though I was skeptical that I could find someone with a sufficient background for the boy.

That night I had trouble sleeping. It wasn't an unusual occurrence. A man of my age typically gets up a lot to do his business, as they say about dogs. But this was more than the usual. Maya had gone to sleep ten minutes after returning from PT, and I was tossing and turning, doing my best not to disturb her as I rolled gingerly out of the bed to make my treks to the bathroom. After the fourth or fifth time, I had basically awakened myself with my peregrinations and gave up on sleep, at least for the moment. I thought about reading but felt somehow too restless, so I put on a robe and traipsed around the back residential area of the synagogue, a man too agitated to do anything useful.

I came to rest at the rear window. It was nearly a full moon, gibbous I believe they call it, and a fair amount of the backyard was at least partially illuminated. As it was still early Fall, most leaves were on the trees, only a few having changed colors.

Just out the window, it wasn't far away, I could see the supine mud figure, although the full contours of its form were not clear in the attenuated light. I don't know exactly what prompted me, curiosity to see it once again, I suppose, but I opened the back door for a better look and walked out. I can't say I was surprised that it hadn't moved. Nor had it grown eyes and ears to appear more humanoid. And yet there was something human about it, like one of those giants out of a children's movie gone to sleep on its back. The head was wide and round at the top and narrow below, where his chin would be, giving him or it, oddly, the aspect of those binocular machines found at vista sites, in which you used to drop quarters for a close-up of a mountain peak. In a certain way, it seemed as if it wanted to talk to me, although I knew in the Golem legend these beings were unable to speak, as if they wanted to be human but couldn't be.

"Hello," I shouted down at it on the off chance that it would stir, but really just for a kind of self-amusement. Of course it didn't. Then I thought to try "Shalom" with an equal result. What was I expecting? Mud is mud. Inanimate. Randomly, I picked up the pointed stick Ed had been playing around with, which was lying just to the side, propped on a rock. I waved it about above the mud would be statue, still in that self-amusement mode, again with the expected no reaction. But then I noticed my hand was shaking as it clutched the stick. Why was that? Was I nervous? Did I somewhere, deep down in my unconscious, believe in the possibility of what was obviously folklore or myth? I was never remotely like that.

I forced my hand to stop, and, in one sense, just to prove to myself I was still of rational mind, G-d may exist, but not on this level, but on another, as a kind of experiment, bent over whatever this was before me. And then, just like Rabbi Loew in days of old, a man of such spiritual eminence and intellectual brilliance I would never think to emulate in any serious way and who probably never really created a Golem himself in the first place—it was just one of those stories that developed—I carved *aleph*, *mem* and *tav*, the letters that spelled the word "*emet*," into what would have been the statue's forehead.

Again, nothing happened, no movement of the mud of any sort.

I checked my watch. It was twenty minutes past one a.m. on October 7, 2023. Yes, that day. Across the world, much was already happening or had happened, but I did not know it at the time. I turned around, walked into the house and went to sleep.

III

I had forgotten about that brief interlude in my life for several days. There was much to think about, obviously, for Jews and everybody else. The stories were horrific and need not be repeated here. Many of our congregants came to visit, seeking consolation and, in some cases, to arrange trips to Israel in solidarity. Others showed their support financially. It was a busy and anxious time, but also one of coming together. Those who were on opposite sides politically were united by a common enemy, at least for a short time. Even the Nussbaums and Tamara stopped their quarrels.

What transpired several days after that, although for much of the world outside Nashville vastly overwhelmed by events in the Middle East, certainly made the local news and, I was later told, the national news as well. It even merited a brief mention on NPR's Morning Edition.

In my life, and that of my family and friends, it would ultimately merit vastly more than that, in essence, determining our futures.

After nearly a year, a suspect in the horrific Allison Carter killing had been caught. He was a Salvadoran national currently being detained at the Davidson County sheriff's headquarters in downtown Nashville in their medical unit.

I first heard this on the radio while driving back from a visitation with a congregant who was, ironically, serving three years himself in a federal facility near Memphis for embezzlement. On an earlier trip, I had given him books to read that I thought might improve his life, including "Man's Search for Meaning" by Viktor Frankl, the Austrian psychiatrist who survived the Holocaust. The man, I had seen from our discussions, was beginning to learn something during his incarceration. It was a rare moment of gratification amidst the world's chaos, almost a respite.

But my thoughts immediately switched to Tamara the moment I heard the broadcast. I pulled over and called her. She had just gotten off the phone with Ed. She had seen the news on her phone just moments before and was still weeping with joy that justice was finally being served. But as we talked, she was already having second thoughts. What if the bastard got a light sentence or even got off? So many did these days, in and out in a matter of weeks to wreak havoc again. And why was he in the medical unit? Did the police overstep their bounds with their weapons to apprehend him, and would pay for their zeal, fairly or not, in the courtroom?

That would be unlikely, I concluded the next day when my wife showed me an Instagram post from the Nashville Nugget. It was one of those internet papers that have popped up in recent years to tell stories the establishment press is often reluctant to expose for professional or ideological reasons, not that these new media, that had biases of their own, right and left, were necessarily accurate either. In this case, however, the Nugget proved one hundred percent correct, even if they insisted on using the tired euphemism "undocumented" for, in this instance, a very obvious alien who could not have been more illegal.

Apparently, the suspect, Antonio Diaz Cabral, had been screaming for help, unable to escape or even move because he had two broken legs before the police even arrived, at what turned out to be, extraordinarily, the very spot Allison Carter had been raped and murdered.

Here, verbatim, I should say "for the record," considering who will be perusing this document, is what I read that morning on Instagram:

ALLEGED MURDERER DISCOVERED BY YOUTH

By Fritz Kaufer (Nugget crime desk)

NASHVILLE, (Oct. 15)—Lucky thing Carlos Espinosa was playing hooky from Antioch Middle School Tuesday, Oct 14.

Without the presence of the 13-year-old, the undocumented Salvadoran migrant Antonio Diaz Cabral may have died of malnutrition because he was unable to move from a secluded area by the Cumberland River due to two broken legs.

Young Espinosa overheard Cabral screaming "Un monstruo! Un monstruo!" (monster in Spanish), he alleged to police, who were in the process of apprehending Espinosa for truancy. The youth had rushed over to help the man instead of immediately going back to school, which had been his original intention, he alleged.

Espinosa led Officer Jason Vaughan to where Cabral was located, with the man still screaming in agony, "Un monstruo!"

Officer Vaughan, who was one of a dozen Metro Nash-

ville Police officers called to the scene when Allison Carter was brutally murdered last year, recognized this as the exact spot where the corpse of the young woman was found.

Checking for weapons, Vaughan discovered what appeared to be the missing plastic top from Ms. Carter's Yeti water bottle in Mr. Cabral's hip pocket.

At police headquarters, the top was checked for fingerprints, which showed matches from both Ms. Carter and Mr. Cabral.

This was corroborated by further prints found on Ms. Carter's belt in police possession.

Confronted with the matches, Mr. Cabral confessed to Ms. Carter's murder, but still complained about being waylaid by a monster.

According to Homeland Security, Antonio Diaz Cabral, sometimes known as Antonio Diaz, was wanted for assault with a deadly weapon and human trafficking in Arizona and auto theft in Georgia. He had been previously expelled from this country three times.

Sources tell Nashville Nugget the current police theory of the case is that Mr. Cabral was a victim of intergang violence between notorious Salvadoran gangs that have relocated to the United States since the controversial crackdown in their country by their new president. Mr. Cabral has several gang tattoos on his back and arms.

As you might guess, the first thing I did after reading this was to walk outside and have a look at you-know-what. To say that my heart was beating rapidly was only one indicator of the complicated emotions and extreme tension I was feeling. Would the "*Monstruo*" or monster still be there? It had been raining two out of the last three days and, as is often the case in Middle Tennessee, the rains were pretty fierce. But now they had stopped, and the sky was clear, a crisp smell of autumn in the air. But a whole new layer of mud had appeared all the way back to the hill behind us the kids used for sledding during the infrequent snows. This made my examination all the more difficult, not to mention the still uncleared detritus from the near-fatal tornado rockslide. I leaned down further to get a better look at what was left of the mud mound. I thought I could detect a bump that might have been his head, but I wasn't sure. I reached down and found a rock instead. If he was still there, the rains had erased him. It probably was the Salvadoran gangs. What did I know?

"Don Benjamin, may I speak with you?" came a voice behind me. I knew immediately it was our security guard, Jorge Estevez, speaking of Salvadorans. He was the only one who called me Don Benjamin instead of Rabbi Golub or just Rabbi or Ben. I knew this was a traditional sign of respect in his culture, so I never commented or complained. In fact, I was flattered, though I didn't like admitting that to myself.

"Hello, Jorge. What a day, huh? No doubt you heard the news of your fellow countryman."

"Yes, unfortunately. How you say—it travels fast? They are already talking about it back home, my brother tells me. They say it is good news for our president that the gangs have gone and bad news for your country.... Don Benjamin, have you been to the safe room lately?"

"Not since the tornado." He was frowning. It was Jorge's job to check every room in the complex at least once a day. He had a tracking device that was supposed to detect explosives, but there were some questions about whether it worked well enough. "I'm guessing you think I should."

I followed him down into the garage where the safe room

stood behind a secure steel door. He pushed on it and it swung open easily.

"Isn't that supposed to be locked?"

"Something broke into it."

"Some-*thing?*" I didn't like the sound of that.

He shrugged. We entered, and Jorge switched on the light. There, lying on the concrete floor in front of us, what would be his head pointing toward the ceiling, though it had no eyes or mouth, was the supine figure of the mud man, just as he or it had been sculpted by Ed. No wonder my attempt to find it outside had been fruitless. It wasn't moving, but given what had occurred, there was no reason to think that it couldn't.

Jorge pulled some new hardware out of a bag he was carrying. "I thought you might want better security, Don Benjamin." Perspicacious man that he is, he had purchased an industrial-strength padlock to replace the broken one. It looked formidable, although it could well not be sufficient to restrain that virtually inexplicable accumulation of mud on the floor, which, for all I knew, could have changed its shape and oozed in under the jam anyway. At least the lock would stop normal human intruders. I'm not sure why, but I was almost certain Jorge realized I had something to do with this or knew something about it. Perhaps it was the look on my face.

We both stood there a moment, silently contemplating a situation that was, to say the least, extremely hard to grasp. As he was, to this point, the only person other than I to have seen the "sculpture" in its present form and since I had known him for nearly a year and judged him to be a genuinely trustworthy person, I sucked it up and went ahead and told him about Golems that, needless to say, he had never heard of before. What else could I have done? To my surprise, he did not seem especially surprised or alarmed.

"Is like El Tabudo," he said, and went on to describe

someone the Salvadorans know as 'The Man with Big Knees," a fisherman who one day came back as more fish than man.

"Do you believe in El Tabudo?"

"Strange things happen in world." It was a diplomatic answer, but hard to dispute.

"For now, let's keep this between us," I said, feeling, as I spoke the line, I was uttering a cliché someone had written for me as if I had become a character in some play or movie.

I felt that way for the rest of the day, as if I were living in a fictional world created by some writer or filmmaker. And yet, like most fictions, it was inspired by real life or, in this case, something that *seemed* real—or was it? How would I explain this if I ever had to? Would even my wife believe what was happening now?

"Forgive me if it sounded in any way like I thought you were hallucinating," Maya said later that evening. I had been showing her cellphone photos I had taken of the supine figure on the storeroom floor. "It's just all so incredible. I wouldn't blame you if you were. Everything's so stressful. Sometimes I feel I am having visions myself... extreme nightmares really...."

"I see you tossing in your sleep. Sometimes I want to wake you, but I'm having them myself."

One of the endless panel discussions on the Middle East situation was on cable TV. Normally, I would listen, but it was hard to pay attention.

"Ben, do you think this really is a Golem?"

"I don't know."

"Did you know the murderer was seen at a convenience store in Mobile, Alabama four hours before he was discovered here with his legs broken?"

"Where'd you hear that?

"Our Max." She gestured down the corridor. "He found it in one of those chat rooms he goes on. That's almost five hundred miles away. He has the exact figure. He computed this Cabral character must've been traveling at about 127 miles per hour." She waited a bit and looked at me with one of those hurt, disappointed expressions wives get when they think their husbands have erred. In this case, she had a point. "You didn't tell me, Ben. Did you carve '*emet*' in its forehead the other night?"

"Well, I...maybe... How'd you know?"

"I looked after breakfast... You should have told me."

"I didn't take it seriously."

"What could be more serious?"

"Okay... I'm sorry."

Why was she, of all people, being so judgmental? Maya's aging parents—her father was already deceased—had been peaceniks who owned the oldest vegetarian restaurant in LA's hippie enclave, Topanga Canyon, which was quite an achievement given the venue. They named Maya after a Hindu goddess, she told me when we first met, for ecumenical reasons. No belief system was considered superior to another, perhaps even especially not the one she was born into. When we first married, part of Maya still believed all that. But those beliefs had long since faded away, as was clear that evening.

"If that is a Golem," she continued, "are you going to do something with it?"

"Do what?"

"What rabbis are supposed to do. Defend our people."

"It's not a Golem," I replied, suddenly overwhelmed by the obvious that I am just a normal man, and this was over my head, miles over.

"Then how did it get into the safe room?"

"I don't know. Poltergeist. Or somebody played a trick."

"Who would do such a thing?"

"One of the students in my class. They don't all like me. Or the teenagers in the neighborhood as a prank. Some..." I stopped, realizing it sounded absurd. "What would you have me do?"

"What would Rabbi Loew do?"

"Rabbi Loew? That's a legendary figure from over four hundred years ago. What relevance would that have? Who knows if any of it is true? I'm just some shlepper in Nashville who ended up with a job because they couldn't find somebody better, if you want to know what I really think... I'm not even a good Jew."

"Because we used to sneak off to eat lobsters when we lived in Maine?"

"Don't forget the oysters."

She sighed in exasperation. "I thought you believed in G-d."

"On a good day." I stopped, realizing how defensive I was sounding. I was beginning to feel as if I were making a fool of myself in front of my wife. "Maya... suppose this, er, Golem is actually real and we... I...as the rabbi... do something with him. I'm not sure exactly how to do that. Give him instructions? Go after the antisemites?... Suppose he hurts somebody? He already did that, if this is real, broke a man's legs. Okay he was a murderer rapist and deserved it. And some of the antisemites deserve worse. But that's not us. We're not violent people. We'll regret it for the rest of our lives."

"Suppose it's G-d's will that you do something?"

"It's hard to believe."

"I know.... It is for me too ... But how could it be otherwise?" She sounded bewildered and had lost the insistence in her voice. "I cannot understand it any other way."

I sat there for a moment, deliberately slowing my breath the way I had learned in a yoga class I took briefly years ago. A million thoughts were racing through my mind, and I was trying to stop them.

"Maybe we should start slowly," I said at length. "Test it out to see if it's real."

"What could be the harm?"

The next morning, after prayers and a cup of coffee, I returned to the storage room. The Golem—I am calling him that because I was assuming he was one, at least until proven otherwise—was exactly as we had left him. I closed the door behind me, secured it and looked down.

I had read that whatever Rabbi Loew asked the Golem to do, it did immediately without question. But I had to make a request myself. On the other hand, if this was a Golem, it wasn't a typical one. It had already broken the rules and acted on its own to avenge a murder. Still, if it existed, it was a creature of the Almighty and laws could be rewritten. Are all Golems the same? Again, if it was real, it was sent for a reason. It might still listen to me. I had a simple test in mind—harmless enough—and I needed at least the feeling that I was being heard.

"Shalom," I said.

He or it didn't register. Perhaps I was doing it wrong.

"Shalom," I repeated. "Please stand."

Again, no response. "Golem, please stand," I repeated three times, each to no avail. Perhaps I needed to be more peremptory, commanding. He was in the literature, in essence, Rabbi Loew's servant, although a servant used for good. "Golem, stand!" I said, affirmation and expectation in my voice.

No response. I was beginning to think this was all a mistake, that I may indeed have lost my mind or simply blundered. This was the modern world, after all. Such things did not happen, except for the most superstitious, and they were always found to be a little daft. I was already starting to figure out an escape route, some way to explain to those few who needed to understand that this was a myth after all, no more reasonable than Jorge's El Tabudo, when the obvious occurred to me. If this was a creature of G-d, he had to be addressed that way.

This gave me a sudden feeling of trepidation. I was going to do something I had done so many times previously but never with such extreme direct intentionality. It was almost as if everything I had said before, every prayer, was merely going through the motions—and maybe it was. I took a breath and bowed my head, waiting over a minute before reciting the fundamental prayer of Judaism, the Shema, in both English and Hebrew, although I had been told that my Hebrew accent left something to be desired. "Shema Yisrael, Adonai Eloheinu, Adonai Echad... Hear, O Israel! The Lord our G-d, the Lord is One!"

For another moment, there was still nothing, but then, very slowly, as if it were an animal or even a human waking up after a long slumber, Rip Van Winkle himself coming back from decades of hibernation, I started to see ripples in the mud. It began to undulate, at first in its midsection and then in its legs and arms. This being, or whatever it was, then started to rise and soon I was confronted with a mud giant I guessed to be about ten feet tall, its head almost reaching the ceiling, with shoulders wider than any football player, even with his pads. Out of awe, I repeated the Shema as it stood there.

I then gave him his instructions, making sure that he followed them under the cover of darkness. To alert anyone to his unnecessary presence at this point would be foolhardy and destructive.

"Ben, look!" Maya awakened me the next morning. She was standing at our window, gesturing excitedly to me. "Is this what you told him to do? He could make a fortune as a landscape architect," she continued, as I shuffled over and peered out.

"I told him to tidy up the back so we wouldn't get slides every time it rains. I didn't say make it look like Versailles." I gazed at the vista. It wasn't quite Versailles, but the artistic arrangement of granite boulders at the bottom of the hill was certainly impressive, resembling those that dotted the desert at a fancy hotel and spa in Tucson, where we once had a rabbinical convention. Normally this would have taken at least a crane and several large Bobcats for a week or more, but the Golem, for that was clearly what he must be, had done it himself overnight. The expanse of what was formerly unkempt piles of mud appeared to have been seeded and aerated in the manner of the most well-tended lawns of the type you might imagine at some Tara-like estate of which we had a few in Nashville in pricier neighborhoods. He (it?) had even erected an ornate gazebo with table and chairs and a Star of David on top as would befit the back yard of an upscale, if not the finest, of synagogues. I could see it all now--the giant driving around in a van, or more likely a Hummer, because a van wouldn't fit him, labeled Golem Landscape Solutions. It almost made me laugh.

"Are you ready to rumble, rabbi?" said Maya. The playfulness of her words was betrayed by a nervousness in her voice I had never quite heard before, except perhaps at our wedding.

"I guess I... I guess I don't have a choice," I replied, wondering if I could possibly have the courage to go through with it, whatever it was.

I kept wondering the same thing throughout the day and the following night —why me? Why had I, the reluctant rabbi, the one who had fallen into the occupation as something of a last resort or even accident, apparently been—I wish there were a less fraught word—chosen for this task? I remembered sitting in my dormitory room, the senior year of my English major, endlessly flipping a coin between law and rabbinical schools. That ambivalence was just one of the causes, both secular and religious, that I recalled years later impelled me to leave the profession to teach in Maine. Another was that I had done things when I was younger that I thought made me unworthy of the rabbinate. Maybe that was the reason, try though I might, I was never able to experience or even get much of a glimmer of the divine Endless Light from above, the Kabbalists say, is visible through the "container" of our daily lives. If we make the effort and do sufficient good deeds, it will be revealed, they said. I was never sure there was something there.

Over the years, I met brilliant rabbis who understood the liturgy far better than I, the parvenu who had spent more time and received more pleasure reading Saul Bellow and Philip Roth than David's Psalms or anything in The Tanakh that still seems, if I am honest, somewhat foreign to me. And yet here I was in the midst of this, with the circumstances for the Jewish people becoming more ominous than ever in my lifetime. Predictably, the horror of October 7 was already beginning to wear off, but days after the terrorist massacres, rapes, and abductions. You could already sense it on the evening news. The victim was not far from being declared the perpetrator, at least by the many who could profit from the switch. The first mutterings of "from the river to the sea" that would soon be a cacophony were starting to be heard with portions of our society, not to mention the world at large, where it was worse, exploding from decades of semi-closeted pent-up antisemitism.

And then there was this guy with a muddy statue in his basement.

IV

The next morning, I went to "The Orphanage" and spoke privately with Ed and Tamara in Ed's back-room studio. I felt I had to tell them what had happened. Neither of them, strangely enough, was as astonished as I was at the reappearance of Ed's work in a new guise but readily understood the need for secrecy. That would make six of us who knew—the two of them, Jorge, Maya, and me, and Max, who had undoubtedly figured it out for himself anyway. For now, maybe forever, I wanted to keep it that way. In fact, I needed to keep it that way if anything were to come of this.

Therefore, I was smart enough to know that I would have to move cautiously. If I were to use this entity for the positive purpose of defeating the enemies of the Jewish people, and I was not hesitant to include, as presumptuous as it might sound, Western Civilization itself, I could not do so in a wanton manner. That would be doomed to backfire, likely in a big way. I had considered giving the Golem an instruction to destroy the Hamas leadership, whether in their tunnels or their luxury hotel rooms. But if HaShem had wanted this Golem to attack

Hamas in Gaza, why would He have materialized him in Tennessee in the middle of America? The Israelis would have to deal with that for themselves, and I had confidence they could do so, eventually. That was what I thought then, anyway. The Golem's mission would have to have its primary impact on the good, old USA. My divine brief for saving—and it seemed to be that, like it or not-- was for what I had heard long ago referred to as the "Big Satan," challenging enough by itself and until quite recently the most welcoming home for the Jews, outside Israel, in history. The question was how to do it. Moving precipitously was not the answer.

Maya and I talked about this for several days. We kept discarding possibilities as too dangerous. Was it my risk aversion rearing its head? Still, it didn't seem the time to send the Golem to deal with the hordes of "river to the sea" demonstrators blockading New York bridges or obstructing Times Square or Wall Street with the attendant violence that would be a certainty.

The person we eventually chose was not universally despised—even the most evil had friends in the society in which we lived-- but it was close, as close as anyone we could think of anyway. When I went to the Golem to explain his mission, however, I emphasized we did not want to see this person physically hurt in any way, even though the individual was notoriously antisemitic, not to mention anti-American, and was riddled with an extraordinary level of ungratefulness toward the land to which she had immigrated. I reiterated in my instructions that if more time were necessary due to safety constraints or the length of travel entailed, he should take it, although it was unclear whether the Man of Clay would have any such concerns, given his powers.

Nevertheless, it was nearly a week before the mission was accomplished. This may have been due to scheduling, as the

Golem appears to have preferred to send his cargo via Emirates Airlines, a carrier known for being among the safest and most luxurious, which flew nonstop to this destination.

So when a large, securely wrapped corrugated cardboard box, about the size of a kayak, covered with shrink wrap and labeled "Fragile—Handle with Extreme Care" in English and Somali, was unloaded from the cargo hold of the Emirates Boeing 787-400 Dreamliner and moved via conveyor to the oversized baggage claim area at Aden Adde (formerly Mogadishu) International Airport, everything seemed completely normal.

Except that no one came to pick up the box for hours. But if you stood close and listened very carefully, you could hear someone screaming and banging on the walls inside, although some form of soundproofing, later found to be two layers of industrial-strength foam insulation panels, made it seem they were far away, as if at the end of a cave.

Finally, late that night, Somali time, morning to us, a couple of maintenance workers, trying to hide behind the box for a smoke normally prohibited in the airport, heard the cries within and, first stubbing out their cigarettes, notified authorities who —after considerable discussion leading to an hours-long inspection by a bomb squad in ordinance disposal suits (OEDs)—the box was opened by one of the two tactical robots in Somalia.

A woman of Somali appearance was carefully extracted from the center of the box where she was ensconced with copious food supplies, including protein energy bars, dried fruit, and several half-consumed bottles of lemon Gatorade. She appeared to be in a near state of shock, although it turned out she was perfectly healthy, and was dressed in a white beekeeper's suit on the back of which was printed in neat black letters, again in English and Somali, the words "RETURNED TO SENDER."

After some incredulity, the woman was almost immediately identified as the controversial Congresswoman Bilan Ali of Minneapolis, Minnesota, by far the most recognizable Somalian immigrant to the United States, who had come to the USA some twenty-five years before at the age of 12. Within hours, Ms. Ali was in first class, a breathable scarf over her face to disguise her identity, on a direct flight back to Minneapolis-Saint Paul International Airport.

Of course, the news spread quickly. This all happened in plain view at Adden Adde Airport. But just as fast, it was debunked; they used that word, by the American networks and on the internet, branded as misinformation and a smear, once again showing the ugliness and willful disrespect of right-wing propaganda. This was especially true when a shaky video appeared to have been pirated from airport authorities. It was then accused of being a primitive form of photoshopping by some, and advanced AI counterfeiting using a look-alike by others. Several months later, such videos would be called "cheap fakes." No one suspected at all what had happened, although Max told me he had noticed a report on a Minneapolis radio station about an airport cleaning woman who claimed to have seen a "beanstalk giant" racing across the tarmac around 4 a.m. But later, when questioned by police, she denied it all, saying she had been on duty for ten hours and was "seeing things." That eleven-going-on-twelve-year-old Max was the one who discovered this report troubled me because he was so young to be involved with something this complicated. But he had been there from the beginning, and there was no choice. Still, due to some stealthy placements by the boy on seemingly obscure—meaning they were constantly surveilled—message boards for young nerds like him, rumors have persisted to this day that have not been contradicted.

As for Congresswoman Ali herself, she dismissed the idea

of a forty-eight-hour trip to Somalia and back as a ridiculous and insulting fairy tale that no decent person could possibly believe. She had been at home the entire time, her husband, a political consultant, confirmed. They were just taking some personal time for themselves, he explained to CNN, deliberately disconnecting from the endless, often obnoxious and personally hurtful social media bullying that can be so dehumanizing. To avoid temptation, they locked their cellphones in the family safe for forty-eight hours.

Maya and I guffawed when we heard that. We were sitting in The Orphanage with Ed and Tamara. Ed had closed it early so we could watch the news together and this called for a mutual fist bump. We knew that tradition began with COVID, but it wasn't a bad one.

"'Returned to Sender,'" Tamara said. "What a hilarious play on Elvis."

"I'm not sure the Golem knows 'Return to Sender,'" I replied, although I knew she was mostly joking. "But since HaShem created the universe and is part of all of us, that means he's responsible for Elvis and every song he ever wrote, from 'Hound Dog' to 'Don't Be Cruel.' We could even include Irving Berlin and Beethoven in the mix." I was feeling a little tipsy.

"I'll drink to that," said Ed, raising his glass. He had brought the expensive bottle of Caymus 50th Anniversary Napa Cabernet, which, luckily, was kosher, for the occasion. Most of it was already gone.

"All I did," I continued as Ed poured what was left in our glasses, "was give the Golem the most general instructions, but he took it from there—'Returned to Sender' and all."

"He sure did," said Tamara. "To the Golem!" She raised her glass and we all toasted life—or was it lives since the

Hebrew word was plural..."L'chaim!"... before downing the last bits.

But I wondered, after all was said and done, if we had had that much, or even anything, to celebrate. Yes, we had made a mockery of a selfish and evil person. Honest people, those paying attention to such things anyway, and who could blame them if they weren't, would know that she and her husband's excuses were nonsense and that something untoward had happened, that someone—a prankster, who knew?—had indeed returned her to sender. Nevertheless, she had bounced back almost immediately, very little the worse for wear except for some embarrassment and only slightly more notoriety as a liar than she already had, scarcely earth-shattering for a politician. Was there even one who had not experienced something similar somewhere along the line? And who would doubt for a moment that the notorious antisemitic and anti-American Rep. Bilan Ali would not be reelected by her Minneapolis district anyway? Her constituency was a perfect witches' brew of an enraged multi-cultural underclass with a sense of victimhood ginned-up by the media, along with the most extreme woke liberal Jews west of New York's Upper West Side.

That latter group was the greatest mystery to me. Why in this post-Holocaust world did they continue to act so unbendingly against their own self-interest? Was it self-hatred, self-preservation, just plain guilt, or all three? I had been wondering about that for decades when I stumbled on a citation from Rashi. The legendary Talmudist claimed only twenty percent of the Jews left Egypt during the Exodus, the rest preferring to remain in the slavery they knew. Could that have been? Though he wrote that a thousand years ago, it explained a great deal about human nature in general when I read it. Were these people, these Jewish Minneapolis Bilan Ali voters, actually the progeny of the progeny of the progeny and so forth down the generations of those who stayed behind, the leftover strands of slave DNA still percolating through their bodies thousands of years later under the rubric of whatever special pleading terminology fit the times, like woke or social justice? For that to have happened, some Pharaoh would have had to have eventually let them go, not because of plagues but for "good behavior" or because their services were no longer necessary. Who knew, really? Perhaps I should have asked the Golem—but he couldn't speak even though I suspected he wanted to. I could only speak to him. Still, it was as good an explanation as any—at least for the moment.

Or maybe their obdurate party loyalty was just a habit akin to smoking and harder to break.

"I want to convert to Judaism." Ed broke through my reverie.

Convert? All of a sudden? Was it the wine speaking? I thought we only had one bottle. "You do? Now?"

"Absolutely."

"You know what you're getting into, don't you? Joining a group that has been the victim of virtually non-stop discrimination for the last thirty-five hundred years."

"I don't care. They were all wrong... Can you do it?"

I hesitated a bit before answering. I had only done conversions twice, and only once successfully. "Yes, I can," I said. "But it's not easy. A lot of work. A panel has to approve you in the end."

"Whatever it takes... I would like to marry Tamara." He took her hand. "And I know she would want me to be Jewish."

"I said I would *prefer* it." She was suddenly beet red. "That's all."

Okay, prefer. But it's still better. You'll be happier, so we'll both be happier." He smiled at her sweetly. "Besides, I feel like I am part Jewish already... from my role in what happened. I feel like I started it with my shovel." He nodded to the news show, which was already off on another story, when Tamara leaned over and kissed him sweetly on the cheek. This was apparently real.

"Well, congratulations. To both of you," I said. " *Mazel tov!*"

"*Mazel tov!*" Maya joined in. "And *siman tov!*"

"*Siman tov*? What's that mean?" said Ed.

"Basically the same thing. *Mazel tov* and *siman tov*. Good luck and a good sign. You just had your first pre-lesson....It would be my pleasure to do your conversion. When do you want to start?"

"Since it's so difficult, the sooner the better. Tomorrow morning. After I open the shop, I'll come over if it works for you."

"That's not possible," said Maya, turning back to me. "The teacher."

"Oh, right... I forgot in all the excitement.... A possible homeschool teacher for Max is *finally* coming. We just got his application this morning out of the blue. I have to interview him... We can start Thursday.... Meanwhile, what a wonderful surprise."

"Why don't we all go back to the synagogue right now?" said Maya. "I have some Bartenura Moscato on ice for special occasions. We're so happy for you both. This is fantastic. We need at least one more l'chaim tonight."

"Maybe five," I said.

So the four of us returned to the synagogue and continued into the small hours discussing what assignment I should next give my charge. I was in no hurry. I didn't want to repeat my mistake of doing something that was merely, in modern parlance, performative. In fact, I had probably done the dreadful congresswoman a favor. All she really ever wanted was publicity anyway and this was a gift to someone with a lulling career. But Tamara cautioned, undoubtedly from the experience of her niece, that if I didn't move quickly, the Golem might well act on its own. It already had. We had seen it. Who knew what that would entail next? I knew she had a point. She had been reading the original legends and understood the inherent dangers of an unsupervised monster running amok, causing the opposite of what was intended and increasing the very intolerance the being had been brought forth to diminish. She had seen such craziness in her own business, but I tried to make light of it. "What? You think the Golem is going to act out like that twenty-year-old client of yours? What's his name—Brent Cody?"

"Cody Brent," she corrected me. "And yours is a lot younger."

"A few years, but he has the wisdom of the ages... I think. Anyway, what should I, given the surreal level of antisemitism these days, tell him to do first?" I asked.

"Everything!" both said, almost simultaneously, Ed adding "Of course."

I laughed. It was easy to see why these guys wanted to marry, yet still I was unsure what to do. As I understood it, once a rabbi created a Golem, the entity was his responsibility alone. Of course, I was kidding myself, since I hadn't really created him. He was, one could say, a group project. Or was I being my risk-averse self?

As we were going to bed, I started to ask Maya what she thought, but she wanted to talk about Max. She had taken him to the Nashville Zoo that day. I wasn't surprised to hear that he knew a lot about primates, but she had something more on her mind. The boy was lonely. He needed friends as well as a tutor if he was going to stay with us longer than his parents had anticipated and, from what we were hearing, not to mention the reality of the situation, he probably would. His fancy private school back in Indy had apparently gone half day to accommodate immigrant kids in the morning who were getting "free rides" on tuition, medical care, and a housing fee. At the same time the usual (paying) students were being given the opportunity—parents were assured it was optional—of viewing a special video series on "The Middle East Conflict and the Amazing History of Ancient Palestina" sponsored by Qatar. Home schooling, my son and daughter-in-law had concluded in response, was the best, probably only, solution for Max. David and Rebecca had two other children, much younger than he, in a Jewish day school that went to the sixth grade. But the eleven-year-old was already on the level of a MIT junior, intellectually anyway, and he made no bones about telling his parents that the day school bored him stiff. But since they both worked full-time, that would leave it up to the grandparents, the Rabbi and Rebbetzin, who, in their eyes, had a more leisurely schedule, or at least no one watching the clock for us. With each passing day, it became increasingly clear that it was up to us.

Maya had already delved into the situation, sending out feelers to homeschool groups. I could imagine all the soccer games with all the scrawny kids tripping over each other, but maybe they were better than that.

As for the issue with what to do with our other charge, or my other charge technically, "Mr. G," as we had taken to calling him, her advice differed from the eager Ed and Tamara.

"Wait. Think. Take your time." Maya replied. "The anti-semites can wait. They'll always be there."

I remembered reading somewhere Carl Jung said that men and women switched roles when they grew older. I could see his point. But somehow I wasn't entirely comfortable with it. What if she was wrong?

I was pretty groggy from a long night when Jack Ripton

showed up the next morning. He was in his early twenties, around six-two, dwarfing me by a half foot or so, lanky, and wore a baseball cap for the Chicago Cubs. It turned out we shared the same birth city, I learned not too much later.

"How'd you hear about us?" I asked.

"Your wife's work."

"You're in physical therapy?"

"No, but I have a friend in PT whose roommate told me about it. You know how it works. Kind of on the grapevine. It was a bonanza because I'm looking for part-time work while I finish grad school."

"What're you studying."

"Astronomy."

"Astronomy?"

"I know. Pretty abstruse. I did my undergrad in math."

"Those are my grandson's favorite subjects."

"Good luck then," he said with a smile. "Maybe he can help me pick my thesis topic. I haven't chosen one yet."

I was about to say that might be out of his range, but maybe it wasn't. I remembered how, when I was a boy about his age, I would go to Chicago's Adler Planetarium with my mother's brother Sydney, a high school physics teacher. We would wander around the exhibitions while he explained to me the infinitude of the cosmos, that there were probably multiple universes, and that they were ever expanding at some incredible pace, faster than the speed of light. The multiplicity of things was mind-bending. There may even be an infinite number of young Bens walking around an infinite number of Adler Planetariums with infinite Uncle Sydneys. When it came to who was behind all this infinitude, what force or deity, Sydney was a self-described agnostic, so at that point, I assumed that was the proper response for adults, intelligent ones anyway. I adopted it as my own for a while. This may have accounted for my lifetime of ambivalence, something I didn't want Max to repeat, especially now with young people alienated from each other as never before, as if they were all living in infinite universes staring at infinite cellphones with an infinite number of identities, devoid of any human contact at all.

Nevertheless, Max needed a qualified teacher to be legally homeschooled. Otherwise, he was in trouble in Nashville and Indianapolis. Though it was all very sudden, and I felt a bit lazy that I was not doing it myself (how could I?), Jack Ripton appeared to be more than qualified, having earned a B. A. in mathematics from the University of the South and being currently enrolled in the PhD program at Vanderbilt's Department of Physics and Astronomy, from the resumé emailed to me early that morning. According to Tennessee law, he would be required to teach Max four hours a day for 180 days a year, which he said he would be happy to do. Attendance records were to be submitted annually to the district's director of schools. Jack would keep them too. Everything seemed promising. All that was needed was for Max to sign off. I imagined that would be simple given Ripton's bona fides. I was right. Max was thrilled to have Jack, not only for his scientific interests, but to have a real human to interact with instead of the anonymous ciphers that populated the dark web chat rooms where he spent the majority of his time under his own pseudonym, which was, he confided in me, betraying his still eleven-year-old essence, Indiana NotJones.

All this success resulted in my spending the better part of the rest of my day shuttling between state offices, filling out forms for an official homeschool, something I discovered was more complex if you had only one student. I was behind schedule with the script for my weekly video, which I send to congregants, and found myself up quite late writing it in my office. Maya kindly came in with supper on a tray. Typically, I discuss the Torah portion for that week and try to relate it in some way to our lives today. For that reason, I keep a television in my office to stay abreast of something relevant. Lately, that hadn't been difficult, and that evening the news was dominated by the growing antisemitic—they claimed they were merely anti-Zionist, of course—demonstrations at Columbia University. At first one might think it peculiar, since that university was the only Ivy League school in the one city that had the second most Jews in the world, roughly twice the number that live in Jerusalem. But it was hardly unexpected since the university had long been a hotbed of virulent Jew hatred, its Middle East Studies department led by Edward Said of "Orientalism" fame, who once went to the Lebanon border to throw "symbolic" stones into imperialist Israel. He was followed in the post by his near-clone, Rashid Khalidi, apparently a buddy of Barack Obama's. I had read an internet report claiming the attendance of the then future president at a celebratory party cum extreme Israel bashing for Khalidi's appointment had been memory-holed by the media. I had no reason to disbelieve it.

Even so, these demonstrations at Columbia were more horrific than anyone could have anticipated. It seemed now half the city's youth, hiding their identities with kaffiyehs or leftover COVID masks, wanted Palestine to be free from some river to some sea with everyone in between paying homage. It was hard to attend to my work, to actually formulate words for my script that would accurately describe what was going on, let alone give my congregants advice on how to react other than to donate money to Israeli organizations, a pallid response under the circumstances, rather like "they're forcing you into the gas chambers, send cash."

So I sat there, staring at the unfolding monstrosities on the screen, stymied by a writer's block I rarely have, when I heard a sudden thud and a crack as if a heavy weight had fallen on the hardwood floor. I turned to see a huge, shadowy figure looming over me.

I was about to scream when I realized it was the Golem. What was he doing in my office? Or was this the same Golem? For a split second, maybe I had Uncle Sydney still on the brain. I wondered if there weren't infinite Golems in the expanding universes battling infinite antisemites. But no, this had to be our Golem. How'd he get out of the safe room? But I realized immediately that was an absurd question. How'd he get in? He went where he wanted, though I was the one who was supposed to tell him where. I didn't tell him anything, and now he was here. Only I couldn't ask him why because he couldn't talk. So, for what seemed like several moments but was probably a lot less, we just faced each other, although he had no face to speak of, not even eyes. I did notice, however, that the letters *aleph, mem* and *tav* for "truth" remained carved in his forehead. If I removed them, he would disintegrate or crumble, so the story went. Or was supposed to. Maybe I should do it. It would be a relief, less risk all around. But I already knew this was not a conventional Golem. He was not conjured up by a rabbi in the tradition of Rabbi Loew but appeared through the happenstance of a tornado and was originally carved by a gentile, albeit one who aspired to be a Jew. When it came to what we might call orthodox Golemology, all bets were off. So what was this about?

The Golem, silent as he was, did not need words to communicate. He raised what one could describe as his arm and pointed to the screen. The demonstrators were breaking into Columbia's Hamilton Hall.

V

The next morning was one of those glorious Spring days that make you thankful you live in Tennessee, and Ed and I elected to sit outside under the recently erected gazebo for his first lesson in Judaism. Not far off, maybe a hundred feet, Max was seated next to Jack Ripton for the beginning of his lessons as well. They had spread a blanket on one of the boulders.

"In the old days," I told Ed, "...and for some still, this was a very formal process, and you had to get approval from a rabbinic court. Lately, it's become a little more lax, like everything else. In the most liberal cases, you can even convert online. I try to find a middle ground...Although, as I told you, I've only done it twice...And the second time didn't go well... This is what the Talmud says a potential convert must be asked." I read him the exact quote I had written on a card. "'Why should you wish to become a proselyte; do you not know that the people of Israel at the present time are persecuted and oppressed, despised, harassed, and overcome by afflictions?'... That was from about seventeen hundred years ago.

"You know why I want to convert," Ed replied.

You told me the reason, and it's a good one. You've got an incredible woman there. You're very lucky, and so is she... But marriage is the reason most people want to convert these days. Sometimes I wish there was another motivation too, something more... theological.

"In my case, there is..."

That was a surprise.

"I don't know how to express this. It's kind of embarrassing... Ever since I've been here in Nashville, I've been impressed by how wonderful all the evangelicals are. They're great people, kind, generous, God-fearing. But every time I'm at one of their events it's 'in Jesus' name.' That had a strange effect on me. I started to wonder why God needed a messiah, a son. Wasn't he, whatever he was, bigger than that, beyond human form and something cosmic that encompassed all?"

"Jews have their messiah too. Mashiach—they're waiting for him." I replied, but he had struck a chord with me. For years I had wondered the same thing. The human form approach seemed primitive, for lack of a better word. "You know what Franz Kafka says about it?"

"Oh, Kafka. Fancy. I never read him. Does that make me stupid?"

"It's not nearly as hard as you think, not like Joyce or anything. He makes sense in his weird way. He said the messiah will come when he is no longer necessary. He will come on the day after his arrival."

Ed laughed. "That does have its appeal. In a weird way. If you believe that, you're probably in trouble with a lot of rabbis. But I do want to convert, for both reasons, but primarily for Tamara. And I will get the required circumcision, as long as I can have total anesthesia."

Now *I* laughed. "You've been reading ahead in your studies. High marks...Look, I apologize. We're going to have to be brief today, but I'll make it up to you." I checked my watch. "I've got to catch the one p.m. to LaGuardia. I want to see for myself what happens this time." I could see from the look on his face that Ed instantly grasped what I was talking about, why I was going, but I added for corroboration, "He's *your* masterpiece, Michelangelo."

"I'm no Michelangelo."

"*His* David never came to life."

Ed hesitated before replying, the look in his eye betraying a confusion—a combination of awe and fear—concerning his own handiwork. "True, in a way," he finally acknowledged. "Good luck on your trip and say hello to my 'masterpiece'."

"If I can keep track of him. Somehow I think I have to."

As we walked out, Jack and Max had taken a break from their lesson and were tossing a baseball, Jack winding up to pitch a harder ball that ended up flying through and over Max's outstretched hands because of his height and limited athletic abilities. The ball bounced near me, and he raced over to retrieve it. "Wow, he can throw!" said the boy, adding in a confidential voice, "But he doesn't know that much about astronomy. He didn't know about the comet that hit Jupiter in 1994."

"I didn't either."

Max looked disappointed. "Well, you're a rabbi. You don't have to know that."

I never felt more like a rabbi, and a vulnerable one at that, standing in the main square of Columbia University that evening when a cop—I don't know how he identified me; I wasn't the only person there wearing a yarmulke or perhaps he called every Jew over a certain age rabbi—said "Move back, rabbi. We don't want you gettin' cold cocked." He gently but firmly pressed on my arm to make sure I got the message. The situation was so chaotic even now I am not sure whether he was campus police or the NYPD. It was bizarre, almost an out of body experience, being in the middle of Columbia then, the last time having been five decades before, when, a high school senior, I was on my college tour. Yet, I remembered the basic layout well enough, the Low Library behind me, Butler Library in front. I declined to apply back then, maybe out of fear of rejection, though I told myself I wanted a more countryfied environment. But the furthest thing from my mind then as a late teenager would have been finding the area become a madhouse of people of all descriptions, though largely in Palestinian garb, real or adopted, living in tent cities and screaming for the blood of my people.

To my left was Hamilton Hall, nominally the home to the Classics, Germanic, and Slavic languages departments, but now where the critical action seemed to have gravitated. Some of the more devout Hamas enthusiasts had barricaded themselves inside, making so many demands on the university and the city that it was hard to keep track, except that they all involved thwarting that human pestilence, the Jews, in some way or another. They were supported, sad to say, by leftist Jewish groups who were doing their best to break the record on self-hatred once held by those of our faith who excused Kristallnacht. Indeed, this was far from the first "Night of Broken Glass" in our country, with, as we would learn, many more to come as spring moved into summer and beyond.

That night, the NYPD, after days of back and forth between the city and the cowardly bureaucrats and terror apologists who for some reason seem to have a lock on the leadership of the majority of our universities, were finally being given permission to enter the Hamilton building and extract the militant pro-Palestinian protestors who had barricaded the entrances with its heavy furniture and whatever else they could find. Few, it turned out, were actually Columbia students. One, apparently their leader, I learned much later, was a 40-year-old white sometime lawyer who lived in a multi-million-dollar home in Park Slope and was a self-styled anarchist, veteran of numerous demonstrations for the last fifteen years, and had not a few arrests. I also learned, although not immediately that night, they were attempting to hold hostage some Latino university maintenance workers who were trapped inside and had been trying to defend the building from the masked intruders.

Had the Golem foreseen all this when he was pointing to my office television the previous night? He was there for barely a minute before exiting. The next morning when I looked in the safe room, he was gone. It wasn't difficult to figure out where. Now I was standing behind a police line in front of Hamilton while New York's finest erected a ramp to an upper floor in order to enter the building through a window. Half the city's police force seemed to be there, but the Golem was nowhere in sight, not that I necessarily thought he would be. From what I had observed, he was remarkably stealthy for a ten-footer as if his mud-formed body included a cloak of invisibility. Still, I felt compelled to find him, to see what he was doing because I thought that in the long run the more I knew of his activities, the more I had witnessed, the better. That turned out to be not entirely true.

Nevertheless, some instinct in me—was it my Seventeenth Century self—did impel me to see what was happening on a different level. I had a certainty that the Golem was somewhere and that my role was to record his activities for what passes for posterity. Whether it would be believed would be another question. Older Golem stories had been recorded by rabbis or authored by those of acknowledged wisdom, like the writer Isaac Bashevis Singer. Bashevis, as he was known, was a literary genius capable of convincing his audience of almost anything. I had recently read his version of the Golem and wondered to what extent he actually believed it, whether, as a prolific author, he was just exploiting another folk tale. It led me to wonder whether the story I was telling, contemporaneous as it was, was actually real, although it very much seemed so to me.

Also the Golem was obviously acting on its own now and, in the literature I had read, the stories from the past, the results of this unsupervised behavior were usually devastating, generating painful, even catastrophic, punishments for the Jewish communities from which the rabbis had to rescue them. Was or would I be inadvertently the cause of some disaster?

Whatever the case, I began to shift to my right in the direction of the neighboring building, Hartley Hall, which I knew to be a dormitory. I did this methodically and with the most unremarkable expression and gait I could summon, as if I had an appointment elsewhere that was relatively innocuous. I also—G-d forgive me—removed my yarmulke, in order to attract even less attention. I also was aware that getting in the building would be difficult, if not impossible, most dormitories these days, like hotels, needing a magnetic stripe card or key fob for entry. That supposition was correct, I saw, when I ducked into the Hartley entryway. It was quiet, almost preternaturally so, with all the noise, shouting mixed with chants of rivers and seas, augmented by police sirens, coming from down the block, a couple of hundred yards or more away. Off in the distance, I could see they had almost finished erecting the ramp. Cops were lining up behind it. Wondering what to do next, I looked down at my cellphone in order to seem engaged in something that justified my loitering when I heard footsteps behind me. It wasn't the Golem because they were far too light.

"Excuse me, please," said a voice. The accent was Eastern European. I turned to see a frail young man standing there, holding his entry card. He was obviously orthodox and had the aspect of what we call a *yeshiva bocher* with curled sidelocks—*payot*—and fringes—*tzitzit*—appearing at the bottom of his jacket.

"How do you do? Shalom," I said, hastening to retrieve my yarmulke and putting it back on my head. "I'm Rabbi Ben Golub of Congregation Bethel in Nashville." I fumbled for my card and handed it to him.

"*Toda raba*," he said, using the Hebrew for thank you very much. He glanced at the card and smiled, almost as if he recognized something, but how could he? "Very nice," he said.

"Where are you from?"

"What was once the Pale. Where you are from, no doubt."

"My ancestors, yes.... You are here to study?"

"You could say that." He smiled again. Who was this person? His skin was milky white, as if he had never seen the sun.

What is your name?" I asked him.

"Akiva."

"Akiva, what? Do you have a surname?" His first was a famous name from the Talmud, a man who was illiterate until he was forty but then became a renowned scholar of great spiritual devotion who was flayed to death by the Romans because he defied their decree against Jewish study. This Akiva had evidently been named after him.

He ignored the question and opened the door with his card. "Follow me. I know where you want to go."

As we entered the building, I noticed in the light that the curls of his sidelocks were golden blond—the color of Botticelli's *Primavera*, Ed no doubt would have noted—not the usual black. The yarmulka the young man wore was white and pulled down nearly to his ears. He led me up the stairs to the third floor and gestured down a corridor. I took a few steps in that direction, then turned back to see if he was following, but he was gone. I did not hear him depart, not a sound on the stairs. I also noticed there were no other students around. Where were they? After a few seconds, I turned around again and continued to the end of the corridor and looked about. I saw nothing, was about to turn around a third time, when I noticed the back wall had the tiniest hole about eye level. It was as if someone had poked through the sheetrock with a teacher's pointer. Not expecting to see any more than insulation, I was surprised to see the pointer, or whatever it was, had gone straight through that insulation and pierced the outer wall of the building, boring a hole in the brick. This formed a kind of telescope aimed directly through a side window of Hamilton Hall, magnifying the view.

I strained for a better look. Inside was chaos. Protestors, most keffiyeh-clad, were breaking apart furniture, pieces of which were already stacked on top of each other by the doors and windows, and pulling two-by-fours from the framing they had evidently exposed to secure the building against the pending invasion of the police. As was later reported, a Latino maintenance man, all by himself, was attempting to prevent the protesters from wreaking this havoc. He was wrestling with two of them when another protestor picked up a hefty table leg and came up behind him, about to club the maintenance man on the back of the head with what surely was a fatal blow. I gasped, knowing I, hundreds of feet away in another building, could do nothing as a truly good man was smashed to oblivion. But at the last second, the Golem appeared, grabbed the man with the club and hurled him across the room. Almost simultaneously, he lifted up the maintenance man and disappeared with him from the room to who knows where. This occurred so quickly, almost instantaneously, that it was hard to realize that it even happened. It was more rapid than the proverbial blink of an eye, more like the universe expanding faster than the speed of light. Did anyone notice? Could anyone have noticed, except for me? Had the hole been punctured so I could witness what occurred? The protesters showed no recognition as their attention was immediately caught by the first police officer, who crashed through the window into the room.

What did I just see? How would I explain this to anyone? At that point, I thought it would be better not to. It would not have appeared in any of the endless news reports of this event, during which the maintenance man, if he had known what happened, when he was eventually questioned, never said a word. Who would believe him anyway? For now, it was between Akiva and me.

I can't say I was surprised that, months later, all the protestors, no matter how violent or destructive of property or, as I had seen, potentially murderous, were let off with nary a legal scratch by the same Manhattan district attorney who convicted a former president of a felony that had never before existed.

At virtually the same time as the DA's generosity, if we could call it that, leaked emails from the Columbia administration appeared complaining of something called "Jewish privilege," an odd construct considering world history, but hardly astonishing in today's America.

I didn't tell Maya I felt a tad jealous of the Golem acting on his own. I wished I could do something that brave. It was an embarrassing, almost humiliating, emotion on my part. He was supposed to take orders from his rabbi. Even Rabbi Loew is said to have had to restrain his Golem when the entity became what we might call overly zealous, destroying state property and threatening to get the Jews of Prague in more trouble than they were in the first place. This was scarcely the case in this situation. The entity's actions were entirely positive to the extent of saving a life, in probability a gentile life, but equally important in the eyes of our religion and, of course, G-d.

Still, I wanted my rabbinic authority back. Was there something wrong with that? After all, G-d had placed the Golem in my hands. It must have been for a reason. Had I been remiss in forgoing my responsibility? Had I been too passive and, in my apathy, unintended as it was, frustrated my charge and inspired the Golem to take matters in his own clay hands?

That I did express to Maya when I returned to Nashville.

"You know the remedy for that," she said, having spent years watching me dither about this and that.

I suppose I did.

But before I did anything else, I checked in with Max to see how his studies were going. He remained frustrated by his tutor's limited knowledge of astronomy. "Not the next Copernicus," he alleged, "But who could be like that?" he added, referencing the sixteenth-century Pole who is said to have been the first to define the heliocentric solar system. But Max was pleased that Jack hit fungos with him in the off hours. His teacher was evidently quite the athlete and could hit a ball the proverbial "country mile." He also knew some Mandarin and was teaching him. "Nix xi huan zhong quo de shi wu ma," Max repeated, grinning proudly as he translated. "Do you like Chinese food?"

"Do you?"

The boy sighed impatiently.

Then I remembered. "Szechwan Palace. Orange Chicken."

Max nodded, seemingly relieved. "You did take me to my first Chinese restaurant... *Grandpa,*" he said, emphasizing the last word as if there were something ironic about it. I decided not to pursue the subject. The boy clearly had no interest in changing tutors.

No further Judaism instruction was in the offing for Ed's

conversion that morning because he and Tamara were house hunting, so I went from Max through the garage to the safe room. Before I entered, I noticed that Jorge had installed not one, but three cameras trained on the door and the surrounding area. Inside, the Golem was in its usual place, supine on the floor like a mummy in a museum's Egyptian wing. I stood over it silently for a few moments, inspecting its body as closely as I could. I wanted to see if it was any worse for wear after its activities in Morningside Heights. But the clay appeared untouched, as if it had never left the safe room in the first place. Finally and after having given due consideration to the escalating number of possibilities, foreign and domestic, before me and given the global epidemic of what I had come to think of not just as antisemitism but baldly as Jew Hatred, Palestinian demonstrations erupting everywhere, even here in Nashville, I knew the time had come to throw away a lifetime of ambivalence and to act. I had settled on the one I knew in my heart to be, despite previously rejecting or fearing it, far and away of the utmost temporal and spiritual importance for our benighted people. To execute this, I knew I would have to enlist the aid of Jorge, but, other than Maya, there was no one I trusted more.

The moment of decision had come. Was I going over the line? I found myself trembling, but reassured myself with the words of a rabbi far more famous than I could ever dream of being, "If not now, when?"

"Golem, stand," I said in a firm voice that eerily resembled how actors playing master sergeants salute their recruits in Hollywood movies. "Stand now," I continued, but the Golem's body was already moving, the clay undulating. I realized I hadn't first recited the "Shema" as I usually did, but it didn't seem to matter. In moments, the Golem was on its feet, looming above me. Nevertheless, I repeated the prayer in Hebrew before issuing the order I was about to give, considering its extreme gravity.

I stood there another moment, gathering myself. Then, utilizing the assistance and advice for which I had drafted Jorge, I took the night vision video camera we had purchased together and affixed it to the Golem's chest. We had chosen that type instead of the kind that were attached to the forehead in order not to obscure the *aleph*, *mem*, and *tav* for truth that, according to a tradition I now firmly believed, might cause the being to abort. Jorge had programmed the camera to stream directly to my cellphone and, as I asked him, to his as well for insurance. I had bought burner phones for both of us for the purpose. We verified that the system was functioning properly. I did so again and was able to see my own face reflected in the phone from the Golem's camera.

Once more I paused, taking a breath to slow my rapidly beating heart that was approaching tachycardia. Then I spoke in English, doing precisely what I had originally told myself not to do. It was too late to turn back.

"Golem, I, your rabbi, Rav Ben Golub of Temple Bethel, have an urgent task for you. According to reports, roughly 120 Israeli and American hostages are still held by the Hamas jackals in Gaza after many months under the worst imaginable conditions, presumably locked away in a labyrinth of underground tunnels the terrorists dug from which to murder as many of our people as possible and then to destroy the state of Israel. You are to go there and liberate those hostages, bring them back, even if dead, no matter what it takes or what adversary you may need to kill or maim in the process... But be careful not to harm innocent civilians," I added as something of what seemed a guilty afterthought, not that I was sure, from polling I had read, that such innocent people even existed.

I stood there and stared at the Golem, standing erect and

motionless in front of me. It was hard to say if he had heard or understood a word I said.

All through this process, the Golem did not flinch or move, although for one split second it seemed he or it wanted to say something, almost to be human. Was it agreement, a warning? It was impossible to say because it remained silent, that urge to speak seemingly an illusion.

Finished, I stepped back and again said the "Shema," adding "Go with G-d," in English, as much for my sake as for his.

"You told him to kill people?" Maya said that night. We were in our bedroom with the door shut.

"Only if necessary to get them out," I repeated with a hint of impatience, since I had already explained that.

"It's not like you... We were once members of 'Peace Now,' remember? You gave speeches for them. Land for peace."

"Nobody believes that anymore. I don't."

"So you're okay with breaking the Ten Commandments?"

"I did before."

"But not the Sixth. Not 'Thou Shalt Not Murder'."

"G-d did. He smote the firstborn of the Egyptians."

She looked at me for several seconds and then exhaled. "Actually, I'm proud of you. You've become the most amazing rabbi." She leaned over and gave me a gentle kiss on the cheek. "What we used to call the sisterhood would frown, but I'd hate to be in your shoes, to be honest. How're you feeling?"

"Okay... Actually, a bit freaked out."

VI

Indeed that was true. I *was* a bit freaked out, more than a bit, especially in the small hours of the morning when the world appears more frightening and paranoia rules the mind. Why was this happening to me? I was finding it overwhelming.

For several days, it was virtually impossible to sleep, and I began taking melatonin, upping the dosage until it finally put me out, creating vivid dreams as that hormone tends to do. It was as if I had fallen into one of Goya's dark etchings, "the sleep of reason produces monsters." I was surrounded by bats, much like those in the etching, flying at me until I woke up, staring into the night, trying to reassure myself that this was a dream, that it wasn't real. I didn't know then these bats were a precursor of something I would actually experience.

After a while the dreams normalized to some extent, one taking me on a tour of my life, way back to my divorce and when my first wife found her new husband, Randall, the CEO of a human rights organization, which led to my ex dividing her time between Geneva and a mansion in Newport, Rhode

Island. Was I jealous? Yes, in real life, but not so much in the dream that continued on for reasons that were not clear to a trip Maya and I took to Israel, her first, when we met some kooky individuals, all American expats, who were helping to breed red heifers back in Texas. They told us that when the heifers were ready for sacrifice, it was a signal for Jews to retake the Temple Mount, destroy Al Aqsa, and build the Third Temple, thus causing World War III. I warned them, even in the dream, but by then these zealots had vanished and I was walking with Max on a beach. I was apologizing to the boy for dragging him into events well beyond his age but Max told me not to worry. He and the Golem could handle things. Oddly, when he did so, he was suddenly 18 or 19 and wearing a uniform.

I was about to ask why when the burner phone on my end table suddenly vibrated, awakening me. Was it a video finally coming through? No, it was a text message from the very Max. "See me quick, grandpa. Emergency."

I said "*Modeh ani*" in a rush. Ten minutes later, I was sitting with the boy in my office. It was 6:35 AM.

"How'd you get the number?" I asked him, holding the phone up to him. He rolled his eyes in the pre-teen equivalent of "Elementary, my dear Watson." I should have known.

"So what is this about?"

"You've been hacked," said the eleven-year-old.

"What? It's a burner phone."

"Stingray."

"What?" I repeated.

"Burners are old tech now," he informed me, responding to what clearly was a clueless expression on my face. "They figured out what to do years ago. The government put up these little towers called 'Stingrays' to monitor calls and texts before they get to the, you know, company towers that are everywhere."

"And we've got one of those... Stingrays?"

"Behind the hill from the synagogue. I hiked over and saw it myself. It's kind of shiny and new."

"So it's reading my transmissions..."

"And blocking them if it wants to."

I looked up at the hills visible from the office window, scanning for a tower that I couldn't see. Was this life or was I still in the dream? It seemed to be the real Max sitting in front of me. My blood pressure must have gone with it. How'd that happen so quickly? Did the government think I was a drug dealer or a terrorist? Or had they already learned about my real activities? That was far more likely. For all I knew, they were probably aware of the phones from when I went through self-checkout to pay for them at Walmart. How sloppy of me to allow my identity to be digitized so readily. There must be plenty of anonymous ways to buy burners. I felt like a fool. Was this the end of any possible communication with the Golem, assuming he still existed? And what was the kid doing checking into my communications anyway? I should have been angry with him. I'm his grandfather. He could show some respect. I could be in jeopardy for treason and God knows what with the other five thrown in as well, of which the boy himself was one.

But I knew better. He was looking out for me. "Come with me," I said and led him down into the garage, where I unlocked the door to the safe room. Not surprisingly, it was empty except for the new tornado paraphernalia Jorge had bought to replace what was destroyed from the original twister, the one that had brought forth *el monstro.*

"He isn't here," I said redundantly.

"You sent him away. To Israel."

"How'd you know what I was doing, you nosey ..." I blurted before stopping myself. I loved him, and it seemed I needed him. "What do we do now? I'm blind," I added, gesturing to my compromised phone that at this point wouldn't even make it as a paperweight because so associated with embarrassing failure.

Max grinned, as if to say, in modern parlance, I got this. He reached into the pocket of his lightly stained cargo shorts, which might have benefited from one more trip through the washing machine, and extracted a white envelope with a rubber band around it. He handed it to me. I slipped off the band and opened it, extracting two small cell phones of the old flip style. They were grimy and looked as if no one had so much as wiped them with a spare Kleenex since the 1990s.

"These work," he said. "They go through Stingrays like water."

"Where'd you get them?"

"Eddie."

"Who's Eddie?"

"One of the regulars in Alpharetta By Night. It's a chat room that opens around two a.m. They encrypt everything. And then I double-encrypt with Japanese software, using a VPN with an IP from New Zealand. Super safe. Alpharetta's the best place to get psychedelics in Fulton County. They're always looking for new chemical combos that aren't illegal. But good luck because the police are there too."

What was this? I didn't want to believe my grandson was taking drugs or smoking dope. I hadn't seen the slightest indication. It would be a very bad sign at his age. I didn't want to think my son and daughter-in-law would allow that to happen either.

"I know it's not true, but I have to ask as your grandfather. You're not... a buyer by any chance?"

"Are you kidding, Grandpa? No way. Your body is your temple. In my generation, we know better. I'd never do anything like that. Some of us anyway."

"Good. I'm glad."

"You guys were different. Dad told me you used to smoke marijuana and eat magic mushrooms in the house. Up until he was ten. Then you quit."

"Well, I..."

"That was a bad thing to do."

"It was. Very. I really did stop."

"You should ask forgiveness on Yom Kippur."

"I have—about twenty times."

Max looked pleased. Or was it relieved? Anyway, he took one of the flip phones from me and turned it on, then pressed a couple of buttons. His mouth widened. "Grandpa, you're going to love this." He held out the phone so I could view it. "You picked a great body cam."

"By accident," I said, before I stared at the screen. My mouth dropped open too. The phone was displaying a remarkably crisp image of the interior of an iron-girded underground tunnel, which appeared identical to those built by Hamas and had been reproduced online or on television for months. Superimposed was a GPS location: *Khan Yunis, Gaza Strip*, followed by a time stamp that was eight hours ahead.

The image was moving forward, as if the camera were strapped to some person or, more likely, some*thing*. It turned left into another corridor, similarly constructed but reinforced with concrete, passing a toilet with a half-open swinging door and then continuing down another tunnel corridor, longer than the first. I heard heavy steps that had the *thump thump* of the Golem accompanied by a static-like sound that might have been from an electrical or air conditioning system. Or was it an alarm?

The camera focused on a thick iron door covered with what I assumed were warnings in Arabic, written in yellow. It paused there for several seconds, as if it were contemplating the painted words, then slammed through the heavy metal as if it were paper. A siren blared. There was a loud rattle of machine gun fire, and the Golem—what else could it be—moved quickly down another corridor where I caught a glimpse of some fleeing figures wearing keffiyehs, hurling grenades as they backed away, flashes of light temporarily blinding the view, until the Golem began swiftly descending a ladder that led hundreds of feet deeper into the tunnel network.

"Holy shit!" was all I could muster, bypassing whatever rabbinic decorum was left in me.

That was just when the video started flickering and went black, the machine gun fire dimming, and then becoming barely audible.

Max shrugged. "Too deep to transmit. When he comes up, it'll be fine."

"Unless he's splattered in clay bits on a tunnel wall."

"He's a Golem, grandpa," said the boy.

I was about to say something from the dark corner of my mind, but I thought better of it and wrapped my arm around the boy. He had more faith than I did. And at least my plan, as outlandish as it seemed to me – a hope and a prayer, as they say – appeared to be working. Perhaps something good would come of it. Praise G-d, it would. The hostages would be freed if any were still alive. The likes of Sinwar and his crew would be no more. I knew it sounded crazy, but it wasn't crazier than anything else.

I went upstairs, sending Max back to his studies, not that he needed them, and making a note to fill in Maya, who was at work. I entered my office to find Tamara standing there.

"Jorge let me in," she explained. "There's something I had to warn you about... in person." I worried for a second something had gone wrong with Ed but she quickly took things in another direction. "The police came around to my office this morning. It was out of nowhere. They've reopened the investigation of Allison's murder."

That was strange. "Still Salvadoran gangs? Or is it Venezuelan this time?"

She shook her head. "Something very odd. They discovered the killer was in Mobile, Alabama, just hours before he murdered Allison. They can't figure out how he got here so quickly. Did you know that?" Yes, of course I did. From Max, a long time ago. I tried to recall if I had told her as well, but Tamara was already moving on before I could ask or remember. "They had a lot of questions. Most of them were pretty meaningless. But, at the end, they wanted to know if I knew you."

"What did you say?"

"I acknowledged that I took a class of yours, since it's easy to find out, but I kept it vague."

"Did they mention the tornado?"

She shook her head again. "There were three of them, a man and a woman from Metro Nashville and a guy who didn't say much. The man and the woman were friendly. But the third guy didn't seem to be paying attention. He was looking down at his hands all the time, as though he were inspecting his cuticles.... He was the one who asked if I knew you at the end."

"And he wasn't with Metro?"

"ATF... He gave me his card and said if I learned anything, I should contact him."

She handed me the card. Ethan Rush, it said, special agent, Bureau of Alcohol, Tobacco, Firearms, and Explosives. Explosives? I, of course, knew of the ATF and its involvement with gun ownership, but didn't know they had added explosives to what we might call their dance card. I immediately learned via my phone that they had. They had recently been made responsible for federal laws on destructive devices, including bombs.

What would the Golem be considered? ATF offices were in D. C., so he seemed to have traveled for the investigation.

"Any idea how long he's going to be here?"

Tamara shook her head a third time. "But he did ask me something after that I thought was weird... He heard the synagogue backyard had a beautiful remodel, and he wanted to know if I knew the landscaping contractor."

As I have mentioned, I am no lawyer and skipped over the one course that might have helped in rabbinical school, but like many people these days, I had come to know that telling a material lie to the FBI is a crime. Would that also be true of the ATF?

Tamara, wise woman, must have suspected that as well because, before I could ask what she had answered, she continued, "I pretended not to hear him and changed the subject."

That was a relief—maybe—but a cold sweat had broken out at the back of my neck. "You'd better go," I said. "You might not want to be seen here for a few days."

"Am I excused from class?" she said with a forced grin, adding, "He was also aware Ed and I are engaged. He congratulated me."

VII

I apologize for the interruption, but I feel compelled to share a brief two-part article I wrote several years ago—long before a Golem or anything similar entered my life—while teaching in Maine. In writing it, I now realize I was searching for relief, or even an escape, from questions about faith but was unable to find it. Now, I am confronting that challenge again. This topic has been a concern for some of the greatest thinkers throughout history, and my contribution is, at the very least, minor, based on the responses I received from about half a dozen online magazines I submitted it to—only one of which bothered to send me a rejection notice.

In full disclosure, I am also appending this because I need a time out from my account of events that, as you may suspect, were about to become considerably more dangerous—physically, emotionally, legally, and every conceivable way-- to my family, friends, and me, let alone the world at large.

(NOTE: I have referred to God in the article with the pronoun He only as a convenience. Also, I have refrained from the orthodox Jewish tradition of not spelling out His name, because I was aiming for mass distribution and didn't want to distract from what I was saying.)

So, without further ado...

Why Doesn't God Intervene in Human Affairs—or Does He?

At this moment, with wars raging in Eastern Europe and the Middle East and the threat of nuclear annihilation greater than ever in history, many are again asking the questions that homo sapiens, and quite possibly their ancestors, have been wanting to know since time immemorial:

Where's God in human affairs?

Why isn't He intervening to save us from ourselves?

Why isn't He, the all-powerful one, snuffing out evil?

Why has He allowed multiple holocausts to happen, not just the Jewish one?

As the creator of the universe, why does He let humanity suffer so much?

Is He fed up with human beings? (Who wouldn't be?)

Why do we even bother to pray if God never answers?

Why is God seemingly so disinterested in human affairs?

That last phrasing may be the most significant because the Supreme Being we are told about in the Bible is anything but disinterested or absent. During Exodus, he is watching the Jewish people like a hawk, judging them badly when they err, as in the Golden Calf resulting in Moses breaking the tablets of the Ten Commandments, and supporting them against their heathen enemies when they follow His path, worshipping Him, the invisible God, in very specific ways (see Deuteronomy) according to his many instructions.

In recent times, though, most of the time, if you think about it, He seems absent—vanished—except in cases when something positive occurs that might seem like divine intervention, but could just as easily be an accident caused by the random flow of events. Theologians and others explain that this is because we really don't know God's plan or His purpose. They are unknowable, or He is working on a schedule beyond our understanding, even beyond good and evil. Others say He wants us to learn righteous behavior, to turn to him, of our own volition. Otherwise, we would have learned nothing. God is teaching us free will.

Still others, Deists, tell us that God created the heavens and the Earth—and presumably the rest of the ever-expanding universe—and then went home (wherever that is) to leave us to our own devices.

Are any of these answers satisfactory? Has God no compassion for all the human suffering around the world? Has He abandoned us because of our sinful behavior?

Who is to blame for this?

Et Tu, Dostoevsky?

As a child growing up, I was aware of the prejudice against Jews, but it virtually never affected me personally. I was living in that era, post the Holocaust and World War II, which was perhaps the best in recorded history for people of my faith.

And yet there were intimations. Around the age of eight I became fascinated with "Ripley's Believe It or Not." It was there I first encountered the couplet "How odd of God/To choose the Jews."

I didn't feel particularly comfortable with being "chosen" and wondered if that didn't make others jealous and hence hostile. It wasn't until I was in rabbinical school that I was really aware of Deut. 7:7.8:

"It was not because you were more in number than any other people that the LORD set his love upon you and chose you, for you were the fewest of all peoples; but it is because the LORD loves you, and is keeping the oath which he swore to your fathers, that the LORD has brought you out with a mighty hand, and redeemed you from the house of bondage, from the hand of Pharaoh king of Egypt."

That didn't reassure me all that much. The discomfort remained. We were reviled, I had learned somewhere in my early teen years, for the Jews having killed Christ. Someone told me that might not be true because the gospels alleging as much were written years after Christ's death, and Pontius Pilate had a greater motivation—the preservation of the Roman Empire- to crucify the would-be Messiah. Who knew? I certainly didn't.

Before I went to rabbinical school, I had thought about being a writer, a career, perhaps out of fear, that I abandoned. Nevertheless, it had led me as a young man to read one of the greatest of all novelists, one who had a more powerful effect on me than any other because of his extraordinary compassion for human suffering beyond any author I read or even knew about, Fyodor Dostoevsky.

He was a man whose depiction of that suffering was even deeper than that of Charles Dickens, and yet I had heard he was also an antisemite. At first I dismissed it—trying to be understanding—but then I read this in "The Diary of a Writer":

"It is not for nothing that over there [in Europe] the Jews rule all the stock-exchanges, it is not for nothing that they control capital, that they are the masters of credit, and it is not for nothing—I repeat—that they are also the masters of

international politics, and what is going to happen in the future is known to the Jews themselves: their reign, their complete reign is approaching! What is coming is the complete triumph of ideas before which sentiments of humanity, the thirst for truth, Christian feelings, the national pride of European peoples, must bow."

It goes on from there, ending with "... from the very lowest Kike to the highest and most learned philosopher and rabbi-Kabbalist: they all believe that the Messiah will again unite them in Jerusalem and bring by his sword all nations to their feet."

Et tu, Dostoevsky, indeed.

I believe none of that, and no other Jew I know has ever mentioned to me that they wished to bring all nations to their feet, by sword or other means.

It almost seems as if the great novelist was one of the original authors of "The Protocols of the Elders of Zion."

What are we to make of this when antisemitism runs rampant on the streets of America and Europe as never before in our lifetimes, except for those few Holocaust survivors still alive?

My only conclusion is that they blame us—the "Chosen"—for the aforementioned God's absence from the world and the consequent enduring man's inhumanity to man—that and a global reversion to tribalism.

VIII

So much for rejected articles. I can see now I was writing on a subject for which I was not qualified. In fact, few are.

Back to events as they transpired.

It didn't take long before I was contacted by Ethan Rush of the ATF. He asked me to come down to an office in downtown Nashville for an interview. I weighed bringing a lawyer but rejected the idea for two reasons. I thought it would seem too suspicious at this point, and I also, to be candid, didn't have one I trusted, even if there could be one. It would be putting the attorney-client privilege to a test it would be unlikely to pass.

Anyway, I had a plan. I had decided to tell him the truth.

The meeting took place in a government building off 2nd Ave. Rush-- a man of medium build I guessed to be somewhere in his fifties with short, grey-flecked hair, dressed neatly in a white shirt with a pale blue regimental tie that nearly matched the color of his eyes, rose to greet me with a firm handshake. "Thank you for coming, Rabbi," he said, while gesturing to a stenographer who looked to be about fifteen but must have been older. "This is Ms. Haddad, who takes notes for us."

"How do you do?"

"Rabbi, my colleagues sent me down here to investigate the murder of Allison Carter."

"So I've been told."

"You have?"

For a second, I reconsidered telling him the truth, particularly about my friends, but he would find out anyway—about everything. My first thought, as the Zen Buddhists say, was best.

"Tamara Klein, a member of our congregation, informed me that you had spoken to her."

He hesitated as if processing that. "What did she tell you?"

"That you had learned the killer had been in Mobile only a couple of hours before he murdered Tamara's

niece, Allison, here in Nashville, that you wanted to speak with me about that as well as about the new landscaping in the back of our synagogue. To save you the effort, I will answer right now that they are related. In fact, the explanation for both is identical."

Rush stared at me, then glanced briefly at Haddad. "What do you mean by that?

"What I said. They come from the same source."

"I'm not sure I understand what you're saying." He looked down at his notes as if to reassure himself of something. "The extraordinarily rapid movement of Mr. Antonio Diaz Cabral from Mobile to Nashville and the overnight creation of this landscape at your synagogue have... a similar cause?"

"Exactly... It was the Golem.":

"The what?"

"Golem."

"Go-lim?" He accented the second syllable, leaning in closely as if he had misheard me.

"Go-lem. It's part of the Jewish tradition, although some say it existed before. A giant made of clay or earth used by rabbis to fight discrimination against our people."

"I see." Rush glanced at Ms. Haddad, who was furiously taking notes. "Let me be clear," he said. "You're saying a clay giant called a Golem is working under your supervision to do these things?"

"Traditionally, yes. They are supposed to obey their rabbis. But this particular Golem seems to act on his own as well. They are creatures of God, after all, as we all are, and He can determine their actions. It was without my knowledge that the Golem went to Mobile and came back with this murderer, Cabral, leaving him in the exact spot where he killed Allison Carter and then breaking his legs so he could not move and would be found there by authorities... Golems typically do not kill. They render evil people harmless, principally antisemites."

I heard Ms. Haddad groan. "And where is this Golem now?" said Rush. "At your synagogue?"

"He has been, but now he is away. On a mission."

"From you... Or from God?" The agent did not bother to hide the undertone of sarcasm in his voice.

"From me, in this instance... Although I can't be sure, as we speak, he is probably somewhere in the Hamas tunnels under the Gaza Strip. He is there to free the hostages, those that are still alive. "

There was a long pause. "Have you been seeing a psychiatrist?"

"Is that a professional question ... or personal?"

"Call it personal for the moment. It's difficult to believe a word you're saying. It makes no rational sense, unless you are lying deliberately."

"I'm not lying. And I have seen psychiatrists in the past, during a divorce. But not recently."

"You might want to reconsider.... So this, um, Golem is under Gaza?"

"Yes, as I mentioned, to free hostages or bring back their remains. Also, to capture the despicable human beings who perpetrated this horrible war in the first place."

"What despicable human beings?!" Ms. Haddad blurted out, her eyes bulging. "You mean the despicable Israelis who bomb innocent children and starve an entire population? It's geno--"

"Miss Haddad," Rush remonstrated. "Please... not your job, remember? Also, under the circumstances, that is entirely unnecessary."

He clearly thought I was out of my mind.

"Rabbi Golub, do you attest that everything you have told us today is true?" He nodded to Haddad, who, calming down slightly, started scribbling away.

"I do."

"You realize this can be entered into the record in court."

"I assume so. Yes."

"That it puts you under possible charges of perjury, not to mention other yet more serious legal matters, including FARA, being the unregistered agent of a foreign power."

"I understand, although I have had no connection with any foreign power in this instance."

"Do you have anything else to add at this time, you think might be helpful to us in the investigation of this crime?"

"No, I don't. I've already told you what happened.... But I am curious how you came to know about our new landscaping."

"I am not authorized to reveal sources and methods. That is all for now, rabbi. Thank you for coming in. I assume you will keep us apprised of your whereabouts in the near future as we resolve this matter."

I was going to mention the obvious—that they were capable of knowing where I was anyway—but thought better of it. I had left the new flip phone at home in what I hoped was a place no one would find but wondered if it was really as secure in its content as Max had led me to believe. Nevertheless, the first thing I did when I returned was to open that flip phone to see what my charge was up to on the other side of the world, but it was still not transmitting.

As soon as possible, I told Maya what had happened. She was naturally anxious but understood what I had done. Putting all of us in such jeopardy was not pleasant, but as my wife immediately realized, we would all be anyway. It was better to assert the truth as quickly as possible, since in the end, there was no other explanation. G-d had put us in this situation by presenting us with this Golem, and He/She or It undoubtedly had a reason. This was for us to discover or, more likely, to live out. If this entailed being in legal jeopardy or even in prison, we wouldn't be the first. It was only young Max for whom I had concern in that regard. From what the kids call a "Spidey Sense," I had long suspected he would prove to be closer to the center of all this than we would have wished. Also, I had the sense that we were being watched for longer than I knew, not just in the now-normal way of our increasingly surveilled society, but specifically. Fortunately, G-d was watching the watchers. What He would do about it was another question.

Ed filled me in on his interview with Rush when we met in a few days for his conversion lesson. He had taken the same tack as Tamara—they had obviously conferred—and was vague in his responses. They hadn't pressed him, although he reported Ms. Haddad gave him a nasty look when he acknowledged he was converting to Judaism. I worried that he was being set up, that we were all being set up, but it is what it is, as they say. So we moved on to the conversion process. Ed had learned a lot since we had talked. Apparently, he had been rooting around online and discovered sites that would make you fully Jewish in three days, with the blessing of some rabbi who would confirm you on Zoom or Skype. In the past, this was a deliberately arduous process that would take years. Ed had already concluded these Insta-conversions were more than a bit silly. Not surprisingly, they had dollars attached.

"I have a few questions though," he said.

"Who wouldn't?"

"These 613 *mitzvot* you're supposed to obey—how many of them do you really have to do?"

"As many as you can, I guess. Not too many people do all of them."

"*Mitzvot* mean commandments, don't they? Some of them seem to be, well, arbitrary. All those rules from Deuteronomy about how and when to worship, even not shaving your head in the morning. Where does that come from?"

"It's a demonstration of faith." I smiled. "You know, showing up for the cause."

"No. 132, also from Deuteronomy," he was consulting notes he had on cards. "'The rapist must marry the maiden.' That's pretty weird. Does that include Hamas?"

"I see what you mean—but it was a different time."

"No. 145, from Leviticus. 'Not to have relations with your daughter's daughter.' We could agree on that, but things must have been pretty wild back then, too. Sounds like something that could happen at 'Burning Man.'"

"Worse. Anything else?"

"Well, kosher laws, actually... like not eating pork or shellfish. That probably comes from ancient times when they made you sick. Today, they're low-calorie proteins and considered extra healthy. And not mixing dairy with meat? Doesn't make much sense."

"Digestion?" I offered, then I added the customary. "By sacrificing something you like, you show humility before G-d."

Ed nodded, then started to smile. "So what do I do? Stop serving Snake River Farms bacon on our breakfast muffins. Everybody loves it... I saw you eating one too not long ago."

"Well, uh, I slip more than I'd like to. Nobody's perfect, as they say in 'Some Like It Hot.'.... You don't have to do this, you know. I mean--"

"No, no. I just wanted to clarify. Jews are supposed to be able to argue, aren't they? ... I'm still with it. Very much."

At that moment, I was not sure I was, when I felt buzzing in my pocket. "Excuse me," I said. "I hope you don't mind." I stood, although I suspected he already had a good idea what was motivating my need for privacy. I walked about fifty feet away into the shadows behind the synagogue, where I took out the flip phone, holding its screen close and tilting it to avoid reflections.

Still, the image was shadowy at best. Before I could make out anything, I was hearing the rat-tat-tat of machine gun fire—or was it assault weapons? I later learned it was an Israeli Tavor, probably a recent X5 model. Then I heard a faint whirring sound that seemed to grow louder. The light came up sharp, almost blinding. I was looking through the iron grillwork constructed in an octagonal Islamic pattern into bright daylight. It was difficult to see because the video camera's exposure and focus were moving back and forth between the black grill and the well-lit street outside. It was clearly Gaza, a small square surrounded by some low Arab buildings, about half of which were bombed out. A half dozen or so Israeli Defense Force troops, their arms at readiness, were grouped near the center around three or four of their comrades who were apparently wounded and on makeshift gurneys. The whirring was approaching a din, even played through the phone's tiny speakers, as one of the troops signaled to what must have been a helicopter that it was okay to land. I could see its bottom now, the ski-like landing gear stirring up dirt. Some of the others began lifting their mates for immediate evacuation. I watched, open-mouthed, as the helicopter settled in the dusty square. It was a large one. Maybe a Blackhawk. Why was I watching this? Where was the Golem? Behind the grill, I imagined. This was the Golem's eye view. The helicopter door opened, and the troops started lifting the wounded aboard. When that was nearly complete, the remaining troops began climbing on with their weapons. It seemed all were being evacuated. The last troops were mounting when two Arab women in black chadors, carrying plastic shopping bags, emerged from a small medical building—at least it had a red cross painted on it—and started across the square, as if headed for another bombed-out building on the opposite side. But at the last second, they veered off and started sauntering casually in the direction of the copter. The last few troops, who were just about to climb aboard, didn't seem to notice. Maybe it was the rotors revving again at high volume. Was I watching a suicide bombing? It was very possible. I wanted to cry out, but it would be fruitless. How could they hear me? This could be the imminent incineration of a helicopter with everyone aboard. Indeed, the chador-clad women began to run at top speed toward the copter. Despite its pointlessness, I started yelling into the phone across six thousand miles, when, suddenly, as if out of nowhere, two intense beams of brilliant white light shot out through the grill straight at the women. Everything seemed frozen in time when an immense explosion rocked the area. Pillars of fire shot into the air in an almost Biblical manner. The screen went white, then black, then white again. There was the sound of an unworldly siren. Then the smoke cleared, preternaturally quickly. Lying on the ground were the two women. Only they were not women. They were men, bearded terrorists. The white light or whatever it was had ripped the chadors off them to reveal two remarkably intact corpses with bandoliers across their bloodied chests. One of them had an arm dismembered, the other half his head blown off. A soldier had jumped out of the helicopter and was photographing them when the grill was pulled back with a harsh grinding sound and left open, dangling on its hinges. Other soldiers emerged from the helicopter and, clutching their rifles, headed cautiously toward the opening, hesitating, then shouting to each other as if they had seen something ahead. But by then, the camera had spun around and was proceeding into the tunnels. It turned a corner and started down another ladder like the one before, when the transmission went black and silent.

The next day, I read the IDF had retrieved the remains of two Israeli hostages from Oct 7, a middle-aged man and a young woman, who had been shot in the head, it was unclear exactly when, by Hamas. There was evidence of torture on their bodies as well as indications that the woman had been raped. They were discovered just inside the entrance to a tunnel near an area I had learned was called the Philadelphi Corridor. Was that where my supposed charge was now? At that point, I had no idea where that corridor was, what it was, or what significance it had. (I would soon enough.)

What had happened to these hostages stirred up the already growing calls for a ceasefire inside Israel because large demonstrations to bring the others home broke out in Tel Aviv, Haifa, and other places in the country immediately after their condition was made known. The U.S. government was echoing the calls. I had tremendous empathy for the relatives and friends of the hostages. Who wouldn't? I could only imagine the pain and anger I would be feeling were I in their shoes. But I wasn't. Something larger had placed me in other shoes, and I knew I had no choice but to proceed with my mission despite whatever doubts would arise.

No mention was made in any of the reports of any blinding light at the scene, whether the primordial "infinite light" of the Kabbalah or one emanating from an ordinary explosion during war, or of the near decimation of a helicopter with a dozen troops aboard saved at the last minute, although there was mention of a strange development, the possibility of a new Israeli superweapon of some sort to have appeared in that area in an article in Qatar's Al Watan daily. The Arab outlet alleged the Israelis may have activated, ahead of schedule, their Iron Beam, a high-energy laser weapon they had been working on for some years at the same company that created the Iron Dome. This next-generation armament, called Shield of Light in Hebrew, was intended to shoot down missiles at a cheaper cost, as well as incinerate drones, artillery, mortar bombs, and just about everything else that moved. It was a science-fiction weapon out of Buck Rogers, the Arab paper called a potential "game changer."

This relatively obscure report was discovered, not surprisingly, by Max, whom Maya was telling me had become quite depressed lately, although he never mentioned it openly. She had witnessed him crying alone in his room. I had sensed the same thing. The boy was almost always by himself, despite our efforts to help him make friends with others who were home-schooled. That wasn't working well. The other children, even the brighter ones, had trouble keeping up with his interests. Max was a victim of his own precocity—I had seen this before in high school when a classmate who had gone to college at 13 ultimately poisoned himself one Saturday while the other students were at tailgate parties. I didn't want to imagine a similar fate for Max, almost all of whose relationships were conducted online —a lonely place to begin with.

And in that regard, it had only gotten worse, I discovered, when I played hooky from my responsibilities and drove down with him to Huntsville to visit the U. S. Space and Rocket Center, partly as a good grandfather and partly to take my mind off things to the extent you ever could. For a while, the boy was enthralled, walking about the giant Saturn V rocket. I was, too, as it took you back to better, more optimistic days. But over lunch, he seemed downcast again. After a bit of prodding, he revealed the cause. He had been canceled by his chat room buddies at Alpharetta By Night and was now blocked from the site. The proximate reason was that he shared a link to how Palestinians purposefully destroyed organic farms left to them intact by the Israelis when they left Gaza in 2005. Although absolutely true, this brought forth immediate cries of Zionist propaganda by a couple of people. The rest of the chat room then piled on within what felt like minutes. Anything smacking of Zionism made its source persona non grata in perpetuity, or pond scum, as Max phrased it.

"Did you show them evidence?" I asked.

"They said everyone knows the Jews controlled the media and it was all lies."

I didn't know how to respond to this other than to say, "They weren't really your friends in the first place. Friends don't do that.... Try to remember in bad times that G-d wants you to be happy."

"He does?" the boy responded, not sounding entirely convinced.

"Well, positive. He wants you to be positive." I was aware it seemed as if I was trying to convince myself as well and added, gesturing to the menu, to save myself as much as him. "How about some killer hot fudge sundaes for dessert?... Don't tell your health nut grandmother."

The sugar high only worked briefly, of course, and it was a long two-hour drive home. He was brooding again, not long after we got into the car. After a few minutes, I said, "Is there something else bothering you?"

"I don't want to talk about it right now."

"Why not?"

"It wouldn't be fair."

"I'm pretty good at keeping secrets. In my capacity as rabbi people tell me a whole lot of things."

"Dunno if it's true," he said and fell silent for a while. I didn't prod him until he continued under his breath, "Jack might be a spy."

"Jack Ripton—your tutor?"

"I'm not sure. He knows Mandarin Chinese but not as much astronomy as I do. It's weird, you know what I mean?"

"Well, there are stranger things in this world, but I do.... We could fire him and get you someone new. It's not —"

No. Don't. It wouldn't be fair. I don't know it's even true. I need proof. And if it is, we need to know who he's working for.

"Max...". I glanced over at him long enough for him to know I was being serious, but not so long as we would have an accident. "That is not your job. You are still very much a child... in your parents' eyes, mine, your grandmothers' and, I might add, the law."

"They're already investigating you. They're probably investigating me."

I didn't know how to respond to that. No doubt he was right. How could that have happened at his age? I felt responsible and protective. "So what would you like me to do?" I finally asked.

"Nothing. Wait. See what happens."

"With the Golem or with Jack?"

"Both.... What choice do we have, grandpa?"

That night, Maya and I did what all couples have been admonished to do for some time—turn off the television and wrap our arms around each other. Only we did it as much out of consolation as out of any romantic impulse this time, and we were soon doing what had become, in our senior years, our version of making love, talking to each other until the small hours of the morning and then paying the price when we had to get up early.

Maya began by telling me Emily Nussbaum had stopped by to inform us that she and her husband were leaving the congregation. "She was very nice, actually. She praised you for trying to be even-handed in class and keeping politics out of it as much as possible. But she said it was getting difficult in their law practice. They were losing clients."

"Can't say I'm surprised."

"But Emily added something creepy as she was leaving. She said be careful. She heard the government was nosing around. I asked what she meant, but she pretended not to hear and headed for her car."

I took that in for a second. Things *were* getting around. But from where? "You know that FARA legislation they talk about all the time on the news. Do you think we really could be in trouble for being unregistered agents of a foreign government?"

"Who knows? I'm more worried about Max, Ben. He shouldn't be involved in this."

"I know. It's bad. I try to shield him but it's hard. He's... a prisoner of his own... extraordinary gifts... Has that Rush guy called you?"

She shook her head. "Maybe we should get a lawyer before he does."

"Who? Harry Merman, who blamed his sciatica for not finishing our wills for six months?"

Maya laughed and then squeezed my hand, as she often did when she saw stress overtaking me. "It's not just Max. I'm heartsick, Maya. The Golem killed two people."

"They were terrorists."

"And all those Israelis protesting against their own government when ... "

"They can't face reality, just like so many here. If Hamas isn't finished off, they'll be back in months. And worse. They never stop."

As usual, she was tougher than I was. "You're right."

"Not about everything. I was wrong to bring up a lawyer. It was a dumb reflex. We already have a lawyer. The ultimate one."

"So we do."

"And you were right about just telling the truth. That's what He would want... He, she, or it, as you would say....Get some sleep. You'll feel better in the morning."

"It's already morning."

It wasn't quite, but I managed to fall out in a short while. Soon I found myself dreaming of my childhood, or trying to anyway, not, as I had been doing more often, sleeping fitfully while lost in all-too-realistic violent end-times fantasies out of Daniel, Zechariah, or the New Testament Book of Revelation, the nations of the world battling for control of Jerusalem's Temple Mount, the legendary Armageddon. In those instances, I would force myself to wake up, reminding myself I was a modern man and did not believe in such prophecies.

IX

At this point, I will jump ahead in the narrative several weeks and explain what you may have already suspected—that I would find myself traveling to Israel because I was unable to contact the Golem directly or indirectly and give him instructions personally, as is my rabbinical duty. He had been on his own for quite some time, inaccessible to my phone, deep under Gaza, and I feared, as had Golems before, he might in unwitting zeal perform acts that would create more problems than he solved, ones so dangerous the ramifications could be, at their worst and difficult as it was to admit, global in nature and reminiscent of the dreams I had been having. I had more than a little evidence of that, which I will get to shortly. You could say it was all G-d's will, but how would I know?

This would be my fifth visit to Israel. At my age and in my profession, it should have been more. So many rabbis led annual tours of the holy sites to enlighten their congregations and, to be honest, augment their often mediocre salaries. But early on, I discovered I had a serious jet lag problem, whether in economy or, later, when I could afford it or someone was paying, in a lie-flat business-class seat. Either way, I would be walking around in a haze seemingly forever, barely remembering my name and address, both on my arrival and my return, when others were fine in a day or two. And the Hasidim standing in the airplane aisles or congregating near the restrooms to pray on a schedule during the 13-hour flight didn't make it easier. So many of them had giant families, with children who never slept. I would try not to notice, but it was hard not to hear them. I always wondered how they knew what time to pray as we swept through time zones. I asked one once, and he told me they focused on their faith and tried not to be distracted by the airline's blandishments. It was weirdly akin to "raw dogging," a new fad, if you could call it that, where men, it was largely them, stared straight ahead on long-haul flights without eating, reading, playing computer games, watching movies, or otherwise entertaining themselves, only gazing directly at the flight map for hours on end.

It was Max who first told me about that trend. He was also the immediate reason I made this trip. It was his loose lip that was sinking the ship, not that I blamed him. It could have been any of us in a way, and it was my poor judgment that put us in harm's way in the first place. Already there were intimations— well, more than that— of trouble ahead when Ethan Rush came to the synagogue himself, this time putatively to interview Maya. He drove up unannounced in an unmarked car, accompanied by two Nashville Metro police cars. Jorge had no choice but to let them in.

Instead of Ms. Haddad, Rush brought Nicholas Peebles, who was introduced as a special agent working with the intelligence community, which I later assumed, when I met him, meant the FBI or the CIA. But at first, I sat in my office while the interview took place in our lobby. As Maya told me, Rush showed her before-and-after pictures of the synagogue backyard, taken three days apart.

"You are still saying this Golem did it?" he asked her, pronouncing it correctly this time.

"Yes. We're very happy with it. We use the gazebo all the time."

"Did this, er, Golem transport the murderer of Allison Carter the 400 miles from Mobile to Nashville in under three hours?"

"I have no way of knowing, but I assume so."

"And this, er, Frankenstein monster is currently in the tunnels under Gaza?"

"I wouldn't call him a Frankenstein monster, but as far as I know, yes."

"As far as you know...?"

"Well, I'm not..."

"Not what?"

"Not the rabbi in charge of the Golem."

At that point, Maya told me, Rush glanced over at Nicholas Peebles, who nodded, and soon enough, I was asked to join the conversation. Maybe that was the intention in the first place. So began a discussion — more like an interrogation, as it turned out — whose result was my aforementioned flight to Ben Gurion Airport. Peebles, a man in his forties with a shaved head, was dressed in what seemed a rather trendy suit for one who presumably worked for one of the three-letter intel agencies. It turned out he did work for one, but not one I had ever heard of, although I knew there were many, seventeen I had read. According to his card, he was a special agent of the National-Geospatial-Intelligence Agency (NGA), whatever that was. He sported slightly tinted glasses with a rounded frame that reminded me of the ones John Lennon used to wear. Perhaps they were coming back. I had seen several people in them at the coffee shop.

He took me aback with the first question once we were seated, but I did my best not to show it. Rush had taken a pad from his pocket and was taking notes. "Rabbi, are you familiar with an internet chat room called Alpharetta By Night?"

"Yes, I... have heard the name, but have never seen it. I don't... do that."

"Do what?"

"Go on internet chat rooms."

"Then where did you hear of it?"

I hesitated briefly before telling the truth this time. "From my grandson."

"Menahem?"

"We call him Max."

"I see... What do the letters RUR mean to you?"

"In what way?"

"Do they call anything to mind?"

"Nothing in particular."

"Nothing?"

"Not that I can think of from the top of my head." What was he driving at?

"You were an English teacher, weren't you? In Maine. You should have heard of the famous Karel Capek, the Czech writer, seven-time nominee for the Nobel Prize in Literature."

"Yes, but... I don't think I ever read him."

"Not very impressive... Menahem... excuse me, Max... evidently did."

"He's a precocious young man." I glanced over at Maya who was frowning.

"He wrote about that work on 'Alpharetta By Night.'"

Was that before or after he was banned for being a Zionist? I was tempted to ask, but I didn't. I simply said "And...?"

"R.U.R. is a play by Capek. 1920. Some call it one of the progenitors of the science fiction form." Progenitors? The Feds had apparently sent their A-team, the man behind the Lennon glasses. He was far from what most of us conceived of as an FBI agent. The National Geospatial-Intelligence Agency evidently had a higher entry level.

"It's starting to ring a bell. Maybe from some college survey. But I still don't recall reading it."

"R.U.R. stands for Rossum's Universal Robots. Capek's play is where the term 'robot' was invented. Since the author was from Prague, the home of Rabbi Loew three hundred years before, critics theorized that the robot, made of metal, of course, was the modern version of the Golem. Some also relate it to the Frankenstein story, the creation of a mad scientist that runs amok, destroying things no one intended to be destroyed."

"Very interesting," I said, trying to hide the fact that my head was spinning. "Of course, the Golem I have been speaking about is made of mud... somewhat dried out, but still mud.... not metal or anything technological."

"You're sure about that?"

"Absolutely."

He nodded to Rush, who handed him a manila envelope from a folder.

"Our investigation into the peculiarities surrounding the brutal death of Allison Carter... the cries of monster or '*monstruo*', to be precise, by the perpetrator when he was discovered... that his movements across the country made no sense unless he had access to a private jet, unlikely in this case... has taken a strange turn that you might be able to help us with." Peebles reached into the envelope, extracted some photographs that appeared to be 8 by 10, and handed them to me. "These are stills taken from a video camera on an Israeli helicopter near the Philadelphi Corridor in the Gaza Strip."

Attempting with only limited success to restrain my hand from shaking, I looked down at the photographs. One, particularly graphic and taken close-up, revealed something I had not been able to see on the phone. While the terrorists' bodies appeared to be intact, all four of their eyeballs were missing, as if hollowed out by some intense beam of some kind. The other photo, which was grainier, appeared to show the Golem, lurking in the shadows behind the grillwork. My hand started to shake more visibly. Why had I done this? Why had I gotten us into this, all of us? It was selfish and naive of me. But then I realized I hadn't done it. It wasn't me at all, and my hand stopped shaking.

"Can you tell us anything about this? Was that your Golem?"

"I'm not sure, but if so, it was the Golem acting on its own. That's not the traditional way. They are supposed to follow the precise instructions of a rabbi, but I only gave him general directions."

"So who gives him precise instructions then?"

"God."

"I see... Are you aware that in the chat room, your grandson discussed how microchips can be placed in humans and even in animals to make them perform specific actions?"

"No... I mean, I've heard that, but wasn't aware Max was discussing it. I assume he was being theoretical. He discusses many things."

"Rabbi, it would be an understatement to say this Golem, if that's what it is, is interfering in an extremely delicate international situation. I hope you have been entirely candid. As you know, telling untruths to US intelligence officers is a crime."

"I understand that. Yes."

"And we wouldn't want to think you were one of those who

had fallen into the trap of dual loyalties. Such things lead to unwanted legal consequences."

"I have only one loyalty—and that is to God."

That came out spontaneously, surprising myself, and for a second, I could see it had startled Peebles. He hesitated before saying, "Of course. You are a rabbi."

Strangely, for the first time, I actually felt like one. I also could have replied "And apparently what's known as a 'person of interest,'" but restrained myself, though he as much as acknowledged it, saying "Just be aware that you have been meddling in things, affairs of state, that are well beyond your competence and understanding and have put you, your family and friends in jeopardy, not to mention the very lives of the hostages you intend to save. These are the most serious crimes with life-changing consequences. You would be wise to reconsider your actions."

"These are not my actions."

Peebles nodded slowly, looking at me with an expression of something closer to concern that seemed oddly out of character, as if for a moment he was abandoning his government role for something more human. "I understand. Thank you for your time. We will be in touch.... Mrs. Golub." He nodded to Maya as he stood.

"One last thing," he said. "Do you know an Arthur Leventhal?"

"An old friend," I replied. "Lives in Israel, so I don't see him much."

"Well, you will soon, evidently... If, as you say, a divine force has entered your life, you will be seeing things the modern world has rejected, though there are explanations. You and others close to you could be harmed through no fault of your own, even if you have the best of intentions. Take care."

He exited. Rush, who seemed bewildered by what Peebles was saying, followed him out.

"What was that about?" said Maya.

I shook my head.

On the flight to Tel Aviv, I tried not to dwell too much on that visit, Peebles' ominous warning, or his final question about Artie Leventhal, with whom I had recently been communicating about my arrival. I wasn't surprised anymore that they knew. I had been emailing my Israeli friend for a while, starting with concern for his and his family's safety after October 7. As time went on, this shifted into something more than a hint that I might have a reason to go to his now-home country during this time of war. My encounter with Nicholas Peebles may have been the last push, along with discussions with those close to me, for what I'd been thinking about. I had suspected all along that my actions could eventually lead me to cross the Atlantic.

And that same encounter with Peebles had no more than reminded me, after all, what most of us already know—human privacy no longer exists. And given what was transpiring, it was also not surprising that the National Geospatial-Intelligence Agency, charged with tracking everybody and everything, was taking the lead —or one of the leads —in the case —even though I had hitherto never heard of the organization that O learned was known by the acronym GEOINT. Its website, in the tradition of government outlets, was deliberately opaque, though one sentence revealed the extent of its power: "*GEOINT goes beyond describing 'what, where and when' to exposing 'how and why.'*"

How and why? It went beyond what the CIA once purported to do. Tracking Golems would be a unique and undoubtedly educational experience for them, even a challenging one. Would they consider the "monster" to be an "adversary" or a "noncombatant person"? I had wondered why, straight away, they hadn't arrested me for sedition or something like that. It occurred to me that they wanted to use me to track down what I mistakenly, in their view, believed to be a divine being, perfectly capable of eluding even the most advanced GPS. And yet I had no choice. So, as the National Geospatial-Intelligence Agency and all the other myriad spooks obviously knew, I was on the flight to Ben Gurion airport. They undoubtedly knew precisely which seat I was in, the wine I would be ordering to accompany my dinner, and what movies I might be watching or what book I was reading.

They likely also knew just who that woman was sitting next to me. She was young, in her mid- to late twenties, and attractive, with a curvy body and her hair cut short in the style Maya had when we first met. Like Maya, she wore little or no makeup and, remarkably, resembled my wife at that age. I had met Maya before my first wife, Ellen Hoffman, and I split due to mutual recriminations. Whatever guilt I might have had diminished when, only a few months later, Ellen started dating and eventually married a man for whom she seemed much better suited, at least if you measured his bank account that dwarfed mine many times over.

During takeoff, I wondered if I was being paranoid, thinking there might have been something pre-planned about the young woman's uncanny resemblance to my wife. She had arrived at the last moment before takeoff, almost as if the plane were being held for her. She smiled at me apologetically as she took her seat. I nodded back, and that was it, as the El Al jet—most other airlines having canceled their flights due to the war—roared forward and taxied to take off.

Thinking it prudent not to engage her in conversation, I turned on my Kindle, where I had downloaded a book that I had never read in all my years as an English major and teacher, though like nearly everyone, I had seen the movie, "Frankenstein: or the Modern Prometheus" by Mary Shelley. My reasons for finally wanting to read it should be obvious, but I found the author's life story, as recounted in the foreword, so depressing that I didn't want to continue. Like me, Mary had left her first marriage for the love of her life, but Percy Bysshe Shelley died prematurely at age 29 in a sailing accident, leaving her a young and indigent widow. I closed down my Kindle and shut my eyes. But thoughts of Maya immediately flooded my mind, or our discussions--ones we had with Ed and Tamara as well--that had precipitated my making this journey. None of us thought we were Dr. Frankenstein, or that the Golem was some kind of Promethean monster who would harm the innocent. But we didn't want that to be the result of its activities, if only by accident. And to be honest, we feared our government, what it might do to us should Mr. G. cross some invisible line. So all agreed that I must go—Maya and Tamara, the two women, promising to keep a close watch on the vulnerable Max, while Ed vowed to take him to every sports event in town. Arrangements were made with the synagogue for me to go on a short leave. And I made my reservations, all the time asking myself the question—did this mean I didn't trust God or G-d? Or was I fulfilling G-d's requirement? I was, according to the great Rabbi Loew, the current man responsible for the Golem's activities, for good or ill. I had no choice but to pursue the being. No one else could do it, no matter the warnings I had from GEOINT or any other agency, governmental or otherwise. Who else could do it? I ruminated on this for what seemed like hours, but was probably a lot less, when the roar of the engines caused me to drift off into a sounder sleep than I had had in years.

X

I woke up as my head slammed into the window of the 787. The plane was banking sharply. People were screaming. I caught a glimpse of water and land, and the plane banked in the opposite direction, slamming me into the young woman next to me. I didn't have time to say excuse me because the plane banked again in the opposite direction, accompanied by more screams of panic, babies crying, and prayers to God in several languages as the jet dipped suddenly and swerved again, sending some people whose seatbelts weren't fastened out of their seats. Out the window, I could see flares shooting out from under our wing. The plane climbed again, then wobbled a bit before starting to even out to everyone's relief. It then began what felt like a slow descent.

"Ladies and gentlemen, please make sure your seatbelts are fastened," said the pilot through the loudspeaker in English and Hebrew. "We are landing."

Landing? That didn't seem like Tel Aviv out the window. Was it an island? The plane went into a steeper descent. I looked over at the young woman. "You okay?" I asked, meaning myself as well. "I guess so. How are you?" she responded, folding the book she, despite everything, had been doing her best to read. Seconds later, we were jouncing on the tarmac in what was far from the most perfect landing I'd ever experienced. Almost simultaneously, my cellphone started ringing, the burner one I kept in my lower left pocket. I had bought ugly cargo pants for the trip even though Maya hates them. I retrieved the phone and glanced at my neighbor, then bent away from her as if checking for valuables beneath my seat while taking the call. It was Max. "Welcome to Cyprus," he said. "How'd you—" I whispered, not wanting my neighbor to overhear. "Real-time commercial flight reporting. It's public," he said. The young woman was watching me with a querulous look. "Call you back," I replied, clicking off and looking up at her. "We're in Cyprus," I said, trying to make it sound mundane. "So we are," she replied, pointing through the window at a sign reading Larnaca International Airport.

As we were deboarding, the news spread among the passengers, later confirmed by El Al, that our flight had been diverted due to a drone in the area. It was unclear whose drone it was, but we would be delayed for a few hours to ensure our safety. Welcome to the Middle East.

"Houthi," Max told me about the source of the drone. I had called him back from a corner of the waiting room, as far from the other passengers as possible.

"Houthis? You mean from Yemen?" This was the first I had heard of their direct involvement, which would soon become incessant.

"Are you okay, grandpa?"

"No Houthi drones have gotten me so far."

"This one's already been destroyed." I didn't bother to ask him how he knew who it was. The Mossad didn't have to sign him. He already knew as much as they did. "Anyway, I'm fine," I assured him. "This isn't my first international flight."

"Please be extra careful, Grandpa. They're trying to get you. They want to arrest you for treason. Don't let them."

"What? I thought you stopped listening to those chat rooms."

"I didn't hear it in a chat room. They want to trap you. I saw."

I realized I was sounding more irritated than I should have. It was probably the jetlag. There was a serious worry in the boy's voice that I had never heard before. "Okay, okay. I'll be careful. I promise... God sent the Golem. He will protect me."

"I hope so."

"Yes, He will... But...who wants to trap me?"

"Washington people.. For treason. In Israel. You're being set up."

"How do you know?"

"I read their texts. But most of them don't think you're important. They think you're just a goofy nutcase who believes in fairy tales. That's what one of them wrote."

"Great. Maybe they're right.... But then why would they want to arrest me?... And which Washington people?"

"I'm not sure. They all use phony aliases online these days, and most of them hate each other. When I find out who's who, I'll let you know."

What a world. When I was his age, my biggest worry was whether the Cubs' Billy Williams would make the All-Star team for the eighth time. Out of the corner of my eye I could see the young woman coming toward me. She seemed upset, trying to hold back tears. "Sorry, gotta get off," I told Max.

"Wait. Look."

The boy pressed, and the screen switched to something resembling a hailstorm.

"What's that?"

"Hamas shooting at the Golem. Don't worry. They're all bouncing off. Bye."

He clicked, and the image went blank. I wondered why I couldn't see that myself. Maybe I could. I hadn't tried. Anyway, it would have to wait. The young woman was five feet from me. "Are you okay?" she said. That seemed to be the question of the day. "I saw you on the phone and you seemed so..."

"I'm okay. You look a little stressed yourself, I must say. We've been sitting next to each other for half a day without talking. I'm Rabbi Ben Golub."

"Half a night, you should say. I'm envious. You were sleeping like a log. My eyes wouldn't close. At least I had a chance to catch up on my reading." She held up her book. It was the Gittin Tractate of the Babylonian Talmud, in English and Hebrew.

"Heavy stuff."

"You should know."

"More or less."

"My name's Olivia Dreben." We shook hands. I think she was worried at first that I might be orthodox and didn't touch women and had hesitated. Or was it the other way around? "I've been doing *daf yomi*," she said, gesturing to the heavy book she was barely holding in one hand. She grabbed it with the other before it fell. "But I've fallen behind. I assume you've done it."

"No, I haven't. I'm probably too lazy," I added with a smile, downplaying the situation given the obligation involved. She was talking about the pledge: *daf yomi*, to study one of the double-sided Talmud pages with its extensive annotations each day until the entire Babylonian Talmud is completed. It usually takes about 7.5 years. I have friends in rabbinical school who tried it, but almost all of them dropped out. If this young woman was an agent sent by someone to spy on me, she was hiding it behind a heavy workload. "What's kept you behind in your studies? The war?"

She shook her head. "Life," she said with a sigh, accompanied by a wan expression. "Anyway, that part's over... I'm on my way to make aliyah."

"Congratulations. What a time to be doing it. You've got guts."

"Thanks. Big changes coming." She smiled hopefully. " You're on... rabbinical business?"

"I guess you could say that... I feel it's kind of my duty to support our people at this time." I gave her the explanation I had given Israeli security at Dulles before boarding the flight. I had had an answer prepared because I was used to their interrogations from several trips. In a way, it was disingenuous but not wholly. They didn't need to know everything, assuming they didn't anyway, at least not now. In any case, they didn't question what I said. As for the young lady who was making aliyah, immigrating to Israel, that had set off the usual twinge, or more precisely, the uncomfortable, guilty feelings in my stomach that it almost always made on my previous trips. Why hadn't I done that? Why didn't I immigrate, or ascend, as was the literal translation of aliyah? At different times, I had different reasons.

The loudspeaker came on, telling us to reboard. I lined up behind Olivia Dreben. It was a 787, and the line was long. There were still quite a few passengers in front of us when Ms. Dreben suddenly looked irritated, spun around, and started slapping her arm. She did this a couple of times, then stopped and shook herself.

"Mosquito?" I said.

"I don't think so. It just felt like someone was touching me, but no one was there. Then it felt like it was taking my hand, as if it was trying to lead me somewhere, as if we were going dancing or something, if you can believe that. Never felt anything like this. Like I have an invisible stalker, crazy as it seems." She shrugged and smiled. "Long flight, I guess. Does strange things to your body. Maybe I didn't hydrate enough." At that point, she stumbled, almost hitting the woman in front of her who was carrying a small child. "*Slicha*... I'm so sorry," she said, trying both languages. She looked back at me in embarrassment. "Jetlag, the enemy of human existence," I said with a smile for lack of something more original. But I wondered if it was something else, though that was so unlikely. I took a step backwards, allowing her to pass onto the plane more easily.

The flight from Larnaca to Ben Gurion was only an hour—with no drones lurking about--but Ms. Dreben and I had become friends of a sort and picked up our conversation with the openness that occurs when you expect never to see the other party again. I shared with her my feelings about aliyah, how on my earliest trip to Israel in 1988, I had discussed immigrating with my first wife. Walking on the Tel Aviv beach, I suggested we do it.

"What'd she say?"

"Not enthusiastic... We were divorced within a year."

"From not immigrating?"

I shook my head. "I could have done it afterwards by myself, but I didn't."

"Maybe you will sometime." She stared at me a moment, then tapped the Talmud volume in her lap. "Gittin, I might have needed it myself... It's the divorce tractate, as you know." She bit her lower lip and looked down at the book, then back up at me again. "We were in grad school, comp lit at Harvard... together for three years, studied *daf* together ... planned to make aliyah as a married couple, have a house full of children...

when he suddenly ran off with a Chinese girl in the biology department... daughter of some high Communist Party official. I thought it was the tragedy of my life then, but I was probably lucky."

"Sounds as if you were."

"Sorry I mentioned it. I don't want to burden others. Maybe because you're a rabbi or we're strangers on a plane. Anyway, I'm much better now ... Look, Israel." She pointed past me at the lights of Tel Aviv and beyond. "Where will you be staying here?"

"I don't know. It's a bit... up in the air. It will depend on others."

She gave me a long look. "You're going down to the Gaza border, aren't you? Be careful."

"Don't worry."

Maybe it was the tone of my voice, but she kept looking at me with concern. "Be extra careful... You're married, you know." She nodded at the ring on my finger this time.

"I know... You too. Good luck in your new life... And watch out for mysterious happenings... invisible stalkers." I cracked a smile, waving in the air to mime what had happened to her at the Larnaca Airport.

She grinned. "I will... I hope to see you again... Can I ask you a question... as a rabbi?" We were coming in for a landing.

"Of course. I can't promise a good answer, though," I smiled again.

"Do you believe in love at first sight—like in Genesis ... Isaac and Rebekah?"

I thought for a second. "Actually, I do. It was that way for me with my wife. She said only a few words when I knew I wanted to marry her."

"So you believe in the old Yiddish phrase *bashert*... that your soul mate can be predestined?"

"It's almost the same thing, isn't it? Why do you ask?"

My old friend Ahava... she made aliyah five years ago... is friends with a guy in the IDF. She says she couldn't imagine anyone more perfect for me, that we were meant for each other. We're having dinner tomorrow night.

"Well, mazel tov for that! I hope it works out."

"Thank you. Thank you so much. *Baruch HaShem.*"

"*Baruch HaShem.*"

The plane had landed, and the passengers broke into applause, as they had every time I had flown to Israel.

When I got off at Ben Gurion, something pulled me, a kind of faithfulness or duty, I suppose, or maybe a moral imperative, to go directly to Hostages Square, the center for supporting the kidnapped of October 7 that had developed opposite the Tel Aviv Museum of Art. I highly doubted I would find the secretive Golem there, but I had my own suspicion, even more pronounced now, that he always knew where I was and would approve of my pilgrimage. It was late afternoon when I arrived, and the square was filled with people, almost all highly emotional, many crying or with tears in their eyes. A singer on a stage sang a version of the national anthem, *Hatikvah*, that sounded more mournful than ever, while a jumbotron above her broadcast the latest news from the front on a local station. Off to my left, a mockup of a Gaza tunnel had been erected to give all a chance to experience what it looked and felt like.

I assumed it was much shorter than the actual tunnels I had read about that sometimes went for miles, but, probably by design, I couldn't see through to the end. I thought about entering, but hesitated out of what I quickly realized was cowardice of the most pathetic kind, and walked in. I began to feel claustrophobic almost immediately. For a split second---was it jetlag —I thought I saw the Golem but then realized it was an exceptionally tall man holding a "Bring them home!" sign above everyone's heads. On the other end, I emerged, shaken, in a crowd of young female soldiers, most with assault rifles clung casually over their shoulders, a sight you never see in America. "*Beseder?*" one asked, repeating "Are you okay?" recognizing me as an American of a certain age. I nodded sheepishly. Even embarrassed, I was glad I came.

I don't consider myself an expert in military strategy or strategy of any sort—I am a mediocre chess player and, not surprisingly, was defeated in minutes by Max the two times we played—but it always seemed to me, and others obviously, Hamas would hold on to as many hostages as long as they could, likely never give the last ones up. Failing that, they would hold on to their dead bodies, or what was left of them. It was the terrorists' only real bargaining chip against a superior army, and they would play it to the very end, keeping the Israelis and the rest of the world guessing how many of the kidnapped were still alive.

On the one hand, the only solution I could see would be to blow the lot of them off the face of the Earth as quickly as possible. Still, on the other hand, I had overwhelming sympathy for the tearful people filling the square waiting for their loved ones or their relative's loved ones or their friend's loved ones or their friend's friend's loved ones. I could only imagine how I would react were I in their shoes. It was hard to think of a word that could describe it, imagining your son, or worse in this instance, your daughter, nearly starving, trapped in a tiny dark room in a tunnel under Gaza with a hideous guard who was deciding whether to rape her or already had. Heartsick? Desolate? Inconsolable? Devastating? None of them fit, nor did anything capture the mixture of rage and despair I saw all around me as I walked. But it was clear at the same time that in all their outrage and frustration with their government, the demonstrators were doing Hamas a favor. The terrorists wanted nothing more than to drive Israeli society apart. It was their secondary, maybe their primary, motive, the desired outgrowth of their hostage harvest. As I crossed the square, wending my way through the passionate demonstrators most of whom appeared not to notice me, catching glimpses of more IDF soldiers and also police, some heavily armed, who were guarding the event, protecting the rights of their fellow citizens who were protesting beliefs that were sometimes anathema to those same soldiers and police, I was reminded of how hard it must be for those soldiers to bring back the hostages, dead or alive—more likely dead since their Hamas guards would almost certainly kill their charges rather than give them up. It would be far easier, in a way, to blow up Gaza in its entirety than to extract the hostages alive. No wonder so few had been freed. No matter how sophisticated the IDF's methods, they faced a simple, primitive strategy that could only be overcome by divine intervention.

But what was that divine intervention? Was it the Golem? That seemed highly unlikely. Why would it make its appearance all the way across the world in Tennessee? And why in the backyard of an ambivalent rabbi with no special following. It made no sense. But nothing did, really.

This and jetlag kept me up all night, thrashing in the bed in my hotel room. I can't say I was surprised. Somewhere around three a. m. I phoned Maya to wish her goodnight. I had been thinking about our last trip to the country, when we had spent four delightful days at a vineyard in the Golan Heights, how different that seemed. We hiked through the hills, one time getting high enough to see down into Syria, what appeared to be Damascus in the distance, then coming back for a delicious meal and glasses of cabernet, a far cry from the treacly Manischewitz of our youth. That was the second time in my life I considered aliyah, always under the easiest, most pleasant of conditions, as Maya reminded me. Talking with her always calmed me down and brought me back to center, even when she was correcting me, maybe especially when she was correcting me, and the phone was soon dangling from my hand as I drifted off into a few hours' sleep.

The next morning, I fueled up on caffeine and went, as planned, four kilometers out of the city, directly to Kfar Chabad, where I would meet—also as planned, and as Peebles and his people clearly knew—my old friend Artie Leventhal. The agreed-upon location was in front of the exact Israeli replica of the 770 Eastern Parkway headquarters of the Chabad movement in Brooklyn's Crown Heights, which had been built, brick by brick, in that small town outside Tel Aviv at the instructions of the long-deceased Chabad Rebbe. It was the natural meeting spot since Artie and I had first met by chance at the original Eastern Parkway nearly a quarter-century earlier. I was there out of curiosity, with a couple of days free in New York, and had journeyed out to the Heights after having seen an interview with their Rebbe that caught my attention. A Brooklyn boy, Artie had shown me around, though he wasn't strictly a member of the Lubavitcher movement. He was his own thing. At the time I met him, he was moving to Israel. Since then, he had married a lawyer, had children, and seemingly become well-connected at various levels of society. I was never sure exactly how, but he appeared to know people who knew people—as people do in small countries, at least so I imagined. Over those twenty-five or so years, we hadn't met more than half a dozen times in person, yet we maintained a peculiarly close email/text relationship that many in our era develop. Rarely did more than a few weeks pass without us communicating across the seas, exchanging links to stories or events we found ominous, funny, or both. He had become a father, and we'd occasionally share concerns for our children—

or, in my case, grandchildren, especially Max, who held a particular interest for him. I was never quite sure what Artie did himself—he had a variety of interests—and sometimes thought he was living off his highly successful wife, but that didn't really make sense given his personality. In one email, it even seemed as if he was starting a tequila business of all things. Apparently, the Negev desert has conditions similar to Mexico's Jalisco region, its official "Tequila district." The agave cactus grows well in Israel's desert, so it wasn't all that surprising when you thought about it.

I hadn't told Artie why I was coming to his country this time, only that it was urgent, knowing he was the kind of person who wouldn't ask questions, certainly not over a computer or cellphone. And there he was, standing by a battered Peugeot parked in front of the building, the ritual *tzitzit* dangling from beneath a loose white shirt resembling a Mexican guayabera covering his ample, almost Falstaffian girth. It gave him the air of a wild, religious bohemian, which was probably accurate to who he really was.

"So there's a Golem alive today. What a relief," he said after I got in the car and gave him the short version. I couldn't tell if he believed me. Maybe he was splitting the difference with a little irony to hedge his bets. "So how've you been, *chaver?*" he continued. "Family good? Life good? Your Hebrew still stink?"

"Worse than ever."

"Only in America. Rabbi with pisspoor Hebrew.... So where're we headed?" He turned on the motor.

"Gaza."

"Of course... Have you got your personal anti-tank gun? I didn't see it in that little backpack you're carrying... Now, where do you really want to go?"

"Gaza."

"*Baduk*," he said, rolling his eyes as he pulled out. As I recalled, that meant 'for sure' or maybe something like 'don't worry.' "Now this Golem," he continued, "he's under your control as rabbi... and I would guess you sent him to Gaza to bring back the hostages."

"And finish off Sinwar."

"A two-fer?" He frowned. "Tough sledding, even for a Golem... Shin Bet says they had chances, but Yahya always keeps twenty hostages with him next to a 25-pound bag of TNT."

"Saw that in the Daily Mail. Didn't know it was true."

"You know the story of the clock being right twice a day... Suppose it was ten hostages and 20 pounds?" Artie turned right onto a southbound highway. Somehow, I thought he knew all along where I wanted to go. In fact, I was sure of it.

I didn't respond to his obviously rhetorical question. He was a fast driver. Within minutes, we were passing Ashdod, and I saw signs for Ashkelon, the southernmost Israeli city, 36 miles from Tel Aviv but only 8 miles from the Gaza border. According to Artie's car's GPS, the whole trip wouldn't take much longer than from Chicago to Wilmette. What a tiny place Israel was. No wonder all those kids went to that fatal music festival down there. You could drive to an evening concert, dance till dawn, and be back for a late breakfast.

"It was the left that was killed at the Nova Festival, wasn't it?" I asked, seeking confirmation for what I long suspected.

"Mostly. The same as those who lived in the kibbutzim down there, except the kibbutzniks don't microdose. Too health-conscious. Who else but lefties would live two kilometers from Gaza under constant threat of popgun missiles? They all wanted to make love, not war. They got a lesson some of them might even learn."

Soon enough, we were reaching Ashkelon, much of which

looked gleaming and white, with attractive modern high-rises, an old town renewed along the Mediterranean across from pristine beaches, as if the whole city had risen in the last ten years —and much of it had. It was attractive in a conventional way. But there were pockets of destroyed buildings —some homes and apartments —visible from the attacks, in various states of repair. Artie nodded to a couple of them as he drove. Now there were more of them, shells of houses along the road mixed with buildings that looked newly repaired, fresh coats of paint popping in the hazy sun, their reflection bouncing back off shiny solar collectors.

We had turned inland, heading a few kilometers east into the Negev. We were entering the area known as the "Gaza Envelope" that surrounded the Strip, the zone whose inhabitants were subject for years to Qassam rockets and even direct mortar fire or snipers. All the while, I had been checking my flip phone for evidence of the Golem, but to no avail. Was he still too deep? Was he shattered into a million pieces of dry mud? I was hoping for a better result from a closer range. I wondered if Artie noticed my continued fascination with the tiny clamshell, but he didn't mention it. Within minutes, we were pulling up at what he identified as Kibbutz Be'eri, ground zero on Oct 7, along with the Nova Music Festival. It was a bigger place than I had imagined from what had appeared on television. Several of the buildings were as they were after the attack, windows smashed, bullet holes unrepaired, furniture tossed about against walls still splattered with blood, as if they were left as a testament to unspeakable horror, and yet the place was still inhabited. I saw a man about my age hobbling on what was clearly a new prosthetic leg. Some children were playing a paddleball game while a woman behind them was cooking, visible through the broken wall of her house in a small modern kitchen that resembled something you might see at

Ikea. Just behind her, the skyline of what must have been Gaza City, what was left of it anyway, was barely perceptible through the haze, two plumes of smoke apparently created by crisscrossing Israeli jets. The black smoke was shooting upwards and then spreading. It reminded me of the tornado back home that had created the Golem. I glanced at my phone yet again, but still nothing was happening. This time, I could see Artie watching. "I hope you bought enough credits for that thing," he said. "Careful or you're gonna run out. No 7-11s near here." I was going to explain it wasn't a burner but a flip phone when another group walked past us, laughing together as they wheeled a young girl in a chair, balancing some toy animals. She had no legs and barely a lap.

"So brave," I said to Artie, my heart in my mouth. "Incredible people still want to live here."

"It's their home. You diaspora *yidden* are going to catch the real hell from what's happening. We're safe here with each other. If we die, we all die together. Only we're not going to die. We're going to fight... You ready to go inside now?" He nodded toward Gaza. "You're not chickening out, are you?"

"I don't have a choice."

"Why not? You're Rabbi Loew yet, worrying your charge will run out of control and bring ruin?... You can deactivate the creature like the Maharal did," he continued with a sly smile. "But do you have a *geniza*, a special attic, in your synagogue to store the remains?" Artie knew the details of Jewish history as thoroughly as most rabbis. He stopped for a moment, as if sizing me up. "You're going to need body armor." Then he added, "You think we didn't know why you were coming? Where's your *yiddishe kopf*? You know as well as I do that there are no secrets in this world. Maybe we wanted you to come, needed you to in a way. What you're going through has a purpose. It always does." He signaled to a soldier who had been standing guard across from us. The tactical vest I had noticed him holding was apparently meant for me. He walked over and started helping me put it on. It dug into my shoulders with a weight that I would take getting used to, and for a second, I stumbled. I was being reminded quickly that I hadn't realized what I was really getting into or, more accurately, whose danger I had deliberately ignored. Almost at the same time, what looked like a small, uncovered tank came around the corner. I didn't know much about military vehicles, but I assumed it was an armored personnel carrier. Two IDF soldiers were standing on its platform behind a machine gun and a grenade launcher. Artie introduced me to them. One was a private who, although muscular, looked about 16 but was undoubtedly older —at least I hoped so —and a second lieutenant who seemed closer to 40 and sported a heavy beard. That probably meant he was orthodox or ultra-orthodox, and I later learned that was a special condition for being permitted to have facial hair in the army. The private, seeing me struggling with the vest, helped me onto the APC. Artie clambered on after us, unencumbered by that Falstaffian girth. He put on a tactical vest of his own, grabbed an assault rifle from under a floor locker, and slung it over his shoulder. Then he reached down and handed me a Glock and several loaded magazines. I balanced them in my hand, unsure where to put them. "*Yalla!*" he cried, as the second lieutenant hit the throttle and started to motor us out.

"Don't think for a moment, *chaver*," Artie said, beginning to explain where we were headed and why, "if the Americans know about what happened at the helicopter, we don't. Those were our boys that were saved.... We're grateful—to you and whoever your mysterious aid might be." The APC started to speed up. "Mythology or not, you get carte blanche until further notice."

Nice to know, I thought, but I wasn't entirely sure I wanted the honor. It was one thing to be over your head, but I felt like someone preparing for an Everest expedition who had never even climbed the hill up the street. We pulled up briefly at a checkpoint where an IDF officer, noticing Artie, instantly waved us through. I was starting to realize how much I had underestimated my old friend, whom I had only met those few times in the flesh. Now it was becoming clear he was part of that clandestine world for which Israel is justifiably well known. Maybe I had suspected that all along but didn't want to admit it to myself. It would have made our relationship strangely unbalanced—with me being open, even recklessly so, while Artie listened silently, filing everything away. It's the kind of situation I'd read about in spy novels. Not even his family knew what George Smiley really did.

By this point, we had crossed into Gaza and were nearing the outskirts of Gaza City. I wasn't surprised by the bombed-out buildings everywhere—they had long been a staple of cable news—but seeing them in person hit differently. Human beings had been living there. Some were still moving around or had set up tents amid the rubble. I knew the history of the Strip, of course. I had to teach it in my classes—how then Israeli PM Ariel Sharon handed over the territory to the Palestinians under the Palestinian Authority in 2005, how there was an election in 2007 that Hamas won, and then ensured control either by tossing the remaining PA followers off roofs or shooting them. When I first read that, I wondered if it was exaggerated. The level of violent hatred implied was overwhelming. I had also read that the Gazans completely destroyed some state-of-the-art organic farms left intact by Israeli settlers. That, too, felt a bit much —more of a legend. But after witnessing what they were capable of on Oct 7, my skepticism disappeared. My sympathies, what was left of it, vanished as well. Still, I was watching, moving as far away from our vehicle as possible, scattering like pigeons from an approaching bicycle. Who knew what they really thought? Maybe they loathed their Hamas overlords, too, but were too terrified to show it. I wanted to believe that. On the other hand, they hadn't rebelled against them for nearly twenty years. As we moved closer, a woman in a threadbare cobalt headscarf gave us the middle finger and hurried into a building. Clearly, she made herself understood. If she despised her overlords, they weren't the only people she hated.

We drove through this post-apocalyptic world for another hour or so, making stops along the way to pick up and drop off troops or for security reasons that were beyond my knowledge or linguistic skills to understand. I did hear the muffled, or not so muffled, sounds of ordinance either going off or in some cases exploding with a loud bang not far away as black smoke drifted skyward. My companions smiled at me for reassurance, but I sensed any questions were inappropriate, at least for now.

We continued through a narrow, winding street lined with walls on both sides, the APC almost touching them as we reached a small square. In the center, a large vehicle resembling a bus, its darkened windows painted a dark brown and a hazard sign prominently displayed, was stationed in the center. A tank was parked in a corner, its turret aimed roughly at the bus. For a moment, I wondered if it might blow up, but then a man stepped out of the bus, looking completely unbothered. The tank was there for protection. The man was about my age, fit and athletic, with tousled hair, dark olive skin, and wearing what looked like a lab coat. He approached Artie directly, shook his hand, and spoke in a mixture of languages with an accent somewhere between French and Middle Eastern. "*Shalom, mon vieux de Brooklyn.*" "Shalom, Omar," my friend replied, gesturing to me. "The famous Ben Golub."

"Ah, the rabbi from Music City. I am Omar Alfassi." He extended his hand.

"Not so famous, I'm afraid," I said.

"You are to us. Welcome to the Philadelphi Corridor. This is your first time here, no, but it should look familiar."

Responding to what must have been a blank expression on my part, he pointed toward the building to my right. It had a wrought-iron grill at a low, basement level. Across the street were the remains of a medical building. I realized then that I was standing in the very square where the Golem had saved the IDF and their helicopter, annihilating the Hamas terrorists.

"Yes... yes, it is," I replied, trying to keep my mind and body together at this revelation. It wasn't as if I was going to faint, but my heart, which had been restless for a while, was suddenly pounding a mile a minute.

"*Beseder?*" said Artie. Okay? There was that word again, apparently an Israeli favorite for obvious reasons. "We have been watching over you in our way," he continued. "Or watching *out* for you."

"Come, come," said Omar, waving toward the bus. "We have something to show you that will be of interest."

Not doubting at this point that he did, I followed him into the bus with Artie right behind me.

The first thing I noticed—it would have been impossible not to—was that most of the seats had been removed. Dominating the center aisle instead were two large robotic dogs lined up one after the other. I had seen similar mechanical canines in television documentaries, but never in person. I always found them creepy and not lovable like their real-life precursors, even those that made attempts to be cuddly, dressed up like a favorite pooch. These made no such attempts and resembled menacing black-metal centipedes with sensors in their legs, laser eyes, and some form of ominous high-tech weaponry where their mouths would have been.

"Scylla and Charybdis," said Omar. "We use them to scout tunnels. They get into all kinds of impossible spaces. You wouldn't believe it. The remote can make them drop down to ten centimeters. They're regular what you call spelunkers, right? Sometimes they leave a souvenir of their visit." He puffed his cheeks and made the sound of an explosion. "Sometimes they bring back a souvenir for us."

"Omar's babies," Artie said. "Built with the help of MIT robotics."

"I was there for eight months, hardly saying a word while I worked on them in their lab," said Omar. "Rumor was I was a relative of the Emir of Qatar... Actually, Alfassi is a Moroccan name... meaning from Fez... usually poor Jews... When a Swedish student looked it up on the internet, I was called out as a Zionist agent ... We had to work through that one," he added with a smile. "Anyway, we got them finished and into the tunnels... Scylla ran into this on her last excursion." He walked over to a shelf and reached into a container. Turning to me, he pulled out a tangled belt with broken plastic fragments attached, its store labels still visible. "Recognize it?"

It was the body camera I had strapped on the Golem, broken into pieces.

My heart started up again. I nodded and exhaled slowly as I had been taught in a meditation class decades ago.

Omar poked his finger through a shredded hole in the belt. "AK-47 or similar. More likely a machine gun. I would have advised you to avoid Walmart next time, but I doubt it would have made a difference."

By now, I knew better than to ask how he knew I had bought the camera at Walmart, but at least the mystery of why I wasn't seeing anything on my phone was solved.

"What happened to the Golem itself?" I asked, hoping against hope it wasn't splattered in a million dots of clay against a tunnel wall.

"We don't know. We don't know if it is a Golem. And even though we would love divine intervention, as modern people in the modern world, I regret to say, we very much doubt it is. Therefore, the most logical assumption is that it has been destroyed."

"You're wrong," I said, not as convinced as I sounded.

"And what brings you to that conclusion?

I looked over at Artie before answering. He hadn't said anything, and I wondered why he brought me here. Was it to prove something to me or to themselves? Or to discover the truth?

"It already carried out missions for me," I said.

"There are other ways these things happen. It's quite amazing what can be done in the world of microchips and artificial intelligence....I understand you have a brilliant grandson, a prodigy..."

"Max would never do that!" I blurted out, suddenly raising my voice.

"Yes, of course." That was Artie. "He's a fine young man, as I explained to Omar. Don't worry."

"I'd appreciate you leave him out of this... And the Golem is not a robot," I added, lowering my volume but not entirely calmed down. I can't say I was 100% positive. How could one be? My ambivalence registered on Omar and Artie, who glanced at each other. "Something wrong?" I continued, repeating, "I *am* sure. Take me inside, and I will try to find him. He's supposed to listen to me," I gestured toward the grate. "I'm his rabbi. Like it or not. That's why I came all this way."

Both men were staring at me.

"Look, what you are going through is natural," said Omar.

"Living in America, far from this war, but as a Jewish man, wishing somehow you could participate. So it's not surprising you would conjure up—"

"I did not make this up." I said firmly, surprising myself. "Suppose, incredible as it may seem to you modernists, that this *is* a divine being." It was becoming clear to me that were as confused about what had happened as I was, probably more so. They wanted an answer too. I took a set forward. "You wear the *tzitzit* of a believing Jew, Artie. The Torah is filled with miracles well beyond this Golem. And yet you believe *them*. Your country is in a war for its survival. Why do you think it can't be happening now?" Off in the distance, I could hear more explosions and what sounded like artillery. I waited for their reply, but none was forthcoming, so I continued. "According to tradition and in reality, more or less, I am the rabbi responsible for this Golem. When I asked what happened to him, you already said you didn't know. At least give me a chance to find out if this is real. As you both know, Golems can cause problems that can be extremely dangerous to our people. What if I'm right?"

"Okay, *chaver*," said Artie. "We'll take you inside. But keep this between us and listen to everything we say. No freelancing," he added, not that I would have considered it. He gestured in the general direction of the iron gate.

XI

I passed through it about an hour later in the company of Omar, Artie, the two soldiers from the APC, and either Scylla or Charybdis. I couldn't tell which robot it was since I was already off the bus when it trundled down a ramp. But whichever one it was led the way into the tunnel first for safety's sake, even though the immediate subterranean area had supposedly been cleared. Otherwise, they never would have taken me there, as they explained more than once, before and after. I walked between the two soldiers, just behind Omar, with Artie in the rear. We proceeded slowly, eyes on our robot that had a blinking green light indicating it was safe to continue. We walked for about five minutes until we came to a bend in the tunnel, leading to another corridor that went on for a considerable distance. We passed a bathroom, a shower, and what appeared to be a storage area. A pair of rats was gnawing at a box of Ritz crackers. After that was an office with some documents still stacked on the desk. The younger soldier picked them up and stuffed them inside his flak jacket. We reached the end of that leg at a corner with one of the ladders I had seen on video; at least it seemed to be the same. It descended roughly a hundred feet to the next level. The robot had pincer legs that enabled it to catch onto the ladder's rungs and head down. The idea was to follow it. When I got to the top and looked down, I felt dizzy. It was a steeper and longer ladder than any I could remember attempting. Making it worse, it went down through a round chute-like tube with the narrowest of spaces on all sides, but I knew I had to go. Gingerly. I stepped onto the treads, testing them with utmost care. I continued down, clinging to the sides of the ladder for what's traditionally called dear life. In this case, it was more than a cliché. I was feeling my age and then some. "*Beseder?*" said Artie above me. "*Beseder,*" I replied, but I didn't sound convincing. I said the "Shema" to myself as I continued, even though it felt like overkill. I should be able to handle this without divine intervention. But just then, there was a loud explosion, and the walls shook. Dirt was spraying down all around me. This was followed immediately by a second explosion. My hands began to slip on the ladder rails. Straining to grab on with my fingers, I was able to prevent myself from falling altogether, but not from reaching the floor in a few seconds, where I collapsed on my back, bouncing off the ground. At first, I was unable to move, wondering whether I had broken my spine. I could see nothing because dust and dirt were everywhere. I heard screaming and shouting, bursts of gunfire. Parts of the wall came crashing down. Where was everybody? I rolled over and started to crawl, managing a few yards, when someone grabbed my arm and pulled me to my feet. I stood there, momentarily relieved that I was able to stand, when I was spun around to see my savior had most of his face, all but his eyes, wrapped in a keffiyeh and a handgun pointed at my forehead. A third explosion went off. Were they caused by us or them? Were we all going to die from friendly fire, or was this guy going to plug me first? I looked around frantically for my group but saw no one but the robot in the distance, turned upside down with its green light still blinking. What had happened to them? Where were they?

My captor didn't say anything but pulled me by the arm deeper into the dust-filled tunnel, gun still at my head. I thought of screaming but restrained myself when he poked the barrel into my lip, jabbing it hard. I felt blood. Now another man, another keffiyeh, had my other arm, and they were leading me down another tunnel corridor now, illuminated by some dim lights. We passed an office and a machine shop with weapons stacked against the wall. Beyond that, I could see a storeroom of mostly American grocery brands that seemed to go on for some distance, but before I could get much of a look, we were going through a door. I heard a bolt being secured behind me. Then I was thrown into a tiny room —more like a closet —that was to be my home, with the door shut and locked.

I lay there for a period of time that I was already losing track of. It's hard to describe how I was feeling because, in a way, I wasn't. I had blacked out, though still conscious. Briefly, I thought about home, about Maya and the others, my children in Indiana, young Max, who was so brilliant and so innocent at once, or so I wanted to see him, but this filled me with an intolerable amount of regret that I had done this and I pushed it away, concentrating instead on my physical being. To what extent was I hurt? I moved very slowly, fearful of making things worse. Not attempting to stand, I tested my legs one at a time. They seemed okay, though the left was trembling with some blood showing through the pants. I was undoubtedly in shock. I felt an intense pain in my pelvic bone where I must have fallen initially. It had been reinjured when I was brutally thrown into the room. Would it prevent me from standing? The ceiling seemed low, almost deliberately so. I leaned forward on my forearms as I sometimes did when getting into pushup position, then brought my feet under me, slowly hoisting myself up. Although I wobbled, I was standing, my head bent to protect it from hitting the ceiling. I felt a crick in my neck. Bending lower, I reached for the wall to feel my way around, and the door slammed open. Another man was standing there, visible from the light behind him in the tunnel. He was more neatly dressed than the others with a green headband. He grabbed my arm and yanked me back out into the tunnel where I could stand straight again. He stared at me for a moment, said something in Arabic, and another man, much larger, maybe six-three with grenades attached to his vest, walked up to me. He patted me down and took out my passport and two cellphones, stuffing them in his vest. Then he unzipped mine and pulled my shirt off, ripping the buttons. Next, he yanked down my pants and underwear, leaving me stripped naked. A slight sadistic smile came over his officer's face as I started to cover my groin with my hands, but I stopped, not wanting to give either of them the pleasure of my shame. He signaled to the large man, who pushed me back into the tiny room, locking the door behind them and leaving a dim slice of light shining in through the bottom. I shivered in the damp, sitting down on the cold earthen floor and clutching my legs for warmth when the door opened again and a threadbare blue smock was thrown in. I stared at it for a second before putting it on. What choice did I have? I thought it would smell. Thankfully, it didn't. For a moment, I could see outside where the heavyset man was sitting with an assault rifle across his lap. Further down the corridor, two others were sitting around a table playing a card game. The nearer man kicked the door shut. Then someone got up and locked it.

I sat down again, leaned against the wall, and tried to take stock of the situation, but I found it almost impossible to focus.

Had I done something to deserve this? Was there something about me, a flaw, indeed I had plenty, that destined me to be, of all things, trapped under Gaza during a war, a war that I had nothing to do with? Why was this my battle when, as I had learned long ago, the real battle was within myself, one that I had been fighting a long time, that tortured me. I tried to resist such thoughts, but my mind in the damp gloom for some inexplicable reason—how could I be thinking of this now; in recent years I had mostly pushed it away, hopefully forever-- drifted back inexorably to the early days of my first marriage. I was still in rabbinical school, and a few of us, thinking ourselves rebels, did psychedelics together. Something similar was done in the ancient days of the Temple, we assured each other. It was all but written in the Talmud, one of my friends said, although I could never figure out where that was. He never gave a citation. It was the same friend who, on a trip to Israel, had taken magic mushrooms that had been growing near the Dead Sea since before Biblical times. He came back with some, and we took them together, several couples, student rabbis and rebbetzins, male and female. We told ourselves we were implementing G-d's will from the Song of Songs. I ended up sleeping with someone else's wife. This initiated a period of infidelity on both sides that one would hardly call rabbinic, although it seemed almost common in those days when even clergy spoke of free love, we reform ones anyway. That was my initial excuse. It didn't last. I had been subject to what they called in Hebrew *yetzer hara*, the evil inclination, so often attached to sex. Besides being the primary topic of psychotherapy I underwent, this behavior came up every year on Yom Kippur like clockwork during *slichos*, the penitential prayers, before and after what became my inevitable divorce. The repentance never felt sufficient. That had a lot to do, more than anything else probably, with my leaving the rabbinate and disappearing to Maine to teach for all those years, another kind of penance. I told myself I had done enough when I returned to take my current position, but maybe I hadn't. Years later, watching a Chabad video—yes, rabbis watch videos, especially those with a lot of making up to do—it was explained I had been in a battle between my Godly self and my animal self. I had always liked animals, especially a dog we had named Winston, and couldn't quite accept the dichotomy. Nevertheless, it occurred to me then that I was wrong. Was this the final reckoning, here under Gaza? I also remembered reading that there was a Jewish equivalent to karma. It translates as something like "measure for measure." Very Shakespearean.

How odd it was to think of such things then, sitting or lying on the ground so far from normal life. I was torturing myself while the world was torturing me. Maybe it wasn't that surprising, though it felt so far away and hardly fair--or necessary. But prayer was, more necessary than ever. I started reciting one of David's psalms as best I could remember it. "Save me, O G-d, for the waters have come up to my soul. I have sunk in muddy depths and there is no place to stand. I have become weary out of calling out." I was starting to hear explosions again. Who was it? Where was The Golem, if he even existed? Was the building going to collapse with me under it? My leg was getting worse without treatment. Was it gangrenous? And then, out of exhaustion, I fell asleep.

This is all a while ago now, and I cannot recall what I dreamt then or if I did. Because they had taken my watch, I had no idea how long I had slept, nor would I for some time. It was at that point that I resolved to write this book, memoir, or whatever you want to call it, though I had no way to do it, no writing implement other than my finger on a hardened earth floor. Recalling books I had read and movies I had seen about prisoners, I knew in some instances they had found a method, but I couldn't think of one. I knew at that point my mind was so addled by adrenaline, cortisol, or whatever else that I would find it difficult to remember anything. So when I started making mental notes, they only evaporated the moment I made them. Realizing this was happening and dreading that it could soon be much worse, I summoned the energy to do some push-ups in the hopes of jump-starting my brain — at least temporarily — with endorphins and dopamine. When the door opened and my first meal arrived —a small bowl of beans and a grimy spoon —I was nevertheless relieved to see it. The heavyset man placed it on the floor as if I were a dog and left.

I'm not sure how many days it was, or even whether it was just hours, when two men I had not seen before crawled into my hutch and yanked me out, each pulling on one leg. Their faces were covered with keffiyehs, so I couldn't be a hundred percent sure they were indeed new. At least it seemed that way. I had had at least two sleep periods of indeterminate length, and a portion of beans came with a small bowl of water that I forced myself to drink, though I feared what was in it. I had asked for bottled water but the heavyset man had paid no attention. I had no idea if he knew what I said, even though I pointed to my open mouth and mimed drinking from a bottle. It was as if I weren't there. The two new men held me up by the shoulders while dragging me down a corridor that was large enough for them to stand. I was in excruciating pain, nearly blacking out, with my bad leg flopping behind me. Was it broken, fractured, what? A woman was screaming somewhere. Who was she? A hostage? What were they doing to her? I could only imagine. Where was she? I looked around but saw nothing.

Eventually, they deposited me on a chair in what looked like an interrogation room with a metal table and a video camera on a tripod. On the table, I noticed a red buzzer button with a wire running off under the door and an intercom. A steel pipe with saw teeth coming out of it leaned against the corner to the right of the table. One of the men tied my wrists and ankles to the chair with zip ties while the other restrained me, although I could barely move anyway. Then they exited, locking the door behind them. I sat there in agony for an indeterminate amount of time, hoping to pass out, when a man with a closely cropped beard wearing clean military fatigues entered. He had a diagonal-shaped scar above his left eye and wore a pistol in a polished leather holster on his belt. From his carriage, I assumed him to be some kind of officer in the world of Hamas. He was followed in almost immediately by another man, taller, wearing a turban above his keffiyeh and carrying a light rig for a video camera. He stood to the side as if waiting for orders. The officer sat there a moment, staring at me, then took out my passport and put it on the table. He nodded to the turbaned man, who turned on the video lights. They were strong, and for a few seconds, I was unable to see. When I could, I saw him press the button that started the camera. I was being filmed.

"Identify yourself, please," said the officer in English that was quite clear despite the accent.

"Benjamin Golub."

"Is that your real name?"

"You have my passport."

"Is that your real name? Do not lie to me."

"Yes, it is."

"Why are you here, Mr. Golub, if that is your name?"

"You wouldn't believe it if I told you."

"Are you CIA?"

"Absolutely not. "

"I said, do not lie to me. Why would you possibly come here? You are not young. You must be officer. Tell me now. You are with American intelligence. Why are you here? You are enemy of Islamic Resistance Movement."

"I'm here to find the Golem." What could I do but tell him the truth as I had done before?

"The Go-lem?"

"A mythical creature."

"Mythical? What does that mean? Fairytale from Disney? When you wish upon star?"

"Something like that?"

"Don't patronize me, American."

"It comes from God."

"And what is it supposed to do-- this mythical creature from God?"

"Stop antisemitism."

"How stupid! Antisemitism is invention of West. You imperialist bring it here. We live happily with Jew for hundreds years." I was going to dispute that but thought better of it. "You tell me you come all way to Gaza in middle of war to look for imaginary being?" He was staring at me again, now with a look of marginally controlled rage. "You insult me and waste my time."

"Your English is impressive," I said, hoping to distract him.

"Ten years Israeli prison. Plenty time learn Hebrew *and* English... And learn weakness of Israeli and American. How much pain you take. Most yammer like little girl."

Through the walls, I could hear the woman screaming again, yet more intensely than before. It was blood-curdling. What were they doing to her? It was unbearable to listen to her without being able to do anything. I was going to say something about it but suspected that would only make things worse.

The officer stood up. "I give you last chance, American, to tell me truth of why you are here."

"I already did. If you want me to make something up, I could."

My interviewer didn't like that even though I had tried to say it in the flattest manner possible. He signaled to the other man to stop the video. For a second, I thought he was going to reach for the steel pipe and start beating me, but he leaned over and said something in Arabic into the intercom. The two men came back into the room.

"Time for you to do some thinking, American. Tomorrow we make nice video for Islamic Resistance Movement. Here is text." He handed me a typed paper.

I didn't read it until I was back in my hutch. The trip back was another not entirely successful exercise in pain management, with my bad leg being dragged across the hardened floor, several times over rocks protruding from the earth. At a certain point, I couldn't feel the leg at all. Was it still there? All the time I could hear the woman screaming nearby. Was she being beaten, raped, or both? I saw a light through a door but couldn't tell what was happening. It wasn't long after that that I almost blacked out when thrown on my threadbare mat. Somehow, the paper was still clutched in my hand. When the men were gone, I strained to look at it in the dim light. With effort, I was able to make out the words:

"My name is Benjamin Golub. I am agent American CIA sent to spy on innocent people of Gaza murdered and starved by Zionist entity and my country. I was captured and assure family I am treated well. I now see error of my thinking. America and Zionist entity are children of Satan. They must stop now with unconditional ceasefire. People of Gaza are dying from starvation and Zionist genocide. Free Palestine. Long live Al Aqsa Flood."

They wanted me to say *this*? Zionist genocide? America and Israel are Satan's children? Free Palestine? The Al Aqsa

Flood? I hadn't heard the latter often but knew it was the label Hamas had given the October 7 massacre. Much of what they did was premised on gaining complete control of that tiny mountain where the al-Aqsa mosque stood —the Temple Mount, or what they called Haram al-Sharif. How absurd that seemed at that moment. This so-called mountain would have been no more than a hill in most places on earth. In the Himalayas or the Andes it wouldn't have been noticed. Even in California, it would be the foothill to the foothills. Yet both sides fixated on it to a degree far beyond what most assume to be rational. The world would explode if the Israelis overly exploited their hegemony over this "mount" that they had recaptured after centuries during the Six-Day War. And yet the more extreme of their citizens, and some not so extreme, very much wanted to rebuild that temple, which was rightfully theirs, for a third time. Years back, it was reported that a zealous jet pilot from the Israeli Air Force was about to commandeer an F-4 and take matters into his own hands. Thankfully, it never happened, yet part of me, I had to admit, wished it had.

During that night —or was it day? How would I know ?—I remained stewing in my own juices in my minute quarters, sleeping or not, listening to the intermittent, terrified screams from nearby while various rodents and bugs scampered across the floor. Logically, I should have been going completely insane. But from somewhere in my conscious/unconscious, I was able to adopt a hitherto unknown, at least for me, calmness. *HaShem* loved me, didn't he? That's what I had been told, in prayer and song. It was simple if I accepted that. Looking for the positive, even in the most extreme circumstances, was an opportunity to learn from them. That was why I had given Victor Frankl's book about the search for meaning to the prisoner in Memphis, which seemed so long ago now. The battle for sanity could be won by planning and then concentrating on exactly how I would behave when the inevitable occurred and was brought back to face my nameless interlocutor, who had spent ten years in an Israeli prison himself. At first, I would be cajoled to read the propaganda I had been handed and, when I refused, undoubtedly tortured until I did so. I deliberately avoided thinking about the obvious: that if I did cooperate to survive, everyone back home would be watching — my wife, my children and grandchildren—including Max—Tamara, Ed, the folks at the synagogue, the gang at the orphanage, and ultimately millions of people. I would be on FOX and CNN, being used for whatever purposes they had that day.

It could have been morning or night when the same two men arrived at my tiny room for my reckoning. The thinner of the two reached in and pulled me out, and then the two hoisted me up by the shoulders again and dragged me down the tunnel corridors. Along the way, I could hear the woman screaming again. I recognized the words "*ezer*," help in Hebrew, and "*ima*," mother. For the first time, I got a look at her through a partially open door that was quickly slammed shut. She couldn't have been much more than twenty and was probably Sephardi or Mizrachi, tears mixed with blood streaking down her darker-complexioned face. Her hair appeared to have been chopped off in preparation for something. An execution? A group of men was behind her. It was hard to tell how many there were, but some of them were laughing. For a split second, I saw the young woman looking at me. My guides yanked hard on me when they saw me looking back, forcing me around a tunnel corner as simultaneously one of them gave me a bone-crushing punch in the back. It sent me sprawling and, with my leg virtually useless, they had to pull me up and half carry me the last hundred feet or so to the interrogation room, where they dropped me in the same chair as before. The interrogator was in front of me—this time with his keffiyeh pulled down so he could smoke. He had a stubble of a beard that was beginning to grow out.

"*Salaam*, Mr. Golub... or I should say rabbi, since we have read your profession on Google? They forgot to write it in passport."

"In America it's illegal to put a religion."

"As if we don't know anyway, *Rabbi* Golub.... Are you ready to read statement? After, we will send doctor to fix leg. It not look good. We do not want to have to cut it off, as happened my cousin Aisha from your bombs. She has one arm and one leg, no husband, no children." He hesitated to let that sink in. "Here. We make other copy for you."

He handed me a paper with the statement printed in large, easily read letters. Down the tunnel, I could hear the woman screaming again.

"Who is that?" I asked.

"Not important. Time to read." He nodded to the cameraman, who switched on the light. It glared harshly in my face.

"Who is that?" I repeated. "Hostage?"

"She is captive of your aggression. Read."

"From where? An innocent dancer at a music festival? A kibbutz? Who is she? She never did anything to you. She was a peacenik for--."

"You are to read statement. Or we make you recite *Shahada*. Become Muslim in minute."

"I will read the statement if you let her free."

He stared at me with a look between rage and disbelief, then turned to one of the men and said something in Arabic. The man picked up the metal rod, took a step toward me and slashed my leg, causing me to topple from the chair with blood splattering against the wall.

"You will read now."

"No."

"Blood makes mess. Read now or we amputate."

"The Golem will defend me. I am his rabbi." What was I saying? The Golem had been nothing but erratic. How could I have any confidence in that? Where was I getting this courage? I was no Rabbi Loew. I was a nobody, writhing on the floor, barely able to think straight while desperately muttering the Shema to myself, all the verses I could recall from Deuteronomy and Numbers that were rapidly disappearing in my swirling brain.

"You have pathetic fantasy, rabbi. I give you one last chance to read statement."

"Free the girl first."

I barely squeezed out the last sentence, but he clearly heard it and ordered his men to pick me up again. Momentarily, they were dragging me along a tunnel artery I hadn't seen before. Up ahead was a clinic of some sort with a couple of beds and some medical equipment that looked well-used. Once more, I could hear the girl screaming. Was she here too? What was happening? The two men hoisted me on a gurney and stepped aside as some others walked up. A couple wore white medical smocks. Another light went on, brighter than the first, as in an operating room. I couldn't focus. My mind was virtually blanking out, approaching a fugue state. Whatever would be would be. One of the men in white moved toward me with a scalpel when I suddenly heard panicked shouts, then more shouts, gasping and shrieking with people rushing from the room.

A shadow loomed over me.

XII

"Can you blink?"

I thought I could hear what she was saying. It sounded like a woman's voice but far away. Very far. On the other side of something, a wall, a mountain...

She repeated: "Can you blink?"

This time the words penetrated, at least somewhat. I noticed my head was throbbing. Where was I? I tried to blink. Several times. Finally it happened.

"*Tov*," she said. "*Tov meod.*" Very good.

Both eyes flickered open partway. I saw sunlight through a translucent white curtain. A nurse was adjusting it. "Shalom," she said, breaking into a smile. "Shalom," I managed back, but she was already on her way out, undoubtedly to report my awakening. Beginning to realize where I was, that I was alive, I involuntarily reached for my groin. It was intact. It seemed so, anyway. My eyes shut again. Sometime later, they reopened. A man was standing there in a medical coat, making notes on an iPad while checking measurements on a screen. I assumed he was a doctor. That proved to be correct when he spoke.

"Hello, rabbi. I am Dr. Aaron Rosenzweig. You have come through quite an ordeal."

I moved my head, which was, I suddenly realized, slightly restrained by a band wrapped around it that I later learned was attached to electrodes. I also could see for the first time that I was elevated in a hospital bed. Several IVs were connected to my right arm. My left was in an L-shaped fiberglass cast. I wasn't sure, but, beneath the sheets, I felt there was something similar encasing my left leg as well.

"How do you do, doctor? Where am I?"

"Sheba Medical Center." He was still checking measurements. He looked around fifty with a scar on his left cheek, probably from one of their wars. "Ramat Gan, east of Tel Aviv."

I touched my cheek. A thick beard was coming in that I imagined was making me seem more rabbinic than usual. "The girl..." I suddenly remembered. "There was a girl. A hostage, I think. Where is she?"

The doctor put the iPad under his arm and stepped closer to me for a better inspection. "At another hospital."

"She's okay?"

"She lost a lot of weight, but she'll survive."

"*Baruch HaShem*... How long have I been here?"

He glanced at the iPad again. "14 days and nine hours."

I gasped, then tried to get a grip on myself. "My wife knows?"

"Yes."

"Where is she?"

"Not far."

"Where?" I tried to sit up but fell back.

"We wanted to make sure you were ready to see her."

"I'm ready. I'm ready."

"Are you certain?"

"Yes!"

He walked to the door.

"You just woke up. Remember not to overexcite yourself. It's important."

He opened the door. Maya entered as he exited, tentatively at first, then she rushed over to me, stopping a foot away as if heeding his words. "Oh, Ben, Ben, my love. We were so worried. All of us. Tamara, Ed ... Jorge." She dipped down slowly to kiss me on the cheek just above the beard line. "I hope that doesn't hurt."

"No, no. More, please."

She kissed me again, ever so gently. "Why did I let you do this?"

"You didn't let me," I insisted. "What about Max?"

"I sent him back to Indiana."

"He'll be in school trouble again. Where's that Ripton guy?"

She gave me a look. "Don't worry about it now. You have other concerns. Max'll be safe in the short run, as you know."

"I do?" But then I realized that, of course, I did.

"Pay attention to yourself instead," she continued. "You have to get well."

My heart started racing again. "I don't even know why I'm alive. The terrorists were about to cut my leg off and I blacked out... Did they tell you why I made it? "

"They said it could be a lot of things."

I sat there a second, waiting for my brain to focus a bit while my heart slowed down. "The Golem?"

"They talked about some new laser weapon they've been testing. Not Iron Dome... "

"Beam?"

"Yes, that's it. Iron Beam. It was in the area."

"I thought that was for drones." Now I was beginning to

feel dizzy again. It would be that way for a while. "Where're you staying?"

"An apartment near the hospital... Are you okay? Your eyes are closing."

"Yeah... I guess... maybe..."

"That's one impressive cast. I hate to think what's under there," she said, looking down at me. "It's going to take some serious work." Spoken like a true physical therapist. I would have responded, but I was too far gone to speak.

I slept another twenty hours, or so I was later told. The painkillers were doing their work.

When I awakened, I felt better, despite the usual fog that comes from those medications. I still felt pain, but for the first time, my brain's thought processes were somewhat clear.

I found myself staring up at a video camera trained on me that I hadn't noticed before. It was no surprise I was being monitored. Not far from that was a TV. I found the remote by the bed and switched it on. A menu appeared with roughly 40 channels. I had just pressed on a local channel that seemed to be in English when I heard a knock on the door. Before I could respond, four people entered. One of them was an elderly rabbi with a fuzzy grey beard and a Hasidic black hat and suit. Another was a dark-skinned woman who appeared to be one of those whose families were rescued from Ethiopia in the 1980s during Operation Moses. I used to teach about it. They were often called Falashas, but that was considered an insult. They preferred Beta Jews. The woman wore a flower-print dress and was much younger, perhaps in her* early thirties. The third was a middle-aged man in good shape, wearing a blue business suit and a white, open-collar shirt in the Israeli style. He wore no head covering and had curly black hair. He looked vaguely familiar, but the only one I truly recognized in the group was the fourth-- Artie.

"Shalom, *chaver*?" he said. "You freed a hostage. Zoya Matsas. Her family is incredibly grateful."

"Is that her name? I didn't know who she was."

"From Ramla. 142 days of the most disgusting torture--sexual violence she is too traumatized to talk about. All for going to a music festival. She went through real Hell. But now she is free. You're a big hero."

"I am?" My voice was strained and weak.

"Of course. Her family is very grateful. We are grateful too. I'd sign your cast, but it's fiberglass and would wipe right off." That last was said with our shared instinct for irony. It was comforting.

"I didn't free her... Something else did."

"Did you see it?"

"No. I didn't see the Iron Beam either... assuming it's visible."

"What *did* you see?"

"I don't know. But whatever it was, I wish it had come earlier."

"It came when it was necessary...Maybe it was what you think it was. Maybe not. We have no evidence.... Anyway, let me introduce my friends. This is Rabbi Shlomo Dessler of the religious court Bnei Barak... Dr. Ednaki Gabaz, vice chair of the computer science department, Tel Aviv University ... and Asher Goldfarb, special adviser to the Prime Minister. "

Special adviser? Oh, yes. No wonder I thought I recognized him. American by birth and said to be extremely close to the PM, Goldfarb was a frequent Israeli talking head on cable news. I had probably seen his face several dozen times but never expected to see him in the flesh. Even with the constant throbbing in my leg, I smiled to myself, recalling my youth when Jewish boys received gag Bar Mitzvah cards reading "Congratulations from the Prime Minister of Israel." But Goldfarb wasn't the PM, just the next best thing, and this was no Bar Mitzvah joke. What was going on?

I found that out, at least some of it, a little later, but first I listened to a discussion, almost an argument but still relatively civil, that broke out between the rabbi and Dr. Gabaz, first in English for my benefit and then devolving into rapid-fire Hebrew I could barely understand, although the bone of contention was familiar by now. It was about the Golem—was he real, or an advanced version of an artificial intelligence construct running on one of the latest Nvidia or Intel chips? I heard the name of Peebles in the midst of a jumble. So they knew about him. Dr. Gabaz, who leaned toward the technological explanation, at least then, cited the latest Intel chip that contained some astronomical number of transistors and could synthesize a robot out of earth capable of practically anything. She theorized this explained what had been happening. The rabbi surprisingly did not dispute this. He spoke instead of something called the Kabbalah of Information, a concept unknown to me and in my present state not especially capable of comprehending, but it was linked to something called Schrodinger's Cat, an experiment devised by the physicist of that name. In it, a hypothetical cat could be considered both dead and alive simultaneously while being locked in a box with a radioactive atom that is in two states at once. But before I could begin to comprehend how that related to the Golem, the rabbi advanced another theory. Since some are saying that AI eventually could evolve into having a conscious brain, in fact may have already, wouldn't it be G-d, an external force, *the* external force that is above us and in us, the unending, who allowed that, who made that happen, who even worked through that? Everything was Him, and He was everything. It was He who gave us free will. Wouldn't He then be the one to have given a machine or device invented by us the same choice? Artificial Intelligence was, in essence, a work of G-d. Further, and as a corollary to that, if a Golem traditionally worked at the express will of a rabbi, couldn't it then be said to have acted on the rabbi's wishes, conscious or subconscious, even if not expressly ordered, even if the rabbi was locked away in a box like Schrodinger's Cat.

My mind was going on tilt as Goldfarb cleared his throat. "Sorry to interrupt, but we are treating Rabbi Golub unfairly. We haven't told him what's behind our visit." I was wondering that myself. "To be direct, from here on we are asking you to be taken into the confidence of the State of Israel and to act in its behalf."

"I'm a US citizen."

"We know that, of course. But you are one of us, nonetheless. By blood and by faith. We have a situation it seems you are the only one who can solve."

"I don't know what you're talking about. To be honest, I didn't understand half of what the rabbi and the doctor were saying."

"That doesn't matter. They work together and argue about this constantly. We know you understand the basic rules of a Golem."

"I thought you guys weren't sure it existed."

Goldfarb glanced at the others. "Yes, we've discussed that. But we have to take into account the possibility. You do know the rules--those that came down from Rabbi Loew and so forth?"

"A few of them."

"That the rabbi who created the being is--"

"I didn't actually do that. It happened in a tornado. It was an accident."

Reb Dessler and Dr. Gabaz gestured to each other.

"Yes, we understand," said Goldfarb. "But you are the one

who activated him.... The one who wrote the word '*emet*' for truth on his forehead. So you are the one who can prevent this being, divine or otherwise, from continuing his actions," the special adviser added. "You can do so, according to the rules, by erasing those words from his forehead. You can stop him."

"And why would you want to do that?" I responded. "He's a force for good. He already freed a hostage. He could free others."

"Yes. That's wonderful.... If that were all he did. Unfortunately, we have a problem, a substantial one."

"What's that?" I asked.

"As I said, this must be totally confidential."

"Okay," I said, as much for him to get on with it as anything else.

"I have your word? There is considerable risk involved—to you and to us."

"Yes." That came out more easily than I expected, almost automatically.

I think Goldfarb realized that, although he added, "Do we have to ask you to sign something?"

"No," I replied flatly.

Goldfarb took note of that too. "Such things are usually not worth the paper they are written on anyway...More importantly, we have a problem with someone from your country."

"Who is that?"

"Jeremy Bogen," he said.

"Our Secretary of State?"

He nodded.

"He's Jewish."

"So was Karl Marx." That was Artie.

Jeremy Bogen? All of a sudden, I was back home at my weekly class, Tamara and the Nussbaums shouting at each other about the man. Tamara was outraged that Bogen kept lobbying for ceasefires that would only help Hamas. The Nussbaums adamantly disagreed. They wanted peace as quickly as possible and at all costs, worried that the world would think badly of Jews if they killed too many Gaza civilians. Tamara argued instead that there were no real Gaza civilians. They had voted for Hamas and then went along with their violent behavior for years. The two sides seemed on the verge of fisticuffs. I remembered my own frustration, wanting to keep the peace between them but unable to, only averting disaster at the last second when nature intervened in the form of a tornado. It had felt as if the argument went on for hours but it was probably more like five minutes.

"We have every reason to believe your Golem may try to kill him." Goldfarb explained. "Or something that could be just as bad or worse—humiliate America's highest ranking diplomat in public."

"Golems do that?" It sounded strange the moment it came out of my mouth.

"Rabbi, you were the one who ordered that dreadful Congresswoman flown home to Mogadishu to embarrass her, 'Returned to Sender' written on the box. Clever idea. Yours or the Golem?"

"Golem, I guess. ... Well, a little of each." Had I been sacrilegious? In the traditional view, Golems weren't supposed to be able to talk, let alone write. That was supposedly my department. G-d was indeed working in mysterious ways. Or was this really G-d? What did I know? Dressler and Gabaz were both frowning, paying more attention to my words than I felt they were worth. "Whoever was responsible, it didn't amount to much," I added. "She was reelected. In a landslide."

"Our problem is this—if it does the same with Jeremy Bogen," Goldfarb continued, having ignored what I said. "Whatever your opinion of this man, the only Jewish state is likely to pay an unfortunate price. Your administration is already withholding arms in our fight against the terrorists. Right now, we're practically out of all sorts of ammunition, including shells for our artillery and tanks. We have to beg for them. Forget about the bunker bombs we requested. A humiliated Secretary of State could shut things down altogether. It would be a disaster for our people, an existential one."

I was supposed to do something about that? There was a knock on the door, and a nurse entered with a tray.

"Your dinner," said Goldfarb. "Get some rest. You'll start rehab tomorrow."

Already, I thought?

"I'll be here to escort you," said Artie, squeezing me gently on the shoulder.

"Please tell Maya. That's her profession. She'll want to be involved."

"We already have," said Artie.

In the morning, I tested my leg. It hurt like the dickens when I put pressure. A wheelchair was necessary to get me to my first rehab session. Artie walked beside me as an orderly pushed me down the long corridor.

"You won't be needing this for long..." he reassured me as we moved forward. "By the way, if your Golem is real, do you have any idea why he chose you or any specific task you're supposed to make him do besides fighting the world's antisemitism? In that case, you'd need an army of about a hundred thousand Golems, considering how things are going."

I managed a smile. "No idea."

"Maybe you should ask that genius grandson of yours. He might be able to tell you. How's he doing?"

"Max?" I frowned. "I'm not sure. I haven't been able to contact him yet."

"I wouldn't worry about him. He's really capable. I've seen it."

"Yea, I guess you have."

Artie had met Max years ago in DC and was impressed that the then five-year-old could operate a slide rule and knew all about logarithms. I had taken him to see the cherry blossoms and accidentally bumped into Artie across from the Jefferson Memorial. We had a bite of lunch to catch up while Max calculated trigonometric functions on his slide rule. Artie wasn't very specific about why he was there, just something vague about a new business that he said was "too early to talk about." He didn't want to jinx it. These days, I was getting a clearer picture of what that might have been.

He was right about the wheelchair, though. My recovery—or a good part of it—was remarkably rapid at first. Because they served a country perpetually attacked by its neighbors, Sheba Hospital personnel had become unusually skilled at rehabilitation, using a variety of methods almost no one else had ever tried. When they removed my cast, the leg certainly looked bad —bits of pink skin barely visible through a conflagration of various shades of black and blue —about as horrible as I had imagined. And yet they immediately made me stand on it, despite the pain that was beyond unbearable.

Maya could only look on in wonder as they put me in an immersive rehabilitation room surrounded by projections that resembled a giant AI-powered four-wall video game. It generated cartoon-like images in vibrant colors like the jungle paintings of Henri Rousseau. I was never good at the standard video games people played on their phones; I rarely even tried. But, alone in the room while being prompted from a booth, I had little choice but to engage. Soon, sweat was pouring down my face as they had me reaching for projected bananas in competition with an imaginary monkey. The monkey almost always got the better of me, but I had to admit it was exhausting fun. Later, gasping for air, they sat me down, put virtual reality glasses over my eyes, projecting programs that tricked my consciousness to distract me from the intense pain I was still almost constantly feeling. That wasn't my leg that was throbbing as if being hit repeatedly by a sledgehammer, causing me to see stars. Through my VR goggles, it became a smiling baby elephant floating peacefully among clouds and rainbows, bluebirds playing on its trunk.

Sometimes it worked. In between I would hang with others being rehabilitated, male and female wounded members of the IDF, some quite seriously, on an indoor/outdoor deck. A lot of dope was being smoked by the young soldiers for allegedly medical reasons. I tried it once for the first time in about thirty years and decided I preferred the VR glasses for my anesthesia. But I liked the soldiers themselves, whose backgrounds embodied the Jewish world—Ashkenazi, Sephardic, and Mizrachi. A Mizrachi Yemenite captain had apparently been there a long time, healing injuries from machine gun bullets to his neck, ribs, and thigh. His wife, he told me, was a nurse who had been shot fatally in the back on the Lebanon border while treating a patient. When I heard stories like that, my head spun. They had a two-year-old daughter in the care of his grandmother. The two came in one day, and the grandmother sang to us beautifully in haunting Biblical Hebrew in what I took to be a Yemeni accent. She turned toward me, sensing I didn't understand her dialect. It was at that moment that I realized she was blind. "Let all that breathes...let all that breathes... praise Hashem," she translated into perfect English.

Maya visited every day, encouraging me, sometimes staying for hours, administering her own, she admitted, more primitive versions of PT. She got to know the soldiers, too, and became a familiar figure. I also contacted home. Tamara was having her problems with Cody Brent. A bartender was suing him for hitting him over the head with a stool. More importantly, things were still going well with Ed. On the other hand, the synagogue board had replaced me "temporarily" with a junior rabbi from the Bay Area who had swapped my usual course for one called "Centuries of Diversity: Jewish History Reexamined". "I know, I know," said Maya, before I could even roll my eyes. I could deal with it later, she assured me. I had the proverbial bigger fish to fry —Mr. G, of course, not to mention my rehabilitation. My left leg still ached constantly. The most minor bone injuries can take years to heal, Maya informed me. It wasn't pleasant news, but she added that not to worry because these tiny breaks almost always got better on their own eventually. I should be patient.

During that rehab I had heard little about my supposed charge nor anything in the way of specifics about his obsession with Secretary Bogen, although one time a giant clay figure—it didn't look much like my Golem, more like the Incredible Hulk, but scary enough-- was projected on the immersive rehabilitation room's wall with the word "*emet*" printed on its forehead. I should erase the "e," the silent Hebrew letter aleph with two dots for the vowel beneath, I was told, so it would become "*met,*" Hebrew for dead. The cartoon monster would then crumble. But just as I was trying to reach it, it morphed into something resembling Spiderman that disappeared so quickly up a wall even the rehab people were baffled by where it came from. No one could figure out who programmed it. Was it AI acting on its own, something many feared? Nevertheless, they had me try again three days later and I succeeded in erasing the aleph, although I felt a fierce shock up my leg that made me grab a bar to stop from falling inches from the floor. I would have injured myself all over again.

Still, I was improving. Within two weeks, I was moving

about with a walker. Four days later, they took that away, and I was making my way with a cane, albeit tentatively. That too continued my improvement. Pain was still there, but it was intermittent. In my last AI adventure, I reached almost every banana in the immersive rehabilitation room, beating all but one cartoon monkey. I was pronounced a graduate and sent for further convalescence to a residence hotel near Tel Aviv's Carmel Market.

Maya and I wandered through the market every day, marveling at the produce. We loved the stall where an Ashkenazi woman sold the best grape leaves we had ever tasted. An Iraqi Mizrachi cooked burek so delicious that I ate too much and got heartburn that lasted most of the week. I also developed a craving for the upbeat Yemenite music that blared from the ubiquitous boomboxes, providing an optimistic soundtrack against the bleak reality in a country where many of its sons and daughters were facing, or worse, stuck in the hands of an incredibly barbaric enemy. We saw signs of this ourselves during our walks. More than once, sirens wailed, and we would dash back to the hotel—if there was time—to hang out in their shelter until all clear, or end up hiding in the nearest doorway.

This was the beginning of the frequent Houthi attacks, speaking of barbarian cultures. Several times, we saw missiles explode in the sky when the Iron Domes fired, hot shrapnel falling to earth. It was during those times I wondered if we shouldn't go home. What were we doing there? There was still no evidence of the Golem, and I wondered if it was still here, if it had returned to wherever it came from, or if it was in another country fighting its eternal battles. During that period, I didn't hear much from the government except for a doctor who would come by to check my progress. They didn't want me to leave, but I was getting impatient, especially since I heard my synagogue was being radically altered by the new rabbi and was rumored to be introducing a Passover Haggadah to the children's program that had Palestinians asking the four questions at the seder. Tamara and Ed didn't go anymore, although they were still together. Tamara told me the Nussbaums had returned and were taking leadership roles. Max was back in his old school in Indianapolis, still having problems and spending half his time in the principal's office. oI spoke with Max on the phone a couple of times and was relieved he had not lost his sense of humor. He gave me a list of people who had won Nobel Prizes in the sciences who were kicked out of school when they were young. Einstein left school in Germany when he was fifteen, he told me, because he didn't like the rigid teaching style. Then he failed the entrance exam to the Swiss Federal Institute of Technology because he didn't pass the language and history sections. "So don't worry, grandpa," Max said. "I'll be fine." I can't say I was entirely reassured. "What about that Ripton guy?" I asked. "He said he was sad to see me go. Said he would help me find a tutor in Indy if I needed one." "Do you?" I asked Max. He laughed.

Several days later, Maya and I were walking through the market again when I heard a woman call out over my shoulder. "Shalom, rabbi." I turned to see it was Olivia Dreben, the young Talmud scholar who had been sitting next to me on the plane. Standing beside her was a handsome soldier sporting ribbons signifying he was an officer of some kind. He also had a beard, indicating he was probably an ultra-Orthodox Haredi of some sort, one of those allowed to have facial hair under the new IDF rules. Was this man, for whom her friend had said she was her *bashert*? It certainly seemed so. I had told Maya about our conversation.

Olivia introduced us to Captain David Cardozo of Sayeret Matkal, the Israeli special forces everyone in the country seemed to revere— the kind of guy they make action movies about. His assignment was unexpected, since the ultra-Orthodox typically wouldn't serve in such a demanding unit that offers little time for prayer and religious study. I wondered how serious the two were already. From the way they appeared together, it seemed they could be. If so, Olivia was making a surprisingly quick recovery from the marital problems she had shared with me. Was HaShem shining His goodness upon her for her devoted study?

She looked down at my cane with a concerned expression. "Sorry to see something happened to you since we met on the flight. It's not easy here. Hope you didn't get that running to a *mamad*," she said, smiling as she used the Hebrew for shelter.

"Thanks, but no," I said.

"What was it then?"

"It wasn't running for a bus either," I said, making a lame joke. She was trying to be friendly, but I wasn't comfortable with the direction the conversation was taking since the source of my injury was supposed to be confidential.

The Captain, too, was staring at my cane with a frown. "I hope you're alright," he said,

"It's getting better. Been doing rehab. Maya's in that business."

"That's good to hear, " he said. His English was perfect, with a slight Spanish accent that could have been Argentinian. "Just be careful. There's a rumor going around. The government is keeping a lid on it but..."

"What's that?" I didn't want to ask but couldn't resist..

"Some soldiers said an American rabbi got wounded in the tunnels. No one's talking about how he got inside. But, praise God, it led to a hostage getting free."

As if on cue, a siren sounded. It was louder than any I had heard before. Did this mean the threat was more serious? People were diving under tables. Maya and I looked at each other, unsure where to go, when the Captain sprang into action and led us and Olivia to a temporary *mamad* set up behind a butcher shop. Then he bravely returned to the market to ensure others' safety. I saw him helping a woman in a wheelchair—someone I might have been just a few weeks ago—and an older man who was anxiously looking around, confused and uncertain of where to go. He then lifted crying twins from their carriage and carried them to our shelter, followed by their grateful mother. Finally, he sat down with us. The siren continued wailing, even louder now. The Captain checked his watch and turned to Olivia.

"Two hours and twenty minutes until Shabbat," he told her.

"We're going to David's parents," Olivia explained to Maya and me.

"Yes, it will be a special time," the Captain added. "They are devout and have been angry at me for leaving yeshiva to fight in the war. They oppose military service. But now they will have something to celebrate. Shall we tell them?"

The Captain smiled at Olivia, who blushed. "Yes, why not?" Then she added, "We're getting married. David asked my father's permission last night on Zoom. Of course, he had already asked me, and I said yes."

Everyone nearby cheered. It was wonderful to have such positive news in the midst of a possible missile attack, and a round of hearty "*mazel tovs*" came from those of us close enough to hear, including the twins' mother, when Olivia began to slap herself several times on the arm just below the shoulder. "Get away," she said in a low but urgent voice. "Go!" But whatever was causing the trouble didn't stop, and she kept slapping, exhaling with frustration.

"Mosquito?" said the mother. "I have spray."

"No, no, it's okay," responded Olivia, embarrassed. "It's nothing. I just get itchy sometimes."

"I know it sounds crazy, but... It's just that once in a while I feel as if an invisible person is pulling at me... as if he wants me for a dance partner."

They were almost the same words she had used on the plane. I quickly glanced around for evidence of the "invisible person," but it was nowhere to be found.

"We're all under tremendous stress these days," her fiancé said sympathetically. "Things will happen. We have to stay positive."

"We sure do," said the mother whose babies hadn't stopped crying. "I have a cousin who's a cognitive therapist," she added for Olivia's benefit.

"I'll be fine. I've been talking with the rabbi at Chabad of Pardes Katz."

"Rabbi Shlomo? I know him. He's terrific."

"He is," said Olivia, who still seemed shaken and was looking around apprehensively. "This doesn't happen often," she insisted. "I promise you. It's abnormal." She turned to me as she said that, and I sensed she was acknowledging our encounter in Cyprus when something similar occurred. I had an idea what was causing it and considered telling her, but Maya touched my hand, the way wives do with husbands to warn them to keep their mouths shut.

Soon, the all-clear sounded, and we all began to get up from our secure positions. I was pleased to see the Captain put his arm around Olivia, ignoring whatever limitations his strict orthodoxy placed on public displays of affection. As we exited the *mamad*, someone with a radio was reporting that the missile had been shot down over Syria. "So nice to have met you both," my courteous wife said. "And *mazel tov* again for your wonderful news." I echoed Maya, and we shared a round of

"Shabbat Shaloms," with the sincere hope that we would meet again.

"He's an impressive guy," said Maya, stating the obvious about Captain Cardozo, "But do you have any idea what's going on with his girlfriend? Is the Golem pursuing her? Why would that be?"

Why indeed? An attraction to young women who studied '*daf yoni*'? Some kind of divine loneliness akin to that experienced by the gods in Greek mythology? Or was that actually not the Golem in the first place and some figment of Olivia's imagination, some understandable reaction to the unrelenting stress we were all feeling that the Captain had so readily acknowledged?

It was then a few days over a year since October 7, 2023. Time was not standing still, despite it being the most painful period of our lives for most Jews, too young to have experienced the Holocaust personally. It was also indeed nearly Shabbat, a time of peace, and Maya and I were invited to Artie and Daria's house for dinner. We took a cab from the residence hotel. You weren't supposed to do that —travel in a car on Shabbat —but I was used to breaking such rules. Almost no one kept them in Nashville, where members of our congregation lived as much as fifty miles from the synagogue. If they wanted to walk only on Shabbat, I would tell them to move to Brooklyn. There would also be more places to get Kosher food than the paltry offerings in Tennessee, most of which came from synagogue kitchens that were not exactly foodie heaven and had trouble making a decent pastrami sandwich. Being honest, I admit I broke kashrut laws often enough myself, usually at my favorite sushi place where I couldn't resist the scallop sashimi. On those occasions, I would try to find a seat far in the corner, hoping I wouldn't be recognized, not even by G-d. Of course, I was kidding myself..

Artie and Daria, I knew, would disapprove even though I was far from the only lax Jew, even lax rabbi, they ever encountered, since they traveled the globe for their work. They lived in an Orthodox community, Artie explained to me, in the center of the country, midway between Jerusalem and Tel Aviv, not far from the Green Line, in Hashmonaim. This was the area inhabited thousands of years ago by the Maccabees of Hanukkah fame, though you wouldn't know it from pulling up to their gated community. No ancient ruins, walled remnants of their bloody battles to rededicate the Temple and save Judaism from being subsumed by Hellenism, were in evidence, only a guard making sure cars wouldn't drive on the premises on Shabbos. We parked by the gate, got out, and walked, meeting Artie, who was emerging from one of the many synagogues inside. These all reflected specific, sometimes minute, tendencies in our faith, one synagogue having been moved brick by brick, including most of its congregants and their families, from Brooklyn when its old neighborhood began to become what is now called "sketch." But this was not a black hat area. That was too extreme. Those ultra-orthodox had their own enclave across the way.

Artie and Daria's hood was much larger than one would have assumed, a hilly upscale neighborhood of large homes, many built of Jerusalem stone, that could accommodate equally large families. Everyone, it seemed, spoke English as a first and primary language. The families, Artie explained to Maya and me as we trod up the hill to his home, came mainly from the US, but also from the UK, Canada, South Africa, and Australia. But unlike in those home countries, kids were playing freely in the street, their parents unconcerned with the possibility of violence, at least local violence. It was at once jolting and reassuring that such freedom existed somewhere. In a sense, it felt as if a part of Great Neck or Kings Point from the

Long Island of the 1960s had been preserved, lifted, and transported intact to today's Central Israel. In a peaceful scene out of a movie from that period, or perhaps even earlier, like "It's a Wonderful Life," well-dressed people were walking to various homes for Shabbat dinner or were already in them, visible through windows, greeting each other warmly in a remarkably benign world. You wouldn't know there was a war on—well, not quite, as events transpired. You also wouldn't know that in many ways Israel was flying apart, just as it had nearly always been since its inception, when its first prime minister, David Ben Gurion, engineered what proved to be a perpetually shaky peace between the religious and the secular to create the state. But walking to Artie's—it was quite a distance, particularly on my leg; I tried to fight it, but basically, I was limping all the way —this strife didn't seem terminal, more like everyday life as it's lived everywhere, or we wished it were. We ran into several friends of his, all Americans, who first stopped us newcomers to greet us and then to ask for news from home, although, via the internet, they already knew as much as we did — or more — correcting me on the latest events while injecting humor into their observations. It was a Jewish enclave, after all. "Our idiot porcine governor wants 40 billion for illegals, as if 20 weren't enough," one of them informed us. He was a lawyer who commuted back to Chicago twice a month for work, hard as that was to imagine. "Pork for the porky," he added. "This is like being in a Woody Allen movie," Maya whispered to me. "When they were funny," I replied.

Along with Artie, we were the last to arrive at his and Daria's house for Shabbat. They had five children, but only two were there because the others were on military assignments in Gaza and at the Lebanon border. Present were Daniela, a girl in her teens and nearing military age, and Reuben, in his twenties, who, I gathered, was with one of the intelligence agencies.

Also present was a lively woman, Ellie Fine, I guessed to be in her fifties. She was introduced to us as the former Canadian ambassador to Israel, still living in the country. She couldn't abide returning to her home country, she told us, after it went terminally woke. After the usual prayers and songs—some of which I knew—and the ritual washing of hands, Daria served a lavish dinner, although I suspected, given her demanding, almost all-encompassing, legal career—she sued financial institutions financing terrorism—she did not often cook this elaborately. We were fortunate in this case. I was also happy the conversation was not solemn and religious but veered to the catty, like many back home, as everyone was dissed from the country's prime minister to several of their pop stars whose names, of course, eluded me, along with some commentators on CNN that I knew well. This was a relief because I often felt tense in the home of truly devout Jews on Shabbos, lest I, putatively a rabbi, be exposed as someone whose background in halacha, Jewish law, was nowhere up to where it should be and whose knowledge of Hebrew was equally thin. Maya always assured me that G-d didn't care, especially about the latter, that He, She, or It spoke all languages and was only concerned about the state of one's soul, their level of righteousness, and if they did good things in the world, but I wasn't so sure. I wasn't sure about the state of my soul, either. I worried that, as a supposed leader in a more than three-thousand-year-old tradition, I was something of a poseur and a fraud. On these occasions, I feared I would be caught or, more frequently, made to feel ashamed of myself for my laziness and ambivalence about righting the situation, some of which could be addressed with a little effort in studying. Worst of all, I could be exposed as an atheist, if not to others, to myself. Still, this particular Shabbat dinner was a relaxed evening among friends, and I was enjoying it.

But just as dessert arrived, Reuben, who had been looking at his cell phone, which was itself violating a well-known Shabbat prohibition, but no one seemed to care, got up and showed his parents the screen. Both looked startled, then excited. "Excuse us," they said, standing and heading with Reuben to another room. "Enjoy your dessert," added Daria, remembering she was the hostess, as she disappeared through a door. The rest of us sat there, puzzled. "Did somebody win the lottery?" the former ambassador said, pulling out what looked like a rumpled ticket of the type I had seen on sale in kiosks, but she seemed skeptical. We all were. Maya and I looked at each other and shrugged. We started passing the dessert around. But just as we began to dig in, Artie ducked his head out the door and gestured in my direction. "Ben, can you join us?"

More puzzled, I stood and walked through the door. Artie was standing there with Daria, their son behind them in a room surrounded by walls of books.

"Yahya Sinwar's been killed," said Artie.

"In Rafa. By our soldiers," Reuben added.

My mouth had dropped open. "Fantastic!" I said. The leader of Hamas is dead.

"*Nehedar!*" said Daria.

"*Baruch Hashem*," added Artie, "the bastard is no more... We should never have let such an evil murderer out of prison in the first place. He was responsible for everything, even after our doctors cured his brain cancer. Think of that."

Everyone murmured in agreement. Broad smiles had broken out when I noticed Reuben was suddenly frowning.

"Is this supposed to be a secret?" I asked.

"It was, but not any longer," he answered, sharing a look with his father whose smile was also fading. "We were trying to figure out how they found him first—it was crazy, almost accidental--but it's all over the internet now. One of the soldiers who shot him must have leaked it."

"How *did* it happen?"

Reuben faced me directly. "They want you to come down to the Institute as soon as possible."

The Institute? That was the translation of a Hebrew word I knew largely from novels, the shortening of a full name I could hardly remember.

"I'll drive you," said Artie.

On Shabbos? He never did that. This was serious. But that was already obvious.

XIII

XVII

"You don't understand how the building came down around him? Wouldn't that be a normal result of constant bombardment?"

I sounded relatively rational, considering I had just been taken through a hidden door in the back of a building in the middle of downtown Tel Aviv and then escorted down an elevator that descended what felt like miles below the surface to what was apparently a secure room in the bowels of what must have been the subbasement of a subbasement.

Besides Artie, who was still with me, Asher Goldfarb was there with two men who were not introduced. Call them A and B.

"We had deliberately spared that building because it housed a kindergarten," replied A. "But when the walls came down out of nowhere, no children or toys were visible... only Sinwar and one other terrorist in full view of our soldiers, who were able to shoot them easily at near point-blank range. They didn't realize who Yahya was until they walked over, and one of them recognized him from a television documentary. It was all seemingly an... accident."

A, who spoke perfect English with a slight Israeli accent, raised his voice a tad on the word accident, inferring a certain amount of doubt for my benefit. It had already dawned on me what he meant.

"You think it was the Golem?" I replied. What was the point in prolonging this?

"We do not know. Do you?"

"No.... But if it's true, I imagine we should all be grateful." I was going to continue to say something banal about being thankful for divine intervention, but the expressions in front of me were stone-faced. Artie rolled his eyes almost imperceptibly and looked down.

"Of course, we are grateful," said A, though his demeanor had not changed. His voice was professionally flat. "But the connection here, if it is what it is, makes the situation urgent."

"I don't understand."

A nodded to B, who reached into a file, extracted about a dozen sheets of printed paper, and handed them to me. I glanced at the top to see it was a document from the US Department of State. It seemed to be a memo of some sort labeled "RESTRICTED DATA."

"Do you want me to read this now?"

"We thought perhaps you already had."

"I've never seen it before."

"You are certain about that?"

"Absolutely."

"It was found in your residence hotel room."

"You—"

"Of course. We check in on you for your protection and ours. It is a necessary precaution. We cannot be lax anymore. October 7 was a disaster for us. Any repetition would be a catastrophe." He gestured to the papers in my hand. "We think these were taken from your Secretary of State's suite."

"From our embassy?"

Goldfarb, who until then had been silent, looked up from his laptop. "Mr. Bogen prefers the King David Hotel," he said. "The Jerusalem Suite. Where most heads of state stay when they visit our country."

The thought that he wasn't a head of state quickly crossed my mind, but given the chaotic situation at home and the fact that he reports to a leader many see as senile, I wouldn't be surprised if he acted like one and took more control.

"So what you're saying," I responded, "is that you believe the Golem took this document from Secretary Bogen and deposited it in my room when Maya and I were out... For what purpose?"

"Perhaps you can tell us."

"I don't even know what's in it."

"It's his draft of their new Rules of Engagement for Gaza."

"Meaning?"

"A disaster for Israel. If they were to be adopted, it would quite simply be impossible to defeat Hamas."

"You're going to expose this?" I asked Goldfarb.

"Not now. We have our ways of handling these matters. We have a more pressing concern, rabbi." He drew closer in his seat. "This Golem, or whatever it is, has extraordinary power to do what it wishes. This is not the first time it has registered its dislike for your Secretary of State. This is, I will say confidentially, understandable. But the Golem is not a diplomat. It's some kind of spiritual... or technical... force. But whatever it is, we fear it doesn't deal in the short-term realities on which the survival of our state depends. If, as we discussed in the hospital, something were to happen to the Secretary... "

What transpired next was highly discomforting at the time, but, in retrospect, predictable. I was asked to put myself in a position not merely of dual loyalty but to become a spy for, or, more exactly, to act for, Israel against the US —a new Jonathan Pollard of a sort. But Mr. Pollard, despite his scientific and technical skills or maybe because of them, ended up spending thirty years in American prisons. I had neither of those skills. I would be risking my freedom and my family's future for reasons that might best be termed spiritual. Or just foolish.

Maya made me wonder about the latter when I told her about my meeting the next morning. We were drinking coffee on a park bench far from onlookers.

"I guess I get it. They don't like Bogen, but they don't want anything bad to happen to him because the Americans will take it out on Israel."

"Something like that."

"And you're being relied upon to stop the Golem from doing that. I thought they didn't believe he or it was real."

"Well, maybe they're having second thoughts. After Yahya. "

Or third or fourth. As the previous evening wore on, I could see those doubts in them and feel them in myself. Doubts about what we were supposed to believe. It was the nature of our, maybe all, religions. We had been told all these miracles had occurred—plagues had been visited on Pharoah, the Red Sea had parted, a bush had burned spontaneously, it's divine self-definition, "I am what I am," preparing Moses to receive the Ten Commandments—but we hadn't seen anything like that in our lifetimes or anything close to them, not by the longest of shots. And people who claimed to have witnessed such things were branded as kooks, disregarded like Seventh Day Adventists who arrived at your door to inform you the end of the world was weeks away, only to be made fun of in movies and television shows. But then there was research that attempted to prove that such supposed miracles did occur in the distant past, that there was some kind of historical justification, an earthquake on Santorini whose aftershocks could have caused seas to divide or at least recede. In Hebrew, the Red Sea was translated as the Sea of Reeds, not so difficult to cross. And most of the ten plagues could be explained scientifically, all, of course, except the death of the firstborn, a plague whose brutality, since childhood, I didn't like thinking about, that turned me against my religion when I did.

Where did the Golem fit in this? Was this the Kabbalah of Information that I didn't have the scientific background to understand anyway? Was this G-d or a computer chip or both? Where was Max when I needed him? Closer at hand than I cared to admit at that moment, but something told me not to reach out to him. Everything would come apart.

As he drove me home in the early hours of the morning, Artie said, "You are a lucky man, *chaver*. You are being shown your purpose."

"What's that?"

"To prevent disasters to our people and the world."

"Oh, good," I said with a substantial lack of enthusiasm.

"It should be everyone's goal... Our Sages say that," he added when I did not reply.

"What did they say about biting off more than you can chew?"

Artie laughed.

"Do they want me involved in this, too?" said Maya, still digesting how that night's conversation had evolved. We had both had much to mull over in recent months, far more than in our entire lives before added together and squared.

"We're a couple. We have to do this together. Also, it's less suspicious, they think."

"*They* think..."

I had already explained most of the plan. Both of our passports were in Israeli hands with photographs, probably already altered to fit the appearances of a different Mr. and Mrs. Benjamin and Maya Golub, who were on the manifest of that morning's El Al flight to Mumbai.

"Suppose it doesn't work?" Maya asked. "We're in deep."

"It'll work. They're good at this." At least I hoped they were. "It's being made to look as if we're headed for a grand tour of India with reservations for the Taj Mahal and the Golden Temple in Amritsar. They've booked restaurants and guides."

"What about the synagogue, your job?"

"I sent the board an email saying we've been under great stress and have decided we should take my two weeks off now to decompress. Everybody and his brother will no doubt be reading that, as Max would no doubt remind us."

Meanwhile, Maya and I were getting new identities and passports for Mr. and Mrs. Charles and Eleanor Baumgarten, a retired couple from Wilmington, North Carolina, where we ran a small hedge fund, since closed. "So we're moving," she continued. "To the King David Hotel?"

"Top floor suite, with its own patio, sauna and panoramic view of the Old City."

"I could deal with that," said Maya, finally relaxing a bit and unable to resist a grin.

"So could, I've been told, our Secretary of State. Apparently, he stays just down the hall in the Jerusalem Suite, where they put heads of state."

"He's not a head of state." She had said aloud what I had said to myself. It wasn't the first time.

"Close enough, these days."

I handed her one of the two new IDF-encrypted cellphones that had been given to me.

"I don't think I've ever done anything this crazy in my life," she said.

"You haven't."

The next afternoon, we were driven up to the King David in a town car that allegedly had come directly from Ben Gurion Airport. Stowed in its trunk was a fresh set of luggage to fit our new identities, including a couple of matching Louis Vuitton suitcases that, as far as I could tell, were authentic. Sitting beside me, Maya wore a Gucci designer suit, her hair, for the first time, bleached platinum blonde. I have to say I found it attractive, though it was on the edge of vulgar, as was often true of the very wealthy who could afford to thumb their noses at the opinions of hoi polloi. I had less luck since it was deemed simpler to shave my head. Also, I was told not to wear a yarmulke and given a British racing cap to match a bespoke Barbour jacket that exuded the intended class, as if I had recently been fly-fishing in Wales. No wonder several bellhops rushed up to assist us when we pulled up.

The interior of the hotel looked even more luxe and distinguished than I remembered it to be when we signed in at the reception. I had been there once before when, as a rabbinical student, a classmate and I decided to splurge on lunch at their outdoor cafe. We went to see how the other half lived and to visit the hotel where a particularly dramatic and controversial event from our Jewish history course took place. July 1946, Menahem Begin's Irgun guerrillas, Zionist militants, bombed the hotel's south wing, which was then headquarters for British Mandatory Palestine. They were trying to destroy some incriminating intelligence documents confiscated by the Brits, but ended up accidentally killing 91 people, Arabs, Brits, and Jews. I wrote a paper on the accidental disaster as a student, condemning Begin for his recklessness. Years later, when he became prime minister of Israel and negotiated the peace with Egypt, I realized I had made a mistake. I was the one who convinced my son and daughter-in-law, despite some resistance, to name their son after Begin. Since Menahem wasn't exactly a popular name in Indiana schools, they started calling him Max practically at birth.

"Is this our second honeymoon?" I asked Maya and kissed her on the lips after the bellhops had left and we were alone in our suite. They had, at our instruction, left the patio doors wide open, yielding the advertised panoramic view of the Old City, including its ramparts and those global matchboxes—the Dome of the Rock and the Al-Aqsa Mosque, with all their potential for world conflagration. We were standing at one end of the living room next to a mahogany dining table that could probably handle a dozen guests, not that we were planning on having any. In the center was a lavish gift bowl filled with an assortment of fruits and pastries, along with two bottles of Yarden Blanc de Blancs, compliments of the manager. Behind us was a bedroom as big as the living room with a king-sized bed, canopied with carved angels, and a private sauna off the bathroom.

"Better than our first in that Myrtle Beach motel with the little green bugs in the bathtub," she responded. "But we didn't need a guard outside the door." She was referring to the man with bulging muscles beneath his white shirt sleeves we saw stationed at the end of the corridor when we emerged from the elevator. He nodded to us. Two others, who, if anything, looked larger, stood at the opposite end, by the door of the Jerusalem Suite, supposedly occupied by Jeremy Bogen. They wore the dark business suits and white shirts one associates with the Secret Service. At the moment, we were told, though it was all over media websites anyway, the secretary was not there but in Doha with Cairo next on his schedule. He was going to be away for at least five days

That meant we actually could be getting a second honeymoon courtesy of Israeli authorities but were disabused of that notion just after three a.m. that morning when a piercing siren wailed across the city. As instructed, we stumbled out of our suite into the corridor, where one of the guards rushed us into the elevator down to the basement, then into a *mamad* marked "Security--Sixth Floor Only" in English and Hebrew. Inside were a couch, two chairs, and a small refrigerator stocked with drinks and energy bars. A video screen dominated one of the walls, but nothing was showing at present. My leg was starting to ache again. It was probably the anxiety. I wondered if I could run if I had to. Sensing what I was feeling, Maya took my hand and we sat on the couch, waiting. After about twenty minutes, an all-clear sounded, and the bodyguard who had escorted us opened the door. "Houthis," he said. "Missile intercepted outside Israel's airspace."

Three of the next four nights, it was the same thing. Somewhere around three a.m., sirens wailed, and we made the trek down to the *mamad*. Getting back to sleep was not just difficult; sometimes it was impossible. The missiles did minor concrete damage, but the Houthis clearly timed them to drive people crazy with sleeplessness. It certainly worked on me and on Maya as well. During the day, we were walking around like zombies. I didn't know how much more of this I could take. At least in the tunnels, I was able to sleep during what I assumed were the small hours of the morning. The terrorists were tired as well then and left me alone. But this was a special kind of torture.

It was Jeremy Bogen himself, back from Qatar or wherever, who had emerged from his suite at almost the precise second we did. He was tall and patrician, even in pajamas, almost like a Jew masquerading as a Boston Brahman. Considering the State Department had long had a reputation for antisemitism, this man must have been a smooth operator to negotiate his way to the top. Or perhaps it was just his fine head of hair, now only slightly greying, and the furrowed brow that gave him the necessary made-for-talk-shows gravitas. We greeted him with polite nods and introduced ourselves as the elevator descended. He was accompanied by one of his secret service men, whom he introduced as Edward. Once inside the safe room, Bogen was outwardly pleasant as we sat together. Still, I thought I detected some irritation he had to share the royal *mamad* with a plebian retired hedge fund manager and his wife. Outside, we could hear explosions.

"Houthis keep doing this," Bogen explained, "when more of their people starve than anywhere in the world."

"Do they get *all* their missiles from Iran, Mr. Secretary?" I asked to avoid sounding overly knowledgeable yet sufficiently aware. A true hedge fund manager, even a retired one, would have to follow global events for his business.

"Almost," he said, checking his watch. "The homegrown ones don't go anywhere."

"Well, good luck with what you are doing. We're rooting for you."

"Thank you. This is some time to be here. What brings you? Family?"

"We wanted to show moral support," said Maya. It was a well-chosen answer.

"Good for you," said Bogen. "It's needed."

I nodded my agreement.

That was the extent of our conversation. I knew better than

to inquire about the hostage negotiations, so we sat there in silence for another five minutes. Out of the corner of my eye, I studied the man, looking for clues to why he was such a target for the Golem. But I was ill-prepared. I had never met a diplomat before, let alone a Secretary of State. By then, I had read his Rules of Engagement, and they were indeed onerous, unfairly restrictive for the IDF, and, in my limited knowledge of war, arguably placed them in harm's way. Bogen himself must have known this, and I wondered why this supremely successful Jewish man whose grandfather, according to Wikipedia, had been a significant supporter of Israel on its founding and whose great-grandfather was a famous Yiddish writer in Poland, seemed to be undermining the Jewish state now. Was this real or a charade of some sort to preserve his power?

A few years ago, in one of my sporadic attempts to transform myself into a rabbi worthy of the name, I had started to make my way through the "*Tanya*," a book published around 1800 by Rabbi Schneur Zalman intended to be a practical guide for life that became the foundational work of the Chabad movement. Called the Alter Rebbe, he wrote of the conflict between the *yetzer hara*—the evil inclination—and the *yetzer hatov*—the good inclination. They are described as two voices inside our heads. The idea was to cultivate the *yetzer hatov* to live a righteous life and bring one closer to G-d. This, the *Tanya* indicated, was difficult for all people and provided another way to view Jeremy Bogen's situation. Which voice predominated in his head? And the *yetzer hara* wasn't all bad, the Alter Rebbe pointed out, at least through its cousin, the ambitious "animal soul" that can give us energy to accomplish things when properly harnessed. And then some people thought their inclinations were good —*yetzer hatov* —when in reality they were *yetzer hara*. Such self-delusion occurred in every walk of life. Why would Jeremy Bogen, a Jewish man, seek to hinder the only Jewish state? Did he have a wish, conscious or unconscious, to hide who he was, as had so many before throughout history? Alternatively, did he think he was doing good, saving Israel from itself, when he arguably was doing the reverse?

When the all-clear sounded and we got up to return to our rooms, there was something about the way Bogen nodded to us that gave me a chill. I wasn't sure—perhaps it was projection on my part—but there was also a hint of suspicion in the way he looked at us as we headed for the elevator. Well-trained, he allowed Maya to enter first.

"Your security guard will be waiting," he said.

Not long after we got back to the room, I got a call from Max on my personal phone, which I had been able to keep. It must've been around eight p.m. back in Indiana. "Hi, Grandpa. Did I wake you?" I must have sounded groggy.

"Not you. I've been up for a while."

"Oh, yeah. Houthis again. I saw on the internet. I had something I wanted to tell you but if you want to go to sleep—"

"Hopeless at this point. Shoot."

"I've been making my own Golem."

"What?!"

"It's been going pretty well. You know how the Chinese are ahead of us in robots?"

"No, but I'm not surprised."

"They've got the fastest one, the L7 from Tsinghua University in Beijing. It looks totally human and can run at 9 miles per hour, not to mention do a zillion other things with AI. I was able to get some of their plans." I didn't interrupt to ask how since I could guess, more or less. Also, it was great to hear his positive voice in the pre-dawn darkness. "So I started to build one," he continued. "I had to borrow some money from my father for parts, but it wasn't that expensive. It's amazing what you can do with two or three used Nintendos. It's in the testing phase."

"A beta Golem...?"

"I dressed it like a Halloween monster and took it to school."

"Which school? Your old one?"

He hesitated a second. "Yeah, they took me back. Provisionally. Anyway, I wanted to check if my programming worked. And it mostly did."

"What was that?"

"To fight antisemites, Grandpa. It's a *Golem*." He sounded a tad impatient. "It ran social media for the whole class in about ten seconds and discovered nine out of the thirty-four had evidence of antisemitism or anti-Zionism for them or their parents. So it pointed to them in class with its robot arm and blinker. Everyone else thought it was funny and wanted the monster to blink at them."

"Parents too? Max, that is not smart. In fact, it's bloody dangerous. Please be careful. It could get you in a pack of trouble that will follow you the rest of your life."

"Grandpa, I am being careful. I'm not stupid. Everyone thought it was a game. They didn't know what was happening... Anyway, I'm doing this for you... as what's called proof of concept. Showing Golems can be built through artificial intelligence, even by me, a kid. I thought you'd want to know. The line between human and AI is very blurry now. We don't know if it exists. An artificial Golem could make decisions on its own, even have feelings like we do. It's hard to tell which is which." The direction he was heading was making me anxious but before I could say anything, he veered off. "How's your leg, Grandpa? I'm worried about you. Everyone is."

I hesitated before answering. "It's not great, but I'm sure

it'll get better. Not to worry. Meanwhile, do us both a favor and ix-nay on the olem-gay. Please. One's enough."

"No one uses Pig Latin anymore, Grandpa."

I laughed, although not really reassured.

"I love you, Grandpa."

"I love you too, Max. Just promise me..."

"I promise."

I thanked him and hung up. "Maybe he could sell them," Maya said with a half-smile. She had been listening intently. "Toy Golems for Hanukkah."

This time, I laughed for real, but maybe it was forced and not that funny. We finally tried to get to sleep for an hour or two, but it was not to be. Somewhere around four a. m., just as we were beginning to doze off again, having convinced ourselves there would be no more missiles, at least for that night, I was awakened again when I heard the suite doorbell ring, followed by someone rapping impatiently on the door. I cautiously got out of bed and trundled over to the door, making sure it was double locked before peering through the peephole. Bogen was standing there in a robe, looking upset. He had his cellphone near his ear as if expecting a call. Since he must have heard me coming, I had no choice but to open the door, but I kept it on its chain latch.

"Sorry to bother you," he said. "Have you seen my bodyguards? They seem to have fled. "

"Fled? What happened?"

"Didn't you hear that weird noise? ...Yours is still here." He gestured behind him, where my security man was slumped sleepily against the wall. "

"Noise? No."

He looked surprised and slightly irritated. "It went on for ten minutes at least... constant ringing in the ears. Like a dozen fire alarms going on next to your head. It was maddening." I glanced back at Maya, who had joined me and was shaking her head. She hadn't heard a thing either.

"My security men just fled," said Bogen, repeating himself, this time more irritated. He turned toward our guard. "What did you see? Did you hear anything?"

"No, sir," he said.

"Who did that?" Just then, his call came through. "Hello, Chris. We got a problem..." Without a word to us, he walked back to his suite.

Maya and I wrestled with this and other matters as we strolled through Yemin Moshe the next morning. Due to the war, few people were around the normally tourist-laden neighborhood, the first Jewish enclave built outside the Old City in the late Nineteenth Century and only a few minutes' walk from the King David. It was famed for its windmill and picturesque homes along narrow hillside alleys. We could walk among them and talk without fear of being overheard. Why had the Golem left Bogen's rules in our room, if it did? What would the being have expected us to do with them? Put them on the synagogue website? Would anybody care? We weren't journalists. I knew a few from the coffee shop but they weren't the type likely to be interested in such a thing. Or was it just the being's way of warning us about the secretary's character, something we might already guess? And what had happened last night with Bogen's guards, who evidently were driven away by that sound? I had noticed them back at their posts when we exited our suite that morning. We both had a good guess what had scared them.

My leg was aching again from walking on cobblestones, and we headed back to the hotel when Maya's cellphone rang. I watched as she said a few words, mainly listening to whoever it was on the other end. Finally, she clicked off and put the phone back in her purse.

"Warner Medical Center in Woodland Hills. My mother has fallen down the stairs."

"Oh my God."

"It sounds serious. Some level of concussion."

"You have to go."

She nodded. There was no point in my adding she was the family PT, first administering physical therapy to her husband and now to her mother. A vision of the adobe house off Old Topanga Road popped into my head, incongruous as it seemed in Yemin Moshe, the same dusty ankhs still hanging in the rear windows that looked out on the dozen or so marijuana plants growing in the rickety greenhouse that somehow survived the fires that burned the canyon every few years. California in the 70s was frozen in time. Nothing had changed there in the decades since Maya was born; her father, in a wheelchair most of the years I knew him before his death, always within reach of bookshelves lined with the works of Meher Baba, Rajneesh, Ram Dass, and others too numerous to recall, even a couple from his own tradition. I once noticed a paperback of Elie Wiesel's "Night," though it was still unread in its shrink wrap.

"Are you going to be okay?" she said, noticing my limp as we walked back to the hotel. My leg was aching, but I was doing my best not to show it, to her and to myself.

"I'll come with you."

She shook her head. "You'll just be sitting around wishing you hadn't... You have to finish this. You'll hate yourself if you don't. Or they'll hate you...Corny as it sounds, this is all happening for a reason."

"If I only knew what it was."

"You'll find out at some point. I'm sure. Just remember you don't owe anybody anything.... The Jewish people will survive without you. They made it this far. Thirty-five hundred years without your help."

I had to laugh, and Maya did too. We stopped for a moment and hugged each other.

"I'll get back as soon as I can," I said.

"Just take care of that leg," she reminded me. "Don't make it worse."

Back in our suite, I checked on flights with the concierge while Maya packed, emptying out her walk-in closet. Maybe it was the urgency in my voice, but he was able to locate a last-minute seat via Frankfort and made a reservation under the name of Mrs. Emily Baumgarten. It would be a long haul from there to LAX. I confirmed with Artie, who double-checked himself, that the Institute's forged passport would pass muster at the other end. They had more than the normal experience at such things. I felt bereft at seeing Maya go, but was comforted by watching her slide her IDF-encrypted cellphone into her purse. I knew I'd be needing to stay in touch a minute after she was gone. Not long thereafter, I saw her off in a cab for the airport.

Our suite, when I returned, was eerily empty, almost too large for one person. I walked around feeling out of sorts, unsure where to sit when I had so many choices. I also felt as if I didn't deserve this, that it was too much, without my wife there. I wondered how Bogen dealt with it, but concluded he was used to being alone in large suites. He was, as my grandmother would say, "to the manor born." I also presumed he traveled with an entourage, though I had not seen any beyond the two Secret Service agents. So I walked back and forth in the living room, my discontent growing, unclear about what I was supposed to do now. I phoned Artie again to inform him that Maya had indeed left, but probably just as much to make contact; he wasn't there. I left a voicemail, but this only increased my sense of isolation. I was becoming agitated. I walked out onto the patio to clear my mind, but, although it was a beautiful day, the Old City and the Temple Mount outlined against a cloudless sky, my discomfort was not assuaged and I returned to the living room, where I continued to pace, actually limping on one foot, although I knew it wasn't advisable. I started looking around, growing apprehensive. I had the sensation that I was not alone. Was I hearing footsteps? Were they in the suite or out in the corridor? What was wrong with me? I was not usually a paranoid person, but my recent life had clearly not been normal. I walked into the bedroom. It too was empty, as was the bathroom, whose door was ajar. The bed was unkempt, the housemaid not yet having arrived. The cover was pushed back where Maya had slept. By instinct, I turned toward her closet. My feeling of being watched had become incredibly intense. I opened her closet door. For a moment, it was almost as if a lightning bolt were flashing in front of my eyes. The Golem was standing there. Terrified, as if I were in a horror movie, I screamed and slammed the door shut. My body shook. Then I froze, almost catatonic. But then I realized this was my opportunity. I could do my rabbinic duty, honor the Israeli government's request, and erase the word "*emet*" from the brow. It would be the end of any possible actions against Bogen or anybody else.

I went back into the living room and found a letter opener in the desk. It should suffice to do the job against its skin of mud. My hand trembling, I returned to the bedroom. I took a deep, calming breath in front of the closet door and opened it. The Golem was standing with what would typically be its head in its hands as if it were sobbing, although there was no sound. What was that about? A Golem in misery? Human emotion? At that moment, it felt impossible to act, and I shut the door, the letter opener dangling in my hand. But then I realized I had a mission, to stop the Golem whose behavior, whatever its intentions, had been dangerously erratic. I could not afford to be sentimental. I gathered up my courage and, instrument at the ready, opened the door again. The closet was empty. The Golem had vanished. Or was it ever there? I touched the bare walls of the closet for evidence of its presence, but found none. I pounded my fist against the door frame. Everything, my life itself, from beginning to end, seemed at that moment to have been an illusion. My leg was throbbing as bad as it ever had been, as if all the rehabilitation had gone for naught. I could barely stand.

I knew that sleep that night would be difficult. Maya's absence was only part of it. I had stayed up on purpose to know that she had landed safely in Los Angeles. When I told her of my brief encounter with the Golem in what was once her hotel closet, she didn't comment with much more than "Oh," but I knew her well enough, knew the multiple tones in her voice, to realize that it worried her and that she was now growing in concern that I was not in my right mind. She told me to really try to get some sleep, the very thing I was almost certain I could not do. She realized that, too. Our conversation was short because her suitcases were just coming down the baggage claim at LAX, so we said good night and good morning, and I turned off the light by the bed. Predictably unable to sleep, my leg throbbing again, I lay there distracting myself by ruminating on why the Golem had not already acted more firmly against Jeremy Bogen. It was odd, considering he or it could clearly do whatever it wanted, be wherever it wanted, whenever it wished. Further, and obviously more importantly, why hadn't it freed all the hostages by now, not just one? I had expressed that quandary to Artie and he had said they were also aware of it. He would arrange a meeting for me to discuss this. But this solved little in the small hours of the morning. The lack of resolution was keeping me awake. My insomnia in this case was extreme. Checking the clock, it was five minutes to 4 AM and I still hadn't fallen asleep. I was busy calling my whole life to question, as one does in the midst of insomnia, starting with the first time I neglected to do my homework back in the fourth grade and lied to my parents about it. It was then that everything had started to go wrong. There was little hope for me now. When would I ever drift off? I kept getting increasingly anxious about things I could not possibly control. Was a breakdown imminent? I had succumbed to the *yetzer hara*.

At that moment, I felt an inexplicable warmth around my bad leg, as if it were being wrapped in a heating blanket from my thighs to my ankles. The temperature started to increase, almost to the point of being too hot, but not quite. I was sweating. A tingling sensation followed, going up and down my side. What was going on? Had my injury metastasized? I knew it made no sense, but was I getting bone cancer? Then I noticed what appeared to be an octopus-like arm wrapped around my leg. The pain was starting to disappear. Within seconds, it was gone almost entirely, back to the state it was in before I had sustained the injury in the tunnel, back to normal for the first time. I looked up to see the Golem lying on top of me, yet I experienced no weight. Briefly, it switched to my other leg, as if it were balancing both limbs out the way they do in rehab. Then it started to withdraw, yet it was still near. I could see the Hebrew letters Aleph, Mem, and Tav for "*emet*," truth, still carved into what would normally have been a forehead. This was a moment I could have erased them, fixed everything, or so I was told. The letter opener was just to my right, on the bed end table. I reached for it, but stopped, changing my mind. It seemed somehow sacrilegious. I smiled up at the divine creature, and it vanished simultaneously. I lay there a few minutes, then got out of bed, feeling remarkably spry, as if I didn't now need any sleep. I walked around the room several times. Still no sign of pain. I did some jumping jacks and push-ups. I lay on my back and pulled back with force on the part of my leg that continued to cause me agony, concentrating on the angle that had resisted PT from both Maya and the squad of doctors at Sheba Medical Center with their high-tech apparatus. Like new, almost youthful. He or it had cured me. Instead of going back to bed, I said "*Moden ani,*" the morning prayer—it was after all morning already--and gave thanks to G-d for restoring my soul within me. Then I rechecked the clock. I was suddenly extremely hungry. It was an hour early for breakfast. I would have to wait. I texted Maya what had happened. "Unbelievable," she texted back. It was.

XIV

An hour or so later, when I arrived at the hotel dining room, it was already crowded. People love Israeli breakfasts for good reason. They are lavish spreads featuring all manners of salads, eggs, fruits, breads, and pastries for which the words copious or maybe bounteous, overly bounteous, could easily have been invented. These breakfasts had originated on kibbutzim and were designed to fuel farm workers for long days of arduous work. The same meals in a fancy hotel were giving the diners about 5000 extra calories a day, and who knows how many inches of girth they didn't need. Nevertheless, I was ready to indulge and was accompanying the hostess to a table when I noticed Jeremy Bogen was sitting at the next table. For a second, I thought this was fine, even possibly advantageous, as I would be able to advance our acquaintanceship under my pseudonym in a relaxed, unsuspicious manner, but then I stopped short. Bogen was dining with Nicolas Peebles of all people. What was he doing here? He could identify me immediately. I could be indicted for treason. I quickly handed the menu she had given me back to the hostess and excused myself as if I had an emergency, turning and walking as swiftly as possible without attracting attention, dodging a busboy laden with dishes, out of the dining room. Out of the corner of my eye, I could see the hostess's look of annoyance as she stared after me.

Instead of returning to my room, I headed out of the hotel in the direction of Yemin Moshe. That spring was still in my legs, and I surprised myself after a minute or two by breaking into a jog, something I hadn't done in years. After some distance, I stopped and sat on a bench to think. My situation had changed once again. Nicolas Peebles was a special agent of the National Geospatial-Intelligence Agency. If there was anyone with the ability to know where you were at any moment, it was he. Therefore, it was more than just possible that he was here because of me and could actually be staying at the King David for the same reason. Should I confront him or try to be scarce? For the moment, I chose the latter. There was still something risk-averse about me. Or was it just common sense?

Being cautious, I called Artie. He had arranged a meeting for me with Rabbi Dressler and Dr. Gabaz, neither of whom I had seen since those first days at the hospital. Apparently, they were working on a book and, for some reason, wanted to interview me for it. That seemed strange, but Artie assured me they were legitimate—it's not their first collaboration—so I agreed, and the meeting was set for the hotel. Now, because of what I had recently seen, that could cause problems, so it was decided we would meet at a café above the Mamilla shopping mall that leads into the Old City. I had been to that mall on a previous trip, so I found it easily and arrived early. With my leg feeling better after a bit, I had started jogging again, then running—a thing I hadn't done in decades. When I was in my thirties, I occasionally ran 10Ks, not as a winner, but not disgracefully either. And here I was, almost to my surprise, able to do it again in my late sixties, which was quite an astonishing side benefit. In any case, because I arrived early, I decided to continue along the mall, which is essentially a modern entrance to the Jaffa Gate into the Old City.

For all that had happened, this was my first trip to Israel during which I hadn't visited the Kotel, the Wall. Did G-d disapprove? Did the Golem? Whatever, I wended my way through the narrow alleys of the Old City to the Western Wall. Again, I was struck by how few tourists were there because of the war. Nevertheless, with a yarmulke placed firmly on my head, I made my way up to Herod's massive retaining wall for the Second Temple, where so many had left their wishes, scrawled on pieces of paper and tucked into the cracks between the bricks. I left my own, praying for the recovery of my hippie mother-in-law. I thought to do others, but that was clearly the most pressing. Maya's latest report was not optimistic. I stood there for a few minutes and prayed, then glanced toward the Mughrabi Gate, the only entrance to the Temple Mount that Jews were permitted to use, and then only at certain hours. They were further not allowed to wear sacred Jewish garments like *tallit* nor carry their prayer book nor, most of all, allowed to enter the Dome of the Rock, once, according to the belief of the three Abrahamic religions, the Holy of Holies, the location of the Foundation Stone, where the world was allegedly founded and G-d asked Abraham to sacrifice his son, Isaac for the Jews and Ishmael for Muslims.

It was forbidden for Jews to go there now, yet I had seen it with my own eyes, many years before, in 1968, when I was about 12 and went to Israel with my parents, not long after the war that made the Old City part of Israel. It was my first time in the country. Going up to the Temple Mount was simpler then—I don't remember any Muslim-only gates as there are now—and my father took me on a father-son expedition to the top. I remember it well because it made such a strong impression being in such a holy, once-forbidden place. Even my father, who was not very religious and had a regular Friday night poker game rather than Shabbat, seemed overwhelmed as we walked directly to the Dome and entered. We were inside the Holy of Holies itself. Just steps in front of us was a railing. We went forward and looked down. Beneath us was a piece of bedrock that I learned was limestone. This was it—the Foundation Stone. I didn't know what to make of it. To be honest, I started not to like what I was seeing all that much. I felt uncomfortable being there, where God asked Abraham to sacrifice his own son. With my father beside me, it was hard for my twelve-year-old self to sympathize with something that seemed so brutal. How could God do that? God was supposed to be this benign figure in heaven, although he evidently wasn't, or it wasn't that simple. Yet, all three religions, Judaism, Christianity, and Islam, wanted us to believe this story. I could tell that it made my father nervous, too. He didn't communicate to me the conventional explanation that God was testing Abraham's faith and obedience. Therefore, the presumption is that God would never have made Abraham actually undertake such a sacrifice. But of course, we don't know. To this day, the story unsettles me. It particularly unsettled me, already a grown man, during that period I decided to abjure the rabbinate and move to Maine to teach. That was far from the full motivation—there were personal reasons, as I have noted —but I know it played a part. Even now, I have not resolved it, though I do my best not to think about it.

When I arrived back at the café, Rabbi Dressler and Dr. Gabaz were already there, sitting with Artie. The Rabbi looked less severe than when we had first met. Maybe it was the more casual blue shirt beneath his Hasidic garb. The doctor was in a chic dark olive business suit, with only a small colorful scarf acknowledging her Ethiopian background. The suit matched her lustrous skin, and if I were thirty-five years younger and single, I would have been fantasizing about her for weeks. But I was neither, so I congratulated them both on their book and asked them what it was about.

"Kabbalah and quantum mechanics," said the rabbi.

I smiled. "Two subjects about which I have, to put it mildly, limited knowledge..." Then I realized I was sounding like a completely fraudulent rabbi from some reform synagogue barely worth its name, and I added, "Well, I am a believer in the Ein Sof," using the Kabbalist's term for the endless light that existed even before creation. The concept had always appealed to me, as had the idea that God contracted to create the universe, another belief I understood to be Kabbalistic.

"And about quantum mechanics?" said the doctor.

"You'd have to ask my grandson."

"Ben has a grandson who's a technology whiz," said Artie.

Dr. Gabaz nodded approvingly. "Then he perhaps can explain to you the theory of quantum entanglements... that quanta, particles, are often linked, behave in the same manner, no matter how far they become separated in space and time, even across continents."

"That's interesting. Amazing actually. Thank you. But I assume you didn't bring me here for science class."

"We have been told you were visited again by the Golem." That was the rabbi. Obviously, they had been talking with Artie to whom I had recounted my experience.

"Twice. The first time I just saw him for a second in a closet."

"And the second time?"

"He came to me in the night and healed my leg."

"So we have heard." I glanced at Artie, who shrugged. "That is very good news," the rabbi continued.

"We're trying to understand how such a miracle could have happened," said the doctor.

"I'd like to know myself. I was lying there at night, feeling some pain, when I felt it hovering over me."

"You didn't do as instructed?" Artie asked, a question he had not probed before.

"Erase the letters? I thought of it. But somehow it didn't feel right to destroy an entity that was curing me."

"Do you have any idea why this entity that, like everything else, comes from G-d had so much loving concern for you?" the rabbi asked.

I shook my head. "Nor why it appeared in the back yard of my synagogue in the first place. It just was."

"Or will be," said the doctor. "It could have been from the past or the future or neither."

"Neither?"

"Well, all at once. Many physicists believe there is no such thing as time."

"I had an uncle who used to tell me that as a kid, but it never really..." I glanced inadvertently at my watch. It seemed to be ticking. "I mean, what do we consider our sacred Torah then. Isn't that the past?"

"Or the present or the future or both at once. As you wish."

The rabbi nodded. "In Kabbalah, we call that *Reisha D'Lo*, the Unknowable Head. The true nature of reality is beyond our grasp."

"In quantum mechanics," the doctor added, "the assumption is we cannot know both the position and momentum of a particle with perfect accuracy. It revises Einstein's saying, 'God does not play dice with the universe.' Maybe He does."

"He is certainly able to," said the rabbi, "if He wishes."

At that point, a siren went off. We all jumped up, automatically looking at the sky with nothing yet visible, when the host rushed up and escorted us around the back to a shelter.

"Amazing, they do this," said Artie, as the door to the *mamad* was shutting. "Shoot at random. They could take out their own Al-Aqsa and the Dome by accident."

"And kill thousands of their own," added the rabbi.

"They don't care," said Dr. Gabaz.

"It would start a race war, wouldn't it?" I offered, having already drawn my own conclusion.

"If not World War III," said Artie. An explosion went off that seemed distant. "That was us. Over Syria, probably."

But wouldn't World War III have already happened, I wondered, many times, remembering our conversation, in the past as well as in the future.

A few minutes later, all clear had sounded, and we were back at our table. In a sense, the rabbi was already answering that question about time, but in reverse, with the past preceding the future in usual fashion—or was it? "We are interested, Rabbi Golub, in the age of your Golem. "

"I have no idea. We're at 5785 in the Jewish calendar so..."

"As you know, God predates Judaism."

"Of course. Millions of years.... Before time or whatever. But I still don't...."

"Your confusion is understandable," said the doctor. "It becomes a question of whether there is a finite number of particles—photons, electrons, and so forth—that were originally formed by the Creator during the Big Bang, or whether they are ever expanding, possibly through repeated Big Bangs. This is an inquiry that has been much debated. For our book, we are interested in discovering why your Golem appeared in Nashville, in the yard of your synagogue, when and where it did, and why those particular particles, originally behaving chaotically, came together there. What is the purpose? Why did that happen? What is and perhaps was and will be G-d's plan? It is something of a test case in the link between Kabbalah and quantum physics we are attempting to draw. They are not common, to say the least. We are grateful to you, Rabbi Golub, for providing us with this rare opportunity."

"So what would you like me to do?" I asked.

"Find out the intention of the Almighty... or perhaps reveal it," said Rabbi Dressler, who had a smile that was somewhere between benign and puckish, as he spoke that extraordinarily weighty assignment that was beyond any reality I could countenance. Was he joking? "Is the Kabbalistic understanding of chaos or *Tohu* much the same as saying this table in front of us is no more than a collection of random quantum particles reorganized by the divine presence? None of us really understands, but do not fear what is in front of you personally," he added, staring directly at me, the smile having disappeared. "You are stronger than you think. Perhaps the Golem cured more than just your leg. Remember—*HaShem* loves you."

Returning to the hotel in something of a daze, I suddenly found myself breaking out into a run again for the pure pleasure of the experience as much as to test Reb Dressler's admonition. Going up the hill toward the King David, endorphins kicked in. I was beginning to feel a "runner's high," and increased my speed as I approached the hotel. My now tranquil state continued right through the front door and into the lobby. *HaShem* did love me. Walking toward the elevator that was unique to my floor, I checked my watch for the time in California to see if Maya was awake for a call when I heard a voice behind me saying "Rabbi Golub," and turned to see Nicolas Peebles standing there. My mood shifted immediately to apprehension, if not dread.

"Don't worry. I'm not here to arrest you for treason or

anything else. I couldn't even do that back home, although I could recommend such action. Here, I have no jurisdiction."

"Did you come here to spy on me?"

"Only partly."

"I saw you breakfasting the other day with the secretary."

"I did see you backing out in a hurry, but with nowhere near the speed I saw you running up the street through the lobby window. Have you had a steroid injection? It's pretty impressive at your age."

"No injection."

"I imagined not... We should talk." He gestured to the back door of the hotel that led onto the expansive patio with its postcard view of the Old City. The man had clearly been waiting for me. That couldn't have been more obvious. And it didn't seem he wanted to apprehend me or get me in trouble, so I nodded. We walked through the back entrance and then down some steps to an area where we were entirely alone. For the last few hours, I had done more than my share of talking in private. Still, apparently, I was going to do more with a man who, ironically, came from the National Geospatial-Intelligence Agency, whose aim was obviously to see all and know all and probably did. This was confirmed by what he said next.

"So you have been talking with Rabbi Dressler and Dr. Gabaz about providing corroborating content for their forthcoming book. Few will read it or even be capable of comprehending it, but those who do will find the work valuable on the deepest level. They are among the most brilliant people in this country, or any other. You should be flattered that they have taken an interest in your story. They clearly sense that you are playing a role of extreme importance."

"I didn't ask for it."

"Who would? I can only imagine how I would have reacted in your place...That is why I wanted to talk with you."

"And not to report on me."

"For what? Because you have been working for the intelligence agency of another country that has given you a false identity and ensconced you in a suite next to one of our highest officials." He had a smile on his face. "No, I have information to impart you may find useful, though it is some personal risk that I do so."

"I guess I'm grateful, but why are you doing it?"

"Because I am, like you, a diaspora Jew."

"You?" I stared at him. Beneath his hip John Lennon glasses and trendy polo shirt from I knew not where, not being au courant on such things, was the very blond, blue-eyed visage of the State Department gentile or goy, to employ a word I disliked using and rarely did.

"Well, not completely, more distantly, but enough, I believe, to become a citizen here through the 'law of return' if I were to go public with the family shame." I naturally thought to ask what that was, but suspected from years of listening to congregants who lived with some private burden that he was about to do so unprompted. "It has to do with my great-grandfather on my mother's side who was Jewish. He was a tailor, like you, in his late sixties but nowhere near the athlete, as far as I can tell, a tiny, hunched-over man with glasses thicker than mine. He was swept up into the Warsaw Ghetto with his family. It was nothing short of Hell, as I assume you know. I first learned about it as a boy from the John Hersey novel."

"'The Wall,'" I said. I used the book several times as I maneuvered our synagogue into more of a Jewish novelist's reading club.

He nodded. By this point, we had both taken a seat at one of the tables. "The book brilliantly dramatized the April 1943 uprising against the Nazis. Unfortunately, that rebellion failed, and most of the Jews went to forced labor or the Majdanek concentration camp, except for a select few who made it out alive, including that distant branch of my family. I had always wondered about that, and because of my privileged access was able to find some documents." He took a deep breath. "My great-grandfather collaborated with the Nazis."

"A kapo."

Apparently, one of his former gentile clients was friends with an SS officer who offered to help him get extra food in exchange for what seemed to be relatively harmless information. He was weak and accepted. Soon, the demands grew, and he was caught between two worlds. Based on my research, this went on for several months. I don't know which of his fellow Jews he eventually betrayed. Maybe I'd rather not know. But there were some people he knew from before. Brave people. He was never caught. After the war, that branch of my family changed its name from Rosenfeld to something Slavic and tried to disappear. Some succeeded and, over the years, did their best to erase any trace of their Jewish roots, eventually marrying into my father's Presbyterian family, the Scottish Peebles. So I owe my existence to my great-grandfather, who collaborated—bluntly, over the bodies of dead Jews. I guess sitting here with you, relaying classified information of the U.S. government, is a form of repentance—what you call *teshuva.*

"I would forgive you if I could, but that's not in my province."

"I understand."

A waiter came over to ask if we wanted something but I wasn't hungry and neither was he. We sat there a couple of minutes without talking, and I sensed, even though his personal revelation could not have been more serious, that it was just a prelude to the gravity of what he was about to say.

"Before I came here," he said, "I did the usual checking on you... old internet posts, private emails, stuff you find only on the Dark Web, although our agency had most of it anyway. You're not a bad guy, compared to most, but, surprisingly, you became a rabbi. It seems to have been something of a fallback, like law school was for so many of my college classmates.... It's mindboggling you wound up in the middle of this. God works in mysterious ways, as they say...Have you read Ezekiel 38 lately?"

"Ezekiel... 38?"

"Apparently, one of his most famous prophesies."

"You read *Tanakh?*"

"Not much. Hardly ever actually. But it's coming up in a lot of Google searches now, so I looked it up. Ezekiel described a future attack on Israel from the North by Gog of Magog. Gog and his forces, including Persia, Cush—"

"That's Iran."

"Yes. He seems to have been right all along... old Ezekiel. "

"You believe these old prophesies?"

"It's not a prophecy in this case. In about twelve hours, Iran is going to be sending missiles and drones all over this country with the hope of eliminating it forever."

"You have evidence of that, I take it."

"We have satellite images of their preparations and have intercepted their communications. This isn't going to be a small-scale operation like Hamas or Hezbollah. Iran's Fatteh-2 missiles have a range of 1500 kilometers, can reach speeds approaching Mach 20, and are equipped with warheads that can change trajectory mid-flight to evade defenses. No one's sure how the Iron Dome or David's Sling will hold up against them. Also, your bunkmate, the Secretary of State, told me that ammunition for the Dome had been 'inadvertently' delayed to pressure the Israelis into negotiations. Now they are short on ammo at the most critical moment... Of course, an emergency supply is being rushed over. Or so I've been told. But the US administration has been semi-boycotting them since October 7th. It's hard to believe it will be enough."

"And you are telling me this because..." All of a sudden I was feeling a sharp pain in the pit of my stomach, as if I were going to be sick. I would have sat down at that point, but I was already sitting. "What am I supposed to do?"

"Leave the country, if you want. But better hurry." He pointed to his watch. "They're shutting the airport in less than an hour."

I was pretty sure he was joking or testing me to see what I would do, so I moved on. "When is this barrage supposed to begin?"

"The End Times? Somewhere between three and four a.m. the coming morning. Probably closer to three... Maybe there is something you *can* do. You seem to have connections that few of us possess. At least, Dr. Gabaz thinks so. These days, physicists are the most likely to believe in God. Rabbi Dressler shares that view. Anyway, according to Ezekiel, 'God will punish Gog and his armies with pestilence and bloodshed... The nations will know that God is the Lord their God... He will pour out His Spirit on the people of Israel, and He will no longer hide His face from them.'.. That's an abbreviated version. Nevertheless, you may be His agent."

"What?"

XV

I haven't dwelled on it too much in my story, but you can be sure I knew that internally Israel was, in simple terms, a chaotic mess—similar to the United States—so divided politically that the two sides barely communicated and spent most of their time hating each other or plotting each other's downfall. Protests were constant over every imaginable issue. Government officials were being fired left and right. The judiciary tried to dominate the executive, and vice versa. The long-serving prime minister was both despised and revered. Many Hasidim—who refused to acknowledge Israel's existence until the Moshiach arrived but still lived there—also refused to serve in the military and were reviled as freeloaders by both religious and secular groups. This had been ongoing for years, since the founding of the state, but the intense disagreements were especially shocking now, given that the nation was at war on multiple fronts, fighting for its very survival. But it wasn't the first time; it's always been like this since 1948, even before. This was the supposed "light unto the nations"? These were "the Chosen"? Chosen for what?

Nevertheless, I had been following all this, sometimes reluctantly because it gave me a headache, on American cable news and in the local English-language press, except, of course, when I was in the tunnels. Internecine hatred dominated the country to such an extent that, later that day, when I reflected on my encounter with Peebles, I wondered if a successful takeover by Gog of Magog—with his boogieman name from a Marvel comic—might not have been doing them all a favor.

That was far from all I ruminated over in the roughly twelve hours between my meeting with the man from the National Geospatial-Intelligence Agency and what he claimed would be an onslaught from the forces of the Ayatollah in the small hours of the morning.

I had not gone back into the hotel but decided to go for a walk to sort things out, though I found myself repeatedly circumnavigating the block lest I have to rush back for some reason. I did not immediately call Maya because I did not want to upset her further. The latest reports on her mother were not good, and the last thing she needed was her freaked-out husband calling to warn her the end times were nigh via the Ayatollah, and he was supposed to do something about it. At this point, given all that had transpired, she would not necessarily think I was crazy, although, being a reasonable person, she would have her doubts. When I told her the Golem had completely healed my leg, I heard the professional skepticism in her voice. So I focused on what was at hand to try to center myself —a virtually impossible task. I gave up on the usual breathing exercises almost immediately. I was feeling oppressed from all sides. Why had I been chosen for this? It seemed both absurd and unfair. I searched backward in memory for a clue as I walked. Why me? My mind drifted back to childhood. I was, for all intents and purposes, an ordinary kid. I enjoyed dodgeball. I cried when the Cubs lost, which was frequently. Like so many boys of my generation, I was fascinated by Ripley's "Believe It or Not," a dog-eared copy of which was part of my family's library. I would pore over it endlessly, trying to decipher what was true and what wasn't. One thing I knew to be true was those formulations called palindromes, when a phrase was spelled the same way forward and back. One was "Madam, I'm Adam," to which Eve replied, "Name no one, man." This appealed to the seven-year-old me, as did the many limericks Ripley's provided that were not palindromes. This one particularly caught my youthful attention: "How odd of God to choose the Jews." Was Ripley an antisemite? I recall having wondered with no conclusion and no one really to ask. I preferred not to know because I so enjoyed "Believe It or Not". But the question of being chosen stayed with me and started to obsess me over the years. Why would God choose one group over another? Yes, there were Biblical answers, but they didn't resolve the issue for me. When, as a young rabbi, I was called upon to explain the concept, I tended to deflect. I began to think the inherent arrogance in the concept was one of the root causes of antisemitism. To some degree, that was yet another inspiration for my leaving the rabbinate and moving into teaching. When I returned to the clergy, I still had misgivings. In some ways, these misgivings were similar to those I had from God's demanding the sacrifice of Isaac, though not as extreme or personal.

As I was recalling all this, I found myself approaching an art gallery of the sort aimed at tourists. Not surprisingly, it was empty, the lights out as if its owners had given up hope. But a portrait of a man I immediately recognized was plainly visible in the window. It was Rabbi Menahem Mendel Schneersohn, the late leader of the Chabad-Lubavitch movement, known to all as "The Rebbe." I had seen his portrait all over the country in various sizes, more than any figure I could think of, even their own politicians and religious leaders, on lonely power poles in the Negev and crumbling flower-strewn walls next to photos of the hostages—all this despite his never having been to Israel even once. Born in Ukraine, the Rebbe was several years dead when I first met Artie at Chabad-Lubavitch headquarters on Brooklyn's Eastern Parkway, but his essence and vision, his teachings, were in every way very much present, still are. Artie took me inside the 770 Building to see where The Rebbe delivered his *farbrengens*, his gatherings, where he held forth for hours to the Chabad Hasidim, but also to others who came from across the globe —Christian and Jew, some of them world leaders —to hear his wisdom. I remember seeing this once or twice on television as a child, being disturbed as he personally handed out fresh one-dollar bills to hundreds of people. Wasn't this just ratifying the cliché about the Jews? It was all about the money. I was too young to realize he intended these symbolic dollars not to be kept but to be passed on, symbols of the paramount importance of charity, *tsedakah*, among the 613 commandments, *mitzvot*, if one wishes to live a life in accordance with G-d's will. I thought of that and the little boy watching on television as I stared through the window at the portrait of The Rebbe, which was fairly large —about three by five feet —and in the style of a black-and-white photograph, to attract the attention of the sophisticated buyer from Miami or Newport Beach. Then I realized I had a job to do and started back for the hotel. But what was it?

I had asked that obvious question to Nicholas Peebles at the end of our meeting but he did not have a direct response. The issue had been discussed by the group that he was apparently part of, though an American agent, and no one had a real answer either. The problem was that my involvement was in the realm of the mystical and the divine and beyond the pay grade, so to speak, of all of them, even Rabbi Dressler. Goldfarb was part of it as well, but only briefly, because he had so much to do on the actual military level, dealing with a potential attack from Iran. I was, I gathered, something of a last resort spiritual backup to the temporal forces, Israeli, American, possibly Jordanian and Saudi, lined up to defend the Jewish state against the Islamic Republic. Still, I desperately needed guidance. Too bad the Rebbe wasn't around to consult.

His writings were, however. I decided to consider my recent encounter with his image, which I was starting to view as somewhere between fortuitous and pre-ordained, even though I had always had a natural suspicion of leaders, spiritual and otherwise, was a message. Nevertheless, real writings from the Rebbe, other than letters, were scant. His wisdom was usually imparted verbally at those *farbrengens,* during which it was discouraged to take notes or record in order, I presumed, to make the attendee more attentive, more present. Fortunately, another, younger rabbi with an impressive memory was able to recall, apparently verbatim, everything the Rebbe had said, and later wrote it down for posterity. I combed through some of this online back in the hotel room. The Rebbe, after all, had been thought by some to be the long-sought Jewish messiah, though he himself had denied it.

Emerging from my hasty research was something reassuring. He was an adherent of a philosophy of positivity even in the worst of times, even during and after the Holocaust, which he likened to the destruction of the Hebrew temples millennia ago and the subsequent exiles. What could missile attacks from Iran be by comparison? I admired the manner in which he shifted the focus: "If you see what needs to be repaired and how to repair it, then you have found a piece of the world that God has left for you to complete. But if you only see what is wrong and how ugly it is, then it is yourself that needs repair." How many times had I been that person, and for how long? I noted some further advice from the Rebbe: "Man can never be happy if he does not nourish his soul as he does his body." This last prompted me to rummage through the desk drawers, where I was able to find a siddur, the Jewish prayer book. This was, after all, the King David Hotel. I opened it and began to pray, something I had rarely done spontaneously before. I started for no other reason than it seemed appropriate with a Shabbat Amida, although this was a Thursday. It began, "Shalom, Hashem, our Father, grant peace and all good blessings to your children, for we are united." Although I still struggled, I was surprised to find the Hebrew came somewhat more easily than it had.

I continued with the prayer book for another half hour or so before putting it away. I was a bit calmer, as might be expected, even as I began surfing the internet for the latest on the supposedly imminent Iranian attack. Apparently, the military airports of Palmachim, Ramat David, and Nevatim, where the F-35s were based, were of crucial concern. The power plants and natural gas fields in the Mediterranean that provided half of the country's electricity were presumed targets, as was, needless to say, and most of all, the Dimona nuclear installation. Also mentioned were the IDF headquarters in Tel Aviv, known as the Kirya, and the desalination plants in Ashkelon and Sorek. Why did I need this information? I could do less than zero about any of it. I was starting to feel agitated again. I checked my watch. There were seven hours at least until whatever conflagration. My watch also told me my pulse rate had risen to 118 bpm, though I hadn't moved from the couch in over an hour.

Maybe I could use more advice from the Rebbe. It certainly wouldn't hurt. But during my web search, another rabbi appeared on my screen. He was giving a talk on the Kabbalah of Action rather than the Kabbalah of Information. Was this the man who, years ago, took down the words of the Rebbe from memory? "We will do and then we will understand," he was saying. When Moses descended from Mt. Sinai with the tablets, he told the Israelites to observe the Ten Commandments immediately without question. They could learn the rationale later. This was a reversal of how we normally behave, this rabbi pointed out—endlessly pondering the terms of a contract—or any decision in our lives—before committing to it. As I watched the rabbi continue his own screen talk, I had the sense he was speaking directly to me. It felt that way, his eyes staring straight at me from the screen as he described a pattern I had followed—if not since childhood—shortly thereafter, and he was challenging me to abandon it. The Kabbalah of Information had been complicated to understand, and I wasn't sure I truly did. But its immediate implications for my life were not personally significant, as far as I could tell. On the other hand, the Kabbalah of Action—do first, understand later—though easier to grasp, was far more straightforward. It was a challenge I suspected I would need to face soon. I did not feel remotely prepared.

Suddenly, a siren went off the likes of which I hadn't heard before. At a decibel level that made me want to hold my ears, it sounded as if it was coming from a hundred directions at once, although I knew that was impossible. I froze in place for a second, trying not to be terrified. The information had been inaccurate. The attack was early, making it something of a surprise and undermining defenses. This wasn't the usual 3 AM alarm, but closer to nightfall. It was, in essence, a sneak attack, just like Oct. 7. Almost reflexively, I headed for the door. There seemed to be no alternative but to take the elevator to the safe room. That was what my life was about, I thought grimly, safe rooms from tornadoes in Nashville, safe rooms from rockets in Jerusalem.

When I arrived in that room, I was alone for about five minutes, listening to the now more distant sirens while doing breath exercises to control panic, when Jeremy Bogen entered with his two bodyguards. The secretary was talking on a cell when he came in, did not look up, did not extend a greeting of any sort, and took a seat as far from me as possible in the small room. I nodded to him, but he did not respond. So I watched, becoming apprehensive on top of my already constant anxiety over the missiles, as his call went on for some time. He was almost exclusively listening to the other end, just occasionally injecting an "Uh-huh" or a "Yup." Outside, the sirens were continuing to wail, no all clear in evidence. I didn't say a word when Bogen finally hung up and looked at me.

"You're going to have to leave, Rabbi Golub," he said in an expressionless voice. For a split second I didn't grasp the import that he had called me by own name and not Charles Baumgarten. I was just too used to it and was unaccustomed to the alias. "This is a secure room for the credentialed only," he continued, "which you are no longer under any name. Good luck in returning to our country or finding safety anywhere." Jolted, I stood, trying to be inconspicuous, which was impossible, and started out without looking back at his bodyguards. I was concerned I would be arrested before getting out the door. Heading to the elevator, I wondered if my suite would still be available. Who knew what was being arranged on that phone call? It had just been implied I could be charged with treason for which the punishment, as a high school student should know, can be death.

Instead of riding all the way up, I got off at the lobby. Patrons of the hotel were still coming out of other elevators or coming down the stairs, headed for another stair to what I assumed was a larger safe area. Many looked freaked out, evidently aware that this was a lot more dangerous situation than they had become used to. Hotel staff were trying to calm them down while directing them. For a second, I thought about following them down, but considering the secretary's words, I decided it would be safer to leave the building. Still, I didn't know what I was supposed to do? I was lost in a situation that was basically chaotic. What was my role in all this? I thought it was to find the Golem, but how would I do that? As always, I had no idea. The Golem always found me. And what would I do if I found him?

I drifted out of the hotel onto the street. Despite the unceasing sirens, it was a bit quieter. I pulled out my phone to call Maya, but since someone had ratted me out, I decided to call Artie first. He would be as likely to know as anyone. But the phone wouldn't turn on. I banged it several times to no avail. It had obviously been disconnected. I felt so frustrated I almost threw it away but shoved it back in my pocket at the last second and continued down the street. I hadn't gone fifty feet when I saw something like a bat coming toward me. It dawned on me it was one of those kamikaze drones the Iranians sold to the Russians, heading straight in my direction. It stopped briefly in mid-air, moving back and forth, lining up its target. Then it locked in, as if focused on my eyes. Was this the end? The drone shot forward. I ducked at the last second as it whizzed past me into a van parked just behind me. The van exploded, and I went flying backwards into a hedge, knocking most of it over. I lay there, eyes shut, seeing stars as I had in the tunnel, wondering if my body was intact. It didn't seem possible. I cautiously began to touch my core and arms.

"You are fine. Do not worry," came a surprisingly calm voice. I thought I had heard it before but couldn't place it. Something was not normal about it. It was close and distant all at once, as if coming from another realm altogether. "You can stand. You can do so without impediment."

I did what he said and started to stand. It was true—nothing held me back. I determined it easily, briefly flexing my hands and feet, then stopped to look at the person in front of me. I couldn't see who it was at first in the dim light, but I was quickly jolted by a shock of recognition that took me back to Columbia's Hartley Hall. It had been only a few months since I had been at the university during the demonstrations, but it seemed like years. It was also half the world away, yet this was the same ethereal young man who had let me into that dormitory, led me to where I could view the Golem saving the life of a maintenance worker and then disappeared. I was sure it was he. He had the same milky white skin and golden blond side-locks descending from a white yarmulke pulled down to the tips of his ears. *Tzitzit* dangled beneath a cloak that was also white and almost luminescent.

"You are Akiva," I said.

The faintest smile signaled acknowledgement. He gestured for me to follow him and we set off past the smoldering van in the direction of Yemin Moshe and then downhill through its narrow alleyways. In front of us and overhead, several missiles at once soared over Mt. Zion like a deadly meteor display. Seconds later, defensive missiles burst into view, pursuing them. The attacking missiles began to zig-zag, eluding the defenders. Akiva ignored all this, not even looking up, and continued down another cobble-stoned street and around the side of the Old City toward the Zion Gate. We proceeded through the gate onto *Or HaChaim*, Akiva, between five and ten feet in front of me on this street so narrow it would be hard to walk two abreast. We were in the Old City's Jewish Quarter, some ten minutes from the Wall, but not a soul was around, the populace hiding in safe rooms in response to the unceasing sirens. Even through the constricted view, missiles were visible flying overhead, one after the other. I heard explosions. Were they interceptions or the missiles finding their marks, doing untold damage? Their number was more than I had ever imagined. Was the city, the country, about to be destroyed? Who knew Iran had so much firepower? Was it Russia or China helping them?

We turned a corner, continuing downward—Akiva easily knew the way through the maze of streets as if he had walked them a thousand times or more—when, just as we were turning another corner, a second of the kamikaze drones buzzed into view, immediately catching us in its guidance system, weaving slightly before redirecting exactly in our direction. But Akiva simply put up his hand, palm in front, much like a policeman stopping traffic, and the drone halted its attack, spun around and disappeared into the night.

To say the least, the man had powers the likes of which I had never seen, but I had already assumed he was not actually a human but a divine entity of some sort, although it remained hard for me to believe in such things despite what had happened to me or even what was in front of my eyes. Later, I learned, through reading, that he was likely to have been what they call in Kabballah an Ishim, the most human-like of angels, intended to oversee the physical realm, supposedly one of the 72 angels representing the 72 facets of the Creator. But at that point, my knowledge of such things was limited. As a student at a reform rabbinical college, it was implied to me by teachers that such aspects of my religion were primitive outliers, almost cultish, though they did not directly say so. I wasn't prepared, due to my youth and character, to question this, though I found, even then, some of these stories intriguing, another world beyond our perception. Still, I didn't know what to make of them and basically dismissed them, failing to see the more profound messages beneath. I suspected I was now about to get a heavy dose of remedial learning as we proceeded down yet another narrow street to emerge on a platform overlooking the Western Wall.

From that perspective, I could see down into the famous plaza, now virtually empty, with only two or three Hasidim praying, davening, their heads bobbing, in front of the mammoth Herodian stones. Just as it had been on my previous visit, the hundreds, or even thousands, of the devout were not in evidence for the most obvious reason. The fear of the missiles still visible in the sky—even more of them it seemed, coupled with repeated explosions—had kept all away from the giant plaza, though I could still see several Arabs milling about atop the Temple Mount. They appeared more resigned to whatever fate had in store for them, even at the hands of fellow Muslims.

I glanced over at Akiva, who appeared to be becoming gradually transparent. The fabric of his cloak was slowly disappearing in a manner that enabled you to see the neighboring wall through it. Soon his features—his midriff, most of his arms and legs —were vanishing as well, and only the hanging strings of his *tzitzit* maintained their solidity.

"Remember your purpose," he said to me in a voice that had become almost disembodied but still had a deliberateness that made me shiver. "Now and always." He pointed with what remained of his right arm toward the plaza, as if it were my mission to go, then began to disappear entirely in a shaft of light that became so blinding after he vanished I could no longer look at it.

I can't say I felt protected as I followed his admonition and descended the remaining steps into the plaza, passing through the security gate that was apparently unattended. I stopped near the location, some distance from the Wall itself, where paper yarmulkes were dispensed to those who had forgotten theirs or, in some cases, never had one. I was already wearing mine, hidden beneath a baseball cap that I removed out of respect, and started forward.

What then transpired was at once so beyond the normal and proceeded at such a pace that it is almost impossible to remember what happened in a short—or was it actually extraordinarily long—allotment of what we call time. I will do my best, but beg the reader's forbearance if I have forgotten, or didn't even notice, all that occurred.

The first thing I remember is a feeling of intense claustrophobia mixed with a stench of garbage so great I almost vomited. I was at the Wall as it was under Jordanian rule before the '67 war – the tiniest alleyway between crumbling, unattended ruins of the Second Temple and

graffiti-laden slum buildings. Next to me was an elderly Arab whose donkey was defecating on the heavily-stained, almost unrecognizable Herodian stones.

I recoiled as shit piled up when it was suddenly overwhelmed by a river of blood. I had been transported to the steps of the First Temple three thousand years ago as the High Priest was slaughtering animals—endless numbers of cattle, sheep, and goats--as more and more blood poured down, King Solomon watching from his throne. He nodded his head in approval as the ritual red heifer was brought forward, the High Priest preparing its sacrifice.

Then it was modern times again, or so I thought, hundreds of Hasidim back at the Wall davening—only the wall itself was no longer stone but a shiny alloy, unbroken to the top. Stranger still, the pious all had prosthetic limbs. These were transhumanist Hasidim somewhere in the future. They had become something approaching robots. They could have been hundreds of years old, preserved by substitute body parts. Within seconds, they were being attacked by robot Arabs on robot horses who, in turn, were being assailed from above by robot

Israeli soldiers standing on flat spacecraft resembling surfboards.

A giant explosion followed, filling the plaza with smoke and then leaving it empty again as it had been when I arrived with Akiva. But the sky now had more stars than in a planetarium with the planets, asteroids, nebulae, meteors, comets, quasars, pulsars, supernovas in an endless cosmic rotation. It was the expanding universe that Uncle Sydney had told me about as a boy, but now enriched and clarified by Dr. Gabaz. We were moving back and forth in time, which she insisted didn't exist or was just another form of information in a constant flow. I was never sure what that meant, but if time didn't exist —if everything were simultaneous, as she inferred —what was I doing there? What was indeed my "purpose"?

But this was only the shortest of interregnums, perhaps ten seconds or even five, before a series of visions appeared—Jesus and Moses walking together, a Pharaoh riding by on a chariot. It must have been Akhenaten because Freud was with him. Maccabees, Artie among them, battling Seleucids. A yeshiva in Babylon. Maimonides treating a patient in front of the Pyramids, Rashi annotating the Torah in Medieval France. Then, even more fleetingly, a kaleidoscope of blood libels, the Talmud burning in front of Notre Dame, the Inquisition, pogroms, Dreyfus convicted, Trotsky assassinated, Herzl, Jabotinsky, the Holocaust, Einstein, the atom bomb, Israel founded, Golda Meir, Shimon Peres, triumphant Moshe Dayan at the Wall, Sharon at Suez, bleeding and wounded, Begin and Sadat making peace, Sadat assassinated, athletes gunned down in Munich, Bill Clinton shaking hands with Arafat, the Intifada, Rabin assassinated, the Second Intifada, Oct. 7, demonstrations at Columbia, the Bibas children returned in coffins, Israelis weeping... Was all this still happening now, or was it the past?

Would it happen again, or was it already happening in the future?

I heard singing in the distance. It was my family coming toward me, several generations including Maya, of course, and my children, and her mother looking very sick plus Max and the uncle that hated me and Tamara and Ed who were like family at this point, Uncle Sydney, also several I assumed to be relatives from previous generations I didn't recognize or knew only from photo albums, everything from Hasids to Bolsheviks, waving to me in a friendly manner while singing the same song I heard over and over in the Carmel Market and elsewhere. "*Hashem Yitbarach Tamid Ohev Oti*. Hashem blessed be He always loves me." It ended with Max walking along with his homemade Golem, a Hasidic R2D2 with Jack Ripton a few feet behind.

It was hard to comprehend what was going on, this was all suddenly so personal. Was this some version of This Is Your Life that was played over and over for everyone, Jews and Gentiles, other faiths too, not just me, in a world in which time was forgotten, assuming it existed, or was I in the midst of a nervous breakdown of a rather severe nature?

As my extended family walked off, the war returned. Reality—or what passes for it—resumed. Missiles flew overhead with an intensity I had not seen before. Explosions could be heard from all directions. Jet planes, I assumed to be Israeli, crisscrossed the sky. The small number of worshipping Hasidim I had seen on arrival had disappeared. Kamikaze drones were buzzing about in front of the Wall like wasps looking for an object, any object, on which to administer their fatal sting.

I stood there in the center of the empty plaza, realizing I was the most obvious, actually the only, of the potential targets. Whatever "purpose" I might have it would be wise quickly to take cover, that is, if I wanted to live to achieve it. I turned, looking for the nearest possibility when I saw a man walking toward me. Clothed in a colorful cloak that reached the ground, he was older and was moving slowly but deliberately with the help of a cane. Now it seemed I wasn't the only target, except he appeared to have no fear despite his evident age. How could that be? But as he drew closer, I sensed something familiar about him that I couldn't place, even though, unless this was a masquerade, he was from a distant era. What was the explanation? Was I still under some kind of protection? I didn't feel worthy of it. He must have noticed my perplexity because he stopped five feet away and stared at me closely.

"You seem confused," he said. "I will identify myself to clarify for you. I am Rabbi Judah Loew, full name Judah Loew ben Bezalel, known as the Maharal of Prague."

I won't bother to describe my precise feeling of amazement, only what I said. "*Baruch Hashem...* I'm so sorry, great sir. I should have recognized you immediately, but the statue at the city hall is—"

"Much taller. Unduly so in my opinion. The Prague city fathers didn't treat me that well when I was alive after what transpired. They despised me when the Golem went to such excess and wanted to jail me even though the same people sought to expel all Jews from the city, but now, as I understand it, I am a tourist attraction."

"Very much so. Your historic gravestone in the Jewish cemetery and the museum..."

"It is a museum of the Golem, not of me. Everyone loves monster stories. I am just the rabbi who happened to be there... I did my best to restrain the Golem, wiping the letter Aleph from his brow to put an end to his over-zealous actions and locking him, I thought permanently, in the attic, the *genizah*, of the Old New Synagogue, but that did not last. Somehow, over the years, it escaped. Now it appears to be following you around."

"I haven't seen that. Every time I look for it, it seems to have disappeared."

"It is there." A kamikaze drone appeared out of the night like a dive bomber headed for us, but the rabbi, unconcerned, just swatted it away with his staff. "Golems can be invisible. They are with you from the moment you create them until you end their existence and even then.... Trust me. I know. They are also desperate to be human, to be like Adam when he was formed by the Almighty from the dust, to speak and express whatever it is they are thinking, to join a *minyan* of the devout. However, that too is forbidden, most of all to find a mate, even to marry, though they will never be able to. They can fall in love—I had eight daughters; it was a big problem-- and be a force for good or a force for ill almost at random, even though we initially conjure them up to fight the most obvious evil toward our people that always seems to repeat into infinity no matter our efforts."

"Into oblivion," I said, trying to make sense of the darkness of it all—a creature we formed or was formed for us to ward off our enemies that was so desperate to be like us, to speak, to love, he would turn against us and himself. How bleakly human in a way—the *yetzer hatov*, the instinct for good, waylaid by the *yetzer hara*, the instinct for bad, a kind of Biblical or Talmudic schizophrenia enhanced by all too human loneliness. But what are we to make then of the initial intent of their original creation, finally to overcome the persistent canary in the coal mine? Was that just another fruitless game of rinse and repeat? Was the hatred something we would all have to accept forever, learn to live with as a fact of permanent existence?

The sky at that point was filled with kamikaze drones reminiscent of the flying monkeys from The Wizard of Oz. Were they all from Iran, or from Iraq, Gaza, Yemen, Russia, China, all of the above—who knew? For the moment, we appeared to be under a protective dome of sorts, more powerful, it seemed, than the Iron Dome by itself. The onslaught was nevertheless unrelenting, and the explosions near and far constant.

"That would make antisemitism yet another aspect of particle physics as it was explained to me," I continued, trying to make sense of "into oblivion" as much for myself as for my interlocutor from a distant era. "More quanta combining and recombining forever in a timeless series of universes without end."

"I wouldn't know about that. I was born in 1512."

"But you were a great mathematician."

"Perhaps for then, like my friend Tycho Brahe who mapped the stars, but everything we knew has been superseded. Nevertheless, I understand the concept in my way... We all have a role to play in this, like it or not. We are trapped in it for good or ill. Now it is your turn."

He stared at me with an intensity that sidestepped centuries as if they did not exist.

I took a deep breath, while shivering as if shirtless in the dead of winter despite it being a mild April night. "What if I'm not up to this role?"

"Take this. It will be useful." He held out his staff to me.

"Can you walk without it?"

I felt it was not mine to take from such an aged person, but he did not answer the question, instead thrusting the staff nearer to me, almost touching my right arm. I had no choice but to accept it as he slowly began to dissolve into the night air, the colors of his cloak fading in the darkness, and then the cloak itself fading. I heard him whispering the Shema to himself as he disappeared, with no evidence remaining of his presence except the staff clutched in my hand. It was made of gnarled wood, with an evil eye and jewels inlaid in stone at the top to ward off harm.

The plaza in front of the Kotel was now empty as it had never been, I imagined, since its initial development and expansion after the Six-Day War. So important then, how almost routine that once-astounding conflagration now seemed, just another episode in a series of unending struggles across millennia. Out of the corner of my eye, I glanced well beyond the security gate for the Wall, towards whom I assumed was a solitary policeman posted almost symbolically for an area no one person could possibly guard. Others had evidently taken shelter. Even at a distance, I could see the glow of his cigarette, as he puffed to calm his nerves in a situation, if any would, that overrode any possible risk of lung cancer. I watched as he tossed the cigarette and lit another.

At that moment, a figure came streaking across the plaza with something flopping over its shoulder that had the appearance almost of an enlarged rag doll. It was headed straight for the Western Wall, but instead of stopping at the base, it began to climb up the mammoth Herodian stones as if it were Spider-Man or even King Kong. Was this the mysterious Spider-Man from the hospital? The figure was large, at least a foot taller than any man, with shoulders that would be the envy of any fullback. This was no Spider-Man. Even at a distance, it was easy to guess that it was the Golem. Could it have been anything else? The something draped over his shoulder was obviously human, kicking his or her, almost certainly her, legs furiously into his back as he continued up the wall, clearly bound for the Temple Mount at a remarkable pace. Even against the constant sirens, I could hear her desperate cries in a voice I had heard before, which I recognized from a plane and later from the Carmel Market when she was reacting to a mysterious wind. Now she was screaming.

Unable to even fantasize climbing straight up the ancient stone wall in pursuit, I set out at a run for the Mughrabi Gate. Thanks to the Golem's cure, my legs responded as if I were still in my twenties. I had little time to contemplate the irony that it was his ministrations—a sign of that schizophrenia of monsters, at once sympathetic and terrifying—that had given me the capacity to track him at my age. I sped up the covered ramp, summoning the strength to leap, staff in hand, over the security checkpoint barrier that had also been closed during the bombardment. Who would be coming this way at a moment like this, well beyond the restricted hours during which Jews were allowed at the location of their old temples anyway, and while a war was on?

Soon I was emerging onto the mount itself, the open courtyard between the Al-Aqsa Mosque and the Dome of the Rock. A handful of Arabs were huddled under an arch in the probably vain hope it would shield them from whatever misguided missile might be coming their way. They didn't appear to notice me as I slowed to a walk. Where was the Golem and the woman I presumed to be Olivia Dreben? In order not to attract attention, I moved behind the ancient hackberry trees from Solomon's time as I searched for them to no avail. They seemed to have vanished. Did I dare to look inside the Dome or Al-Aqsa, where I would undoubtedly be set upon? They were the only places they could be.

I was summoning the courage when I heard the woosh of a rocket streaking toward the firmament. It must have been one of ours because it seemed bound for some incoming missile. It couldn't have been more than three seconds before I saw it collide with a missile many miles away but seemingly directly overhead, a kind of optical illusion from the emerging space war. I learned later that its target was the Dimona reactor. The overhead location became more immediate moments after the missile exploded because a large part of its shattered fuselage appeared to be plunging directly at the Temple Mount. I knew more often than not such visions were indeed optical illusions, and the burning shard, no matter how substantial, would end up falling harmlessly tens of miles away, but in this case, its path was not wavering. It was as if it were homing in on us through some demonic plan and would soon crash into the top of the Mount, crumbling the holy sites, including the mosques, the Wall and possibly blowing apart the very Foundation Stone itself. In that split second, it could not be clearer that the global implications of such a disaster —all Abrahamic religions undermined in one devastating explosion—were massive. Was this Ezekiel's prophecy of the End Times materializing before my eyes? And was this my "purpose" after all, to help save the Temple Mount and avert global catastrophe? Little me? It was beyond conception. It had to be. Hashem had so many better from whom to choose.

Yet I seemed to be playing a role here. And as the deadly remnants were hurtling their last meters to potential Armageddon, I finally saw the Golem standing athwart the Dome of the Rock at the very top. He was still clutching Olivia with one arm while, a half-human monster with dual intentions, reaching for the flaming fuselage with the other. Just as it was about to hit the Dome, he grabbed the burning metal object in midair with his free arm. He threw it, as if he were a missile launcher himself, high over the walls of the Old City and the vast Jewish Cemetery on the Mount of Olives to the East and beyond out into the Judean Wilderness from which, it was said, the Jewish messiah would eventually emerge on his way to Jerusalem. Not tonight, I thought.

Then, Olivia, still kicking and screaming on his arm to the best of her now-waning ability, he began to descend the slippery, gold-plated aluminum of the rounded roof of the Dome without the slightest stumble. The Arabs who had been lingering in the arches stared up at this monster with a mix of wonder and open-mouthed fear. When he reached the edge of the roof, he leaped to the ground and started running toward the Moghrabi Gate with Olivia. What was he going to do with her? I chased after him, shouting, "Golem! Stop! I command you! It's me, your master, Rabbi Golub!" I also tried the Shema, hoping it might reach the godly part of his soul; it had worked before, but the Golem ignored me. By this point, I was running behind him, barely able to breathe, across the Wall plaza, past the lone policeman who, panicked, tossed his cigarette and urgently spoke into a phone, and up the steps into the Jewish Quarter, weaving through its narrow streets, with no idea where he was headed.

I thought I had lost them when, gasping for breath, I stumbled out onto the plaza in front of the Hurva Synagogue. A couple of hundred feet in front of me, the Golem was carrying Olivia through the doors of the rebuilt Ottoman structure. It appeared this magnificent monument was also not being guarded this night, or that the guards were also sensibly in hiding from the constant bombardment. Crouching low, I ran across the plaza as best I could and followed the pair through the entryway into the large Prayer Hall. I hadn't been inside since the synagogue's reconstruction more than a decade before. I was momentarily distracted by its dome and walls artistically festooned with frescoes in Ashkenazi and Ottoman styles.

But impossible to ignore, in front of the Torah ark, constructed out of palm fronds and wood, was a temporary marital *chuppah*. Olivia Dreben stood beneath, clutching her stomach and sobbing uncontrollably while the Golem restrained her movements with his arms. If his eyeless head could have had an expression, no doubt it would have been a forced smile to save face. He turned Olivia around and faced her toward the ark. Was someone going to marry them? Who? I shouted at the Golem again to let go, to leave her, but he ignored my presence. I drew closer, clutching the staff in my hand, when an old, bent-over man wrapped in rags who looked to be in his late nineties shuffled in from the darkness in front of me. In his shaking hand, he was holding a *ketubah*, an official Jewish wedding contract. Where had this character come from? He was not a force for good. In the Jewish tradition, there was no such thing as an actual Devil. Still, there were so-called dybbuks, ghostly creatures that possessed the living in the midst of yet another outbreak of antisemitism or personal infidelity. This dybbuk, or whatever it was, faced Olivia and the Golem and began reciting the Seven Blessings from the traditional marriage ceremony in a hoarse, barely audible voice in Hebrew. I knew it in English, having performed enough weddings myself. Olivia screamed over his incantation in something approximating the cry of a wounded animal while sobbing so deeply I feared she would give herself a nervous breakdown, if not a stroke. "Blessed are you, Lord our God, king of the universe," I recognized the words, "who has sanctified us with His commandments and commanded us concerning forbidden unions..."

Forbidden unions? I had one of the most extreme ones imaginable taking place under the *chuppah* in front of me. I had to stop it. I clutched the staff and rushed at the Golem, aiming for the letters where his forehead would be. But he barely flinched and swatted the staff away. It went shooting across the floor. I ran for it, just managing to prevent it from sliding out into the entryway, while Olivia continued to wail in desperation, all but drowning out the dybbuk's recitation. Was this marriage actually taking place? Who would believe it happened? Clutching the staff in my hand, I headed back toward the Golem for a second try. But he beat me to it this time, taking a step forward and, without dropping Olivia, lifted me with his other arm and hurled me backward into one of the pews. I landed on the floor between benches, my head ringing and an intense pain running up my spine. The Golem was stronger than the Hamas thug in the tunnel. Far stronger, like nothing I had ever experienced. I could barely move or breathe. Leaning on the staff, I struggled to stand but fell back again, supine on the synagogue floor. Could I summon any strength? Did I have any left? And what was I supposed to do if I did? Tell the Golem he could be human, he could find love, he could be one of us, he could see, he could speak, sing and dance? None of that was possible. I could thank him for preventing the decimation of the Temple Mount, praise him for saving humanity. Would he even understand me?

But then something curious happened. His attitude seemed to shift as I lay barely conscious on the ground. The Golem bent over me and gradually began to caress me to alleviate my pain. I started to feel better. It was almost as if he recognized he had gone too far and was experiencing some form of guilt. Either that or it was a form of schizophrenic behavior, the *yetzer hatov* making a comeback against the *yetzer hara*. Olivia stared down in wonder at the spectacle, for the first time relenting from her constant cries. For a brief moment, that most fleeting of concepts, everything seemed quiet, restrained, almost strangely normal. The staff rested in my hand, the grip relaxed, the Golem leaning over me while continuing to gently stroke my other arm. I realized then that this was my opportunity, perhaps my only one. It seemed almost unfair to take advantage of his empathetic behavior, but in the larger sense — the macro, as it is called — it was *carpe diem* or nothing. The moment had arrived. With all the remaining strength in me, I thrust upward with the staff toward the Golem's forehead, the staff's evil eye smashing straight into the letter *aleph,* driving it into the clay and erasing it. The letters for Truth, the Hebrew *emet*, were no more, leaving just *mem* and *tav*, pronounced *met,* that Hebrew word for Death.

The Golem crumbled instantly into a pile of dust on the ground, which was immediately caught up and lifted by a swirling wind that resembled a more compact version of the Nashville tornado in which he or it was formed or born. The swirling dust continued to revolve faster and faster, rising up above me, until it blew through an open window just below the dome and disappeared into the infinite.

Outside, a new series of sirens wailed. I realized later it was a couple of dozen Jerusalem police, maybe more, arriving a bit late for the nuptials. They would find no evidence of the Golem. The dybbuk, too, was gone. Olivia sat in one of the pews, her hands covering her face, praying as women do on Shabbat after lighting the candles.

XVI

I was having trouble remembering to call it the Gulf of America. After decades of referring to the blue waters in front of me as the Gulf of Mexico, supposedly the original name—what had the Indians called it—had been drilled into my brain all my life, not that I cared what it was named one way or the other. It was the same beautiful sea, the same pure white sand at my feet under whatever moniker, as I sat in a lounge chair under a parasol, pretending to work on this narrative. I like to think I can write in the most romantic environments—Hemingway at the Deux Magots—but usually end up getting nothing done and eventually have to retreat to a solitary office, preferably without windows.

But that doesn't stop me from beginning my day with my feet in the sand here in the demi-paradise of Santa Rosa, Florida, in an area known as the 30A for a road that runs along the water at the very northern tip of the Gulf of America. (I got it right that time.) We first came here many months ago for a little R&R after Maya's mother's funeral at a Jewish cemetery in the

San Fernando Valley. She certainly deserved it, considering how that event went down. Only two days before, a homeless encampment had been routed out of Balboa Park and ended up pitching their tents within yards of the funeral home. They shouted, sometimes antisemitic, comments all through the ceremony. One toothless blonde dude who looked like the typical heroin, or now I suppose fentanyl, addict kept repeating the familiar "river to the sea" calumny at the top of his lungs as if he were a Columbia student on steroids. I thought about going to have it out with him, but realized that would be a pointless endeavor if there ever was one. I consoled myself by imagining what the Golem might do to this character. However, I doubted the mystical being would consider him worth the effort, even though he was soon joined by three other like-minded lost souls, providing a chorus of Jew hatred that had become so trendy it had permeated the misbegotten. Welcome home.

It was not entirely a depressing event, however, because, though ineffably sad, there was a mitigating factor at the end. Maya's mother's concussion proved to have been more severe than had been hoped, with near total amnesia, repeated convulsions, complete loss of balance, and virtually non-stop nausea with little or no prospect of improvement. The Kundalini Yoga postures she had done every day for the last fifty years had become impossible without falling over and clutching her stomach in extreme agony, followed often by uncontrollable vomiting. Still, she insisted on doing it daily and consequently, according to the doctors, contracted pneumonia, aspirated in her sleep, and never woke up. You could call it Death by Kundalini if you were being cynical, but It was ultimately a form of liberation for her and for Maya.

I was the one who insisted on the R&R after the funeral, although I needed it more than my more resilient wife. I didn't realize this vacation would evolve from a short respite into a life-transforming experience, with the possibility of a permanent change of venue and lifestyle. I had my own issues to deal with. I had been confronted with a dilemma on my return from Israel that was neither entirely surprising nor easy to resolve.

But first, the immediate aftermath of those events of the fateful date April 13, 2024, when Iran tried to destroy Israel with missiles and drones but achieved only minor damage to a military airfield. They were repelled by a combination of the United States, United Kingdom, French, Jordanian, and Israeli forces and, I would argue, the Golem. I didn't mention that addition initially that night with the Jerusalem police, assuming they would think me a lunatic. I was taken into their custody and cited for illegal presence on the Temple Mount outside the permitted hours for Jews and locked in a cell with a very drunk Bedouin. But I could see they were unsure what to make of me, an evidently middle-class American, a rabbi yet, who for some reason wound up in the Hurva Synagogue in the midst of a missile barrage. Telephone calls were being made, I couldn't hear much less understand, though I did recognize my name being mentioned, Olivia Dreben's as well. Where was she? We had been led off by the police in opposite directions. I counted about a half dozen such calls, going back and forth. After about an hour, a policeman opened the cell and beckoned to me. I followed him out to a squad car where he told me he was taking me back to the King David. I asked what would happen after that. He didn't know. He didn't know what happened to Olivia either. By the time I walked into the hotel, it was 4 AM. The Iranian bombardment was over. Exhausted residents were trickling back to their rooms. I dreaded heading up the special elevator to mine. The last person I wanted to run into was Jeremy Bogen. But thankfully that was not to be. When I arrived on my floor, the secretary's security personnel were nowhere to be seen. No light was visible under his door. He appeared to be gone, at least for now. I went into my suite, collapsed on the bed and called Maya in California. "You're alive," she said. "*Baruch HaShem*," I replied. "How's your mom?" "Not great. You've been all over the news." "I have?" "Not you personally. Israel... Where were you during it all?" "You're not going to believe it," I said, summoning up the last of my energy to recount the seemingly incredible events I knew she would understand if no one else did. I didn't worry that our conversation was being monitored, as all are, because what I was saying would undoubtedly sound like the ravings of a madman.

The next afternoon, I was ushered once again down the lengthy elevator beneath the anonymous building in Tel Aviv, but this time to a larger conference room to accommodate more people. Goldfarb was there, and Artie, plus A and B from my previous visit, as well as two others I will call C and D. I was never good at remembering names anyway, not an especially good trait for a rabbi. Also present, seated near the end of a long table, were Dr. Gabaz and Rabbi Dressler. Next to them was Omar Alfassi, the MIT-trained engineer whose robot I followed into the tunnels and hadn't seen since. His left arm was now a prosthetic.

"You do realize," A was saying, "that we had been tracking that missile, a Khorramshar-4, from when it entered Iraqi airspace. We shot it down over Syria with David's Sling. It's almost impossible that the fuselage would land anywhere near the Temple Mount, let alone on the Dome ."

"Not so!" Omar interjected. "Would you like to see my calculations?"

"I certainly would," A responded, before breaking angrily into Hebrew.

I had been telling them all substantially what I had told Maya twelve hours before. At first, there was quiet, but I could see beneath the surface that the group was split in its response, with varying levels of belief and disbelief, mostly leaning toward the latter. I had also asked about Olivia Dreben, but no one seemed to want to talk about that for unclear reasons.

"I want to remind everyone this discussion does not leave this room," Goldfarb said, looking at all of us. "Not even the slightest leaks to any of your journalist buddies. It's not the kind of publicity we want. It's obvious how it could be used against us. Makes us seem crazies in the world press," he added for emphasis.

"When are we not?" Omar muttered under his breath. I glanced over at Artie, who shrugged. Then I took a covert look at Rabbi Dressler and Dr. Gabaz, both of whom betrayed no reaction. The doctor was the only dark face in the room, another reminder of what everyone knew—that Israel, like the USA, was a divided country, that the Ashkenazi still were in charge despite all, despite many, if not most, of them, realizing it was wrong, despite efforts made to correct it. Yes, mixed race people were everywhere now, but the face of the state was still what it was and therefore more easily hated and accused of imperialism, phony as that was. Gabaz—from a family of semi-literate desert dwellers, as most who emerged from the back country of Ethiopia--was obviously a remarkable person. My admiration for Mizrachi Jews had grown, not just Dr. Gabaz, but the soldier in rehab, whose extraordinary grandmother had flown out of Yemen on a rescue mission as a six-year-old blind girl. Since they were Middle Eastern, it was arguably better if they were running the country. It might generate less anti-semitism, modify it anyway, although Gabaz herself would likely describe it — and all the other good and bad in the universe — as a matter of particles —protons, neutrons, and quarks, whatever they were—combining and recombining into infinity. Skin color was the least of it.

"I know some of you are troubled by what I told you," I said. "You don't want to believe it. I can understand that. But I wasn't alone in the Hurva. I have corroborating evidence. I assume you have interviewed Olivia Dreben."

Again, there was silence. "That's the problem," Goldfarb said at length. "Ms. Dreben has other concerns." He paused and looked around the room another time. Everybody but me seemed to know what he meant. "It was not just the trauma you described, horrifying as that was. She had a still greater tragedy in her personal life. She is at Sheba Medical Center. Her fiancé... he was on a secret mission in Lebanon when his tank got hit by a Soviet Kornet." In the midst of everything? That handsome young man of the Sayeret Matkal, the Jewish prince? I gasped and held my breath, feeling momentarily almost as if I had been shot myself. In the dark comedy of life, it now seemed the Golem was within his rights, at least arguably. He or it was attempting to marry a woman who was no longer spoken for, or so it seemed. "They had to amputate. They're not sure if he is going to make it," Goldfarb continued.

"They're doing everything possible," Artie weighed in. "It's touch and go. Pray for him to pull through."

"I will... Be sure of it."

I was relieved, at least for now, that my most negative assumption—that the man of Olivia's dreams, the one for whom she was *bashert*—was already gone, and that she would never have a house full of children. Still, what a potentially tragic occurrence.

Goldfarb spoke to the others in Hebrew too rapidly for me to understand, then turned to me again. "And now, our American friend, we have one more thing to tell you. We have made reservations for you to return to your country tonight. It is dangerous for you to remain here, for you and for us. One more day in that suite and you could be the next Jonathan Pollard."

"30 years for spying. I didn't do anything."

"You incurred the enmity of your Secretary of State."

"I did? I tried hard to—"

"I imagine you were careful. It was our mistake putting you there. Of course, we laid the groundwork for a background check on Charles Baumgarten and his spouse, but that may not have been enough. From what we have determined, Bogen became suspicious of you when something was making a piercing sound you claimed you didn't hear."

"I didn't."

"Well, he is convinced he heard something, and it came from somewhere."

I looked around the room. Everyone had their eyes on me.

"Nevertheless, from what we have gleaned, Bogen thought you were lying and has taken an active dislike of you. Even worse, he thinks you're responsible for passing his Rules of Engagement to the press. They were leaked yesterday."

"That's ridiculous!"

"Of course. Unfortunately," Goldfarb continued, "he suspects you're responsible. We have seen communications. Fortunately, he won't be in office forever and will soon be out of power, though they are never entirely without influence in your country. Be careful of Bogen. When they *are* out of office, they become most dangerous and vindictive. I have experienced that myself. You may have made an enemy without realizing it, your own personal Inspector Javert. That happens... Just some friendly advice from someone who has spent too long in politics... Your buddy Artie will drive you to the airport. We made sure no one's going to question this." He handed me a fresh version of my real passport for Ben Golub. It had stamps from several nations, but not Israel, as was done to avoid uncomfortable reactions or even entry refusals from customs officials in unfriendly countries, a number that was increasing again. "And one last thing. Your grandson might be endangering himself with his new invention. Admonish him to be careful. He is needed."

New invention? How'd he know about that? I didn't dare ask. At that moment, I wasn't prepared to deal with Max having gotten himself into some deep trouble. It would have been the most difficult for me to deal with of everything that had transpired.

"Take me to Sheba Medical Center," I told Artie, as we pulled out of the hidden parking garage and turned onto a feeder road. "The flight's not for a few hours."

"I'm already headed that way," he said. Artie knew me better than anyone, except for Maya.

Like so many of the biggest hospitals, it was easy to get lost in Sheba, but my friend knew how to navigate the various twists and turns to our destination, a room at the far end of what seemed the longest corridor. Inside, Olivia Dreben—her eyes bloodshot, a book in her hand-- was sitting in a chair next to Captain Cardozo, lying on his back in bed. You could see a depression in the sheet where his leg had been amputated. Thick bandages wrapped his left arm, shoulder, and top of his head. He seemed to be asleep. After Olivia welcomed us with a graciousness that belied the situation, I said I had come to explain, as best I could, what had happened. I recounted how the Golem had appeared in Nashville, how it behaved so erratically and mysteriously, and how I became confused by the purpose of it all, how astonished I was when the being took a romantic interest in Olivia.

"I can understand that," said the Captain, speaking for the

first time. His voice was weak, but there was a twinkle discernible in his eyes despite the fact that they were nearly closed. "And you know what the purpose was, to save the Temple Mount."

"You were part of it too. You and Olivia. We all did it together... with the Golem."

The Captain seemed momentarily overwhelmed by what I had just said. Tears started to stream down his face as well as Olivia's. I may be naïve, but they appeared to me more of joy than of sorrow. Then Cardozo reached out with his hand toward his fiancée. "Read them what you were reading to me.... From the *Tanya*... the Alter Rebbe...there's an English translation."

She opened and read, "*Therefore, first of all, man ought to be happy and joyous at every time and hour and truly live by his faith in G-d, Who animates him and acts kind towards him at every moment.*"

"Beautiful, no?" said the Captain. By this time, he was holding hands with Olivia.

"Yes, very," I said

"Thank you, rabbi," said Olivia. For a second, the name fit.

Shortly thereafter, we bid them good-bye and left.

"I knew you'd never make aliyah," Artie teased as we arrived at Ben Gurion. "You're an American boy at heart. It will never be any other way."

"Well, you just kicked me out of your country. What choice would I have?"

"Not forever."

He smiled and gave me a bear hug. "Our best to Maya. We know what she's going through."

"Thanks," I said. "Keep me informed about Olivia's

boyfriend as well. It's even worse what she's going through... so much life to live."

"I have an idea for you that might help with that. When you get to JFK, don't just change planes for Nashville. Head over to a place in Queens and leave a note. Who knows? Sometimes it works."

I knew exactly what he meant. "Good idea," I said. "I'll do it," even though part of me still regarded such things as superstitions. My doubts would never end, even though to an extent I had seen it all. He released me after a final hug, and I walked into the terminal, my heart in my throat. Soon, I was passing the flower-strewn photos of the hostages that decorated the walkway on the way to the planes. It appeared it would take more than a Golem to get them out, maybe an army of them. Some of the hostages, it seemed likely, might never survive. Perhaps they would fare better in a future life—or a previous one—with particles rearranged.

When I arrived at Kennedy, I downed some coffee and jumped into a cab to Montefiore Cemetery in a part of Queens that was once a Jewish neighborhood but now is largely African-American. It is where The Ohel is located, the tombs of The Rebbe, Menahem Mendel Schneersohn, and his father-in-law, Rabbi Yosef Yitzchok Schneersohn, the two most recent rebbes of the Chabad-Lubavitcher dynasty. As the resting place of The Rebbe, other than The Wall itself, The Ohel was arguably the most important holy place for Judaism, at least in the contemporary sense. More people congregated there than even the tombs of the patriarchs. It was also considerably humbler, less prepossessing than the Jerusalem site. Next to the tombs is a small, rather austere brick building, with communications to the outside world, because so many are sending messages to The Rebbe —by letter or digitally through an app —in the hopes that their prayers will be answered or that some salient advice will be given. Also available were some perhaps deliberately austere tables and chairs for writing, along with the humblest of snacks—chocolate chip cookies and apples.

I walked through to The Ohel itself, where I had been before. It was less busy than my previous visit, no politicians in evidence, looking to be photographed, leaving their messages for whatever part of the electorate they sought to impress. Nevertheless, the pile of torn white paper in front of me was so large no single person could possibly read them all in a lifetime. And this was only one batch. That did not deter me, however, and I scrawled a message asking for the sufficient recovery of the wounded soldier David Cardozo so he could live happily with his betrothed Olivia Dreben and have many children together. I wasn't sure they were technically betrothed yet, but I took that upon myself as matchmaker. I mentioned too that Olivia was a Talmud student devoted to *daf yomi*. Then I said a prayer as I tore the paper into pieces and tossed it onto the unending pile. It has been said that the righteous, like The Rebbe, remain spiritually potent after death. I was more prepared to believe that now. It wasn't just The Golem. All those myriad notes piled at random reminded me of something. Then I remembered Rabbi Dressler and Dr. Gabaz and all those particles—photons, quarks and so forth—continually flying apart and coming together again to make a whole, not just to fashion a table or a chair but to allow us to survive.

When I finally arrived back in Nashville, I had that surprise I mentioned earlier. I learned my job as rabbi of Temple Bethel was hanging by the proverbial thread. Since it had been that way before, it wasn't that much of a shock. This time, however, it wasn't about Sigmund Freud and Akhenaten, although that came into it. A man I remembered from my class, who had been quite enthusiastic about the book and had found it fascinating "anthropologically," was now on the board and had changed his tune dramatically. He was now outraged that not only had Freud theorized that the original Moses was Egyptian, but in fact claimed there were two Moseses from different eras, the second to explain apparent contradictions in the Biblical original. I made clear I didn't believe any of this, but the mere fact I had allowed such "unnecessarily provocative material" to brave the halls of our temple was apparently anathema.

But that was the sideshow. The real problem was demography. The synagogue board had two new members, both of whom thought I might be too conservative and too "overtly pro-Israel," given the makeup of "the community," and recommended that a replacement be found. I had to laugh when I heard the news. How could I be too pro-Israel when that nation had just ejected me? Not surprisingly, I didn't bother to express that as I was certain to be misunderstood and knew it was pointless. What I was attending was the result of a previous private board meeting that was supposed to be top secret, though my excommunication was, I was told, virtually a fait accompli, only to be ratified by a final vote with a payout decided upon. Battling this would be futile. Apparently, the new board members had fat checkbooks.

It was Tamara who first gave me the news. Among her publicist skills was having an ear close to the ground. In this case, one of the new board members was married to the owner of a new record company that was trying to sign Cody Brent. Cody was playing hard to get, and the owner's wife thought that by ingratiating herself with Tamara, she would give her husband a leg up. She knew Tamara and I were friends, so she intimated she might change her vote in my favor if Tamara would put in a good word with her client. What she didn't realize was that Tamara was done with Cody.

"I've had it with the little putz," she told me. "One more

phone call to bail him out at three a.m., cause he threw a beer bottle at the bartender and hit a patron or whatever, and I'm changing my phone number. More than that, I'm getting out of the business. Thirty years of this is more than enough. No one over fifty should have to attend the Grammys and listen to the blather from those egomaniacs. I'm out. Seriously."

"Seriously?"

"Yes, seriously."

"Did you tell Ed?"

"Of course."

"What'd he say?"

"He's a hundred percent supportive. He says we should get out of town. Start over. Didn't he tell you?"

"I haven't talked to him yet."

That was when she told me their plan. They would open a branch of The Orphanage—at that point, it would be Orphanage 4—in one of the towns along the 30A. So many people from Nashville vacationed down there the name recognition of the coffee shop wouldn't be a problem, and they could develop a clientele quickly. With luck, they could eventually spin off the original locations, franchise them, and relocate down there in the Florida sun. "Sounds like a great idea," I said. It was a particularly dismal day in Middle Tennessee, even though it was almost May first. "Why don't you join us?" said Tamara.

"So what'd you say?" said Maya, who was still in California, when I spoke to her that evening.

"I didn't say anything. I wanted to talk to you."

"You are.... So what're you thinking?"

"The curious thing is how I felt, like a weight was being lifted. I think it would be a relief not to be a rabbi. I've always felt..."

"A bit of a fake? I don't think you are, but you always feel that way, probably for a reason."

"It's not that I don't feel religious. I feel more religious."

"You can be religious down on the 30A. I vote that we do it. I'm going to need a change after all this." She must have known or sensed something. It was only three days before her mother died.

So that was a few months ago now. At first, when we moved down to Santa Rosa on the 30A, I didn't know what to do with myself. I had lost my purpose, as they say. Maya, who had quickly gotten a job doing rehab, was annoyed with me as I skulked around the house. "Go exercise," she told me as I sat around surfing on my computer, as if I could learn something from it. "Just because Max can't come down to visit is no excuse. You dote on him too much."

She was right. I had invited the boy several times—what kid wouldn't want a trip to Florida—but he was always too busy with his projects. When I asked about his AI Golem, he essentially laughed me off, as if he were beyond such things.

His reluctance to visit depressed me. That very night, I dreamed Jeremy Bogen, out of office at this point and replaced by someone much better, was knocking angrily at my door. Dressed like Javert as a mid-19th-century French policeman in a roadshow *Les Misérables*, his repeated knocks startled me awake. I sat there in the dark, Maya sleeping soundly, unaware of my nightmare. It was another of those moments when one doubts everything about one's life. Maybe we had made a mistake with the move. I should have fought for my rabbinical position rather than just giving up as if it meant nothing. I even began to doubt what had happened with The Golem, even though I remembered every moment of it with great specificity. Was it all some kind of fairy tale I had made up for myself to deal with the rise of antisemitism I was seeing around me, my anesthesia through self-hypnosis? Ed had offered me the opportunity to be the manager of the new coffee shop when the remodel was finished, something I had accepted for lack of anything better to do, but that it was taking longer than expected, as it always does, only added to my malaise.

So I was sitting at home a lot in our rented condo, watching the world go by from the balcony. Every morning, while I was drinking my coffee, I watched the local parade. First would come the dog walkers, followed by the swimmers, followed by a group of runners who looked middle-aged but were nonetheless eager and relatively quick. Later, I learned they were called the "30A over 40 Running Team." That was several days after I joined them for the first time. Basically, it was on a whim, but I must have been in a good mood. Max had called to say he was finally free of whatever was holding him and could come down for a visit. I was excited because I hadn't seen the kid in some time. He always made me happy, even though I worried about him more than anybody. In this case, that worry was centered on his "invention," the one Goldfarb spoke about in his final words to me. The last thing I wanted was my talented grandson to upend his life for what most people would regard as a high-tech toy. With his abilities, it was likely considerably more. I wondered what he had been doing with it. He hadn't exactly been forthcoming when I had asked him on the phone, only saying he was continuing "in the interest of science," then he added, "Don't worry, Grandpa. I'm not about to market them, toy Golems for Hanukkah. Every family needs a monster." "Mel Brooks, yet." He was developing a Jewish sense of humor. "Mel Brooks?" he replied. "'Young Frankenstein' is my favorite." I wasn't surprised. "Great," I said. We'll watch it together when you get here." But I wondered why he could come. Wasn't this the school year?

Nevertheless, he had put me in a better mood. When I saw

the runners that day, I was already in my shorts and had a pair of old Hokas on, so I set out maybe a fifty yards behind them just to see if I could keep up. It turned out I could. In fact, I was a bit faster than the group and started to catch up, even though I was about twenty years older than most of them. A couple saw me coming and waved me forward to join them, and I did, not only then but most weekdays after that. Much of the group, I discovered, were evangelicals and seemingly pleased to have a Jew, a self-described retired rabbi, running beside them, one of "the chosen" yet. I welcomed their acceptance and the inherent goodness.

By the third week, their de facto leader jogged up alongside me and said, "Someday you'll have to explain to me why so many Jews dislike Israel. .. I was there and thought it was fantastic." "One of the mysteries of our time," I responded, and he laughed, then continued, "You're in amazing shape for your age. Were you on your college track team?" "Not close," I replied. "I wasn't an athlete at all. I got into it... a bit later." I didn't tell him how much later, or how it happened, that I was so speedy approaching 70. But it was on those runs I started to ignore my residual doubt and acknowledge to myself that the Golem could only have been real—otherwise, why was I possibly able to run like this when I had barely broken into a jog in twenty-five years? Now I even participated in a 10K again. I didn't come in first, but I ended up in the top ten out of 100 or so. In the old days, Maya would have been astonished—didn't I have flat feet when we were married and a back that went out every few weeks—but she clearly knew the proximate cause and just shook her head in wonder.

In the midst of this it became clear to me as well what more of my "purpose" was. I had to write down the details of what happened, tell the whole story of the modern Golem from beginning to end, even if few ever read it, even if those who did

did not believe me. That was their problem. I would only say this to them: If we are, as the particle physicists insist, composed of the most minute quanta moving about almost at random, eventually to form for whatever reason something concrete like a table or even a ladybug, why wouldn't this chaos form a Golem at some point, or almost anything else? This seemingly random event would explain many phenomena that most people, including me, had dismissed as fantasy. All it took was a higher power as organizer.

I set about my renewed purpose with an intensity I had never felt after decades of being essentially uncommitted. It was a new thing for Maya to see me so obsessed, as it was, to a lesser extent, for Tamara and Ed, who were commuting from Nashville to help establish the 30A branch.

I only broke off when Max flew in. I drove over to the Destin-Fort Walton Airport to pick him up. The boy had shot up, as they tend to do at his age. "You're a basketball player now," I said, sounding like an uninventive grandpa. "When're you going to join a team?" "No time," he scoffed. He did have the sallow look we associate with nerds, up all night coding while stuffing themselves with pizza and Cheetos. "Anyway, the NBA sucks now." "Agreed," I said, but something about his tone disturbed me. He wasn't his usual upbeat self. He had a glum expression as he got in the car. It signaled something was wrong. "What's the matter?" I said, nodding out the window. "See all that blue. The Gulf of America's out there. Two minutes in that and all your troubles wash away." "Not this time," he said. "I'm suspended." "Suspended? I thought they just skipped you two years."

He launched into an explanation. It was an oddly familiar story. His mechanical Golem, actually his third iteration, had gone out of control twice, breaking into the girls' locker room at his school. The first time it was treated, more or less, as a joke, but the second time it unmasked a hitherto unknown trans boy masquerading as a girl who happened to be the star goalie of the girls' soccer team. This created a scandal at the school that, although it technically opposed men in women's sports, suspended Max anyway on the advice of its board.

"For how long?" I asked.

"Two years."

That was draconian. It basically erased the two years he had skipped ahead. "How're you going to deal with it?"

"Home school again. I don't have a choice because I'm underage."

"Finding a tutor with your skills won't be easy."

"Jack Ripton said he'd come up. He's working on his thesis, so he's not stuck in Nashville."

"I thought he didn't have the background."

Max shrugged. He didn't seem to care. In truth, nothing about academics bothered him. He was more than capable of learning just about anything by himself, including foreign languages like Farsi and Greek that he told me he had already embarked upon. What had really gotten to him, it emerged, was something else entirely —the oldest of stories, a love lost. His first potential girlfriend had turned him down, but in a particularly unsettling way that was a sad commentary on our times.

It had begun, he told me, when Tamara sent him tickets to a country music concert in Indianapolis. He didn't have someone to go with, so he went by himself and ended up sitting next to a cute, but slightly nerdy, girl (his type) who was there with a friend of hers. They started talking, discovered a mutual interest in software and computers, and went off together during the intermission. It was puppy love at first sight. That evolved into a young relationship of sorts—they met at a Starbucks, though they both hated it—but on their third meeting, she announced out of nowhere she could never see him again.

When he asked why, she didn't want to say at first, then reluctantly admitted it was because he was Jewish and her friends found that "extremely upsetting now." She asked if he approved of the genocide in Gaza, and when Max answered that there wasn't any genocide—it didn't remotely fit the definition—she got up and walked out. He never saw her again.

That had happened to him—so young. For a moment, I couldn't say anything. Sure, rejection was a routine part of growing up—most had it at one time or another—but the girl's reason was so depressingly horrible.

"It's okay," Max said, almost as if he were reassuring *me.* "We're just kids. We weren't really dating."

"She wouldn't have been right if you were. When you get older, there'll be plenty of fish in the sea," I added, sounding more avuncular than I would have liked. I wondered if that was true. The seas were getting fished out, with the remaining ones suffering from an age-old poison worse than mercury.

"It's happening in sports, too. They don't want to play with us. I mean, some do and some don't."

Worse and worse. "It wasn't that way when I was a kid," I said, trying not to sound depressed but knowing it was because I grew up in that rare post-War period when Jews were accepted, even sympathized with, because of the Holocaust. I played ball with everyone and dated gentile girls in high school and college with no problems. \"I'm sure it'll change," I said, "it always has." But I wasn't sure I wanted it to. Bad as that girl's attitude indicated things were, it could be a benefit in the end, if you cared about the survival of the Jewish people. The number of mixed marriages would dwindle significantly. Maybe there would be more of us in the end.

By this time, we had arrived at the condo, and the boy looked to be feeling better for having unburdened himself. "I love you, grandpa," he said.

"I love you too, Max. Big time."

"So how was Israel?" he asked.

"I'm writing a book about it. Israel and what happened in Nashville with the Golem."

"I didn't know you wanted to be a writer, grandpa."

"A long time ago, my father discouraged me, worried I couldn't make a living at it. So I became a rabbi kind of through the back door. Maybe I didn't want to be a writer enough or didn't have anything worth writing about until... this recent adventure."

"Adventures are my favorite books," said Max, brightening. "'The Three Musketeers'... 'The Man in the Iron Mask'... Are you going to do a sequel? 'The Golem Returns?"

"I hadn't thought of that ... though maybe, if it does... But I'm not counting on it."

"They can be really popular," he continued, "Like J. K. Rowling. Although that's kind of exceptional." He frowned. "Just to be on the safe side, you'd better change everybody's names."

"I already did. I call you Max after Menahem Begin."

"Menahem Begin? Cool. He was a great prime minister. Made peace with Egypt.... What do you call grandma?" he added as Maya, who had just joined us, was giving the boy a welcome kiss.

"Maya."

"Maya?" said my wife. "I'm not sure I like that. A little too hippieish."

"I can change it, if you want."

"No, no. It's your book," she said.

"Is everything actually true in the story?" said Max, suddenly a bit suspicious. "Or did you embellish the facts the way Dumas did in 'The Man in the Iron Mask'."

"You're going to have to read it to find out. And yes, sometimes I had to glamorize things a bit, add to the suspense, and all that. It's instinctive, but I stuck to the facts as much as possible, still do... But listen, kiddo, this is just one little book. Who knows what will happen with it? But your grandfather has a suspicion that you will be involved in affairs of great significance throughout your life. I'm proud of you, and I know your grandmother is too."

"I am," said Maya. "Very much."

Max went home a couple of days later. I was sad to see him go. While the world continued its unceasing *sturm und drang*, my once-intense life evolved into a calmer routine of writing and walking on the beach, most often with Maya, who was starting to like her literary name or at least to adapt to it. "The only name you couldn't change was The Golem," she said.

"That and Rabbi Loew," I said.

"*The* Rabbi Loew from that old statue in Prague?" Of course, she knew, but she enjoyed teasing me to keep me on the straight and narrow while supporting me in every way possible. I had long realized I was married to a true Woman of Valor. "*She opens her mouth with wisdom and the teaching of kindness is on her tongue.*" I had always admired those words from King Solomon. Could it have been that way too more than three thousand years ago? We strolled down the sand. Maya continued, this time with a wan expression. "It's sad what you say he told you—that Golems so wish they were human, they could speak... find love..."

"I saw it happen."

"I know. You gave *them* good names—Olivia Dreben and David Cardozo... Wasn't Dreben the name of your fifth-grade teacher?"

"It was." She stopped, frowning. "But you could have given Jorge a different name... Something less routine, more memorable like Alejandro or Santiago."

I laughed. Just the previous day, I was with our Salvadoran former security guard, who had joined our group down in Florida and was doing the lion's share of the construction for the coffee shop. He had even more contempt for the new regime at Temple Bethel than I did and had resigned at the first inkling of a change, even before my return. I watched as he installed beams matching the Nashville originals, although this time white-washed for a beach look.

"Do you think El Tabudo is out there?" I asked him, nodding toward the Gulf of America, a sliver of which was visible through an open window. "Why not?" he replied. "The ocean is big. Many things exist we do not know about." The man was prepared for anything. It was great to have him with us.

Another time I was walking along the sand with Ed. The news from Israel was bad. The Houthis had somehow been able to land a missile near Ben Gurion Airport. There were injuries. Flights from all over had been canceled, leaving the only Jewish nation once more isolated. Ed commiserated. "How does that make you feel?"

"I try to remember that old saw about worrying only about what you can control," I said, not entirely convinced I could do that, maybe not even remotely so. I changed the subject. "I never apologized to you for fleeing the rabbinate before we could complete your conversion. Others can do it."

"We've both been busy," he responded. "Anyway, I'm not sure it's necessary. You believe what you believe in the end without making it official, and Tamara doesn't really care. I asked her." I nodded, gazing out at the sea that was more choppy than usual. "But I do have one request," he continued. "Marry us. We both would like it. Are you still able?" I hesitated before answering because I wasn't entirely certain. But then I remembered the obvious. The country was filled with all kinds of religions, fake or otherwise, that could marry people. You could make up your own faith and be ordained online in minutes. But none of that mattered because I had never formally resigned as a rabbi, only as the rabbi of my Nashville synagogue.

'Yes, of course. I will. I'm honored and delighted. When do you want to do it?"

"As soon as possible."

"We could even do it today, if you wanted."

"Well, maybe tomorrow—so we can arrange a little ceremony, have a party. I know Tamara wants Maya to be her maid of honor."

"Tomorrow then."

We stood, smiling at each other, when a wave rolled in at our feet, causing us both to look down. The sea was apparently getting choppier. The wave went out and then came in again, leaving deposits of sand in our sandals. We watched as it retreated.

"Are you seeing what I'm seeing?" Ed said.

"Yes." Indeed, I was.

Something resembling a supine human body, a large one, had formed in the wet sand. It almost seemed to have actual arms, legs, and a head, although they were somewhat vague in shape, like the beginnings of a Henry Moore. Was it the wave that created it? It hadn't been *that* strong. Nothing around it had risen up in the slightest, no piles of sand, only this eerily familiar form, all by itself.

"I can improve it... sculpt it... if you want... the way I did the first one."

"And then?"

"It's up to you."

I detected understandable trepidation in his voice. I didn't know how to reply, a welter of thoughts overwhelming me. Was it all beginning again, particles coming apart and together in infinite repetition, or, as I had also come to view it, a never-ending battle against antisemitism that seemed hardwired somewhere in the DNA of much of our species, some indelible gene tragically interlocked to some indelible chromosome? The influence of this gene ebbed and flowed, but, so far, no one had been able to destroy it, not for thousands of years, finally. Indeed, the hatred of our people was clearly flowing yet again in places high and low, metastasizing across the globe. We were constantly being blamed for defending ourselves and then pitied when we didn't, our suffering making us palatable again. What was my role in fixing this, small as it would be? What was my purpose? I think I finally knew, but would I follow through?

I glanced heavenward for a glimpse of the Endless Light. It was always there, even when deliberately hidden as a test of faith. I had to strive to find that light, to look beyond or through the impediments. Perhaps then it would tell me what I should do, whether I should go forward at this moment. There was much work to be done, much unfinished business, only one part of which was the sad tale of Olivia Dreben's fiancé, whom I had been informed was doomed to spend his life in a wheelchair. A divine force, if that's what it was, could repair that just as it had my leg. But that was only a minute part of the equation, a small part. The problems were endless. Europe was behaving in a manner reminiscent of the 1930s. My own country was being infected as well. Demonstrations were back at Harvard and Columbia. And Jeremy Bogen and his ilk were out there, with people like me in their sights. What was I waiting for? Was I being risk-averse again? What was The Golem? In some ways, it might have been G-d teasing or testing us, offering only erratic salvation. It was that old, seemingly unresolvable question of His involvement — or lack thereof — in human affairs, coming back to haunt us.

But as I continued to look up, hoping to draw inspiration, hoping to steel myself to act even if it meant suspending my cushy existence here at the Gulf, another stronger wave crashed at my feet, spraying water up to my waist.

When I looked down, the figure in the sand was gone, washed away. No more Golems... for now.

Directorate of Intelligence

Institute for Intelligence and Special Operations (Mossad)

ANALYSIS REPORT

Subject: Golem Manuscript

Reference Number: [XX-####]

Date: [25/08/2025]

Analyst: [Redacted]

Division: [Relevant Division – e.g., Counterterrorism / Political Affairs / Cyber Operations]

Summary of Contents:

This report provides an analytical assessment of the attached document, its provenance, authenticity, and implications for Israeli national security interests.

Distribution:

- Director, Mossad
- Prime Minister's Office (PMO)
- Working Group

Classification Notice:
This document contains information affecting the security of the State of Israel. Unauthorized disclosure is prohibited by law. Handle only within secure channels.

ANALYSIS — "EMET"

This approximately 79,000-word document was provided to us as a courtesy by its author, who writes under the pseudonym Rabbi Benjamin Golub (no middle initial in the text), and will be referred to here as "author."

We have no legal control over the manuscript's contents or its publication, whether through a commercial publishing house or via self-publishing on online outlets such as Amazon or Apple Inc. Nevertheless, the author has verbally informed us that he would consider revisions if requested for security reasons, subject to his approval [**recommendation at end].** In fact, significant edits were made to the manuscript during its creation in consultation with a member of the working group [**redacted**]. This was done for security reasons concerning actions already taken with implications for the future, which will be explained in this analysis.

Generally, the document recounts events, some of which are true,

some fictional, and others whose truthfulness is unclear. Most of the intentionally fictional details are trivial and of the type commonly found in manuscripts of this kind to prevent identification. An obvious example is that there is no Temple Beth El in Nashville, Tennessee, USA, although the city has several synagogues. Similarly, there is no coffee shop named "The Orphanage" or "Orphan" in the area, even though businesses of that type are common.
In the category of occurrences with a factual basis, it is noteworthy that a tornado passed through Nashville the night of October 5, 2023, roughly two days before the events of October 7, allowing for time differences. Any connection is indeterminate, but also noteworthy as actual events, are the curious details surrounding the murder of 21-year-old Allison Carter. The ability of the perpetrator to move with astonishing rapidity across extraordinary distances, only to be apprehended at the scene of his original crime, has never been adequately explained by authorities, nor has an explanation been given for his reported cries of "*monstruo*" in the press.

"Rabbi Golub's" journey to Israel veers to the more fictional, but it is difficult to dismiss in its entirety. He did meet an Olivia Dreben [**redacted**] on his flight, and she did become affianced to David Cardozo [**redacted**], an officer with Sayeret Matkal under rehabilitation for severe injury.

Whether a Golem, legendary or not, became attracted to her is unknown, although remnants of a wedding *chuppah* were found in the Hurva Synagogue several days after the night and early morning (April 13-14, 2024), when Iran launched its direct attacks on Israel.

The author's entry into the Gaza tunnels remains a matter of dispute within the working group. Several adamantly opposed it for justifiable reasons. Nevertheless, even though it went far beyond what was anticipated, the result was largely positive. A hostage was freed, although the author, for a period, was severely wounded. His remarkable recuperation is another matter of dispute. Whether it was due to our rehabilitation skills or divine intervention remains also indeterminate, although such an extreme recovery of physical abilities, well above previous levels, is beyond the normal range and worthy of study until an explanation can be found.

Also of note for the future is the apparent dislike for the author taken by Jeremy Bogen, the now-former U. S. Secretary of State, currently employed by the international consulting firm [**redacted**] in Washington, DC.

But regarding long-term significance, the most important part of this manuscript concerns the young man (**redacted**) known in the text as Max or Menahem. In discussion, the Institute pre-approved the disguise the author used here for the protection of all parties, and what is about to be disclosed, it will be obvious, must go no further than the working group. It will also offer a potential new perspective on the mystery of the Golem.

As the author, "Rabbi Golub," writes, he first met with [**redacted**], "Arthur 'Artie' Leventhal," a member of this working group, at the 770 Eastern Parkway headquarters in Crown Heights, Brooklyn, New York of the Chabad Lubavitcher movement roughly 17 years ago.

The author told "Leventhal" then that he was blessed in his middle years, his wife [**redacted**], "Maya" in the manuscript, was pregnant with a boy. The author was about 50 years old, and his wife was 47. That child was Max or Menahem, in reality [**redacted**], who was and is the author's son, *not* his grandson.

The author and "Leventhal," who had become friends, corresponded frequently about the boy. The author was exceptionally proud of his new son because the child was remarkably precocious, particularly in math, able to do quadratic equations by the time he was four and calculus by the time he was six.

At the same time, the author was deeply worried about his son, concerned his very precocity would make for a lonely life. "Leventhal" shared that concern. "Artie" was also aware that this young person was one of those who would soon be determining the future of the world—and he was of Jewish faith and background.

So when he was twelve, he was invited four or five years earlier than the usual age on a Birthright tour of our country. It was one of the special tours for the scientifically gifted, given by students at the Technion and by soldiers from the IDF's Central Collection Unit of the Intelligence Corps —the esteemed high-tech Unit 2800, most of whom are between 18 and 21. The students and soldiers loved "Max" and planted a love of Israel in his fertile brain.

At the same time, they took him around Jerusalem and Tel Aviv, and one of the things that fascinated the then twelve-year-old was the public statue called "*HaMifletzet*" or "The Monster," which looked like a black-and-white dragon with three red tongues protruding that could be used as slides.
Actually, the statue was an interpretation of the Golem legend by the avant-garde artist Niki de Saint Phalle. Back home, "Max" researched the Golem and started building one himself. Actually, he built several as he had become captivated by the burgeoning field of artificial intelligence, at which he rapidly developed expertise. He was getting into trouble at school because he was so far ahead, which made it boring for him.

We had sent over The Institute's [**redacted**] Jack Ripton, one of our more capable agents who happened to be youthful enough in appearance to pose as a graduate student and help keep an eye on young "Max" for the future, but as it happened at the age of fourteen, three years and a half ago and before the narrative of this manuscript begins and well before Oct. 7, 2023, he was admitted to the Technion and, with the approval of his parents, decided to make aliyah.

"Max" is now a senior at the Technion and is about to graduate, joining Unit 2800, where he has already been functioning on an ex officio basis, having monitored guidance systems during the recent attack from Iran. He is currently part of the team evolving the next-generation laser weapon, the "Iron Beam." He has also been appointed to a new American-Israeli joint artificial intelligence counter-terrorism program, being supervised from the American side by [**redacted**], Nicholas Peebles of the National Geospatial-Intelligence Agency, as mentioned in the text.
It should be further noted that uploading top secret U. S. government files on "Max Golub" was the last action performed by Jeremy Bogen on his final day as Secretary of State.

None of this is related in the manuscript for reasons of confidentiality, nor does the author mention that he and his wife flew to Israel twice to visit "Max" in Haifa while he was a student at the Technion. Additionally, we do not know how much Max's prior construction of artificial Golems influenced his father's interest in the subject, but it is possible that it did.

As members of this working group undoubtedly understand, due to Israeli national security interests, "Max's" current whereabouts and activities are now classified.

As for the author's return to the USA without the risk of indictment for any possible crimes, that was arranged without incident with our American partners. Nevertheless, as a precaution, the author has disguised the city where he now resides.

The above is a more or less technical analysis of issues arising from the manuscript, none of which, in the judgment of the working group, should impede its publication.
It is hereby cleared.

What remains are the more critical overriding questions of whether the Golem existed and, if it does, what should our response be? This raises the eternal mystery of the degree to which God, or more properly G-d, intervenes in human affairs. This conundrum is not generally within the purview of the Institute, although, as appears in the manuscript, some of our members have investigated the relationship between Kabbalah and particle physics, which, at least circumstantially, addresses that issue. If, as the quantum physicists posit, a chair is composed of unstable atoms appearing and disappearing at random, who or what makes it a stable object on which we can sit? Is this the work of a transcendent force? Do we take the path of religion or the path of science? As the working group is also aware, the Spectrum Warfare Battalion has managed to disable enemy missiles at launch using forces that may be similar to electromagnetic forces. Specific details remain classified.
But neither approach finally explains that last-second salvation from a massive explosion at the Dome of the Rock by a Golem athwart its roof, an explosion with ramifications of biblical proportions for all humanity, such that they evoke comparison to Jeremiah and the Book of Lamentations. Such cosmic questions have not historically been the Institute's to answer, concerned as we are with more quotidian matters. In the event of the reappearance of this or other

Golems, it may become incumbent upon us to change course. This is for the working group to review in a timely manner.

Submitted by [**redacted**], Sep. 1, 2025/8 Elul 5785

Acknowledgments

I would like to thank Rabbi Yitzchok Tiechtel of Chabad of Nashville, whose classes set me on the path to writing this book and also helped center me during this time of turmoil. I am also grateful to Avi Rossenfeld, Mark Plastryk, Avi Leitner, Or Hickry, Jon Davis, Michael Patrick Leahy, Aaron Hanscom, Matt Margolis, for the cover and layout, as well as my longtime manager Justin Silvera and publicist Jules Wortman, who gave me advice and encouragement along the way.

Most of all, of course, I thank my wife, Sheryl Longin, always my first and last editor, who has inspired me as a writer and thinker more than I could ever imagine over the now more than thirty years of our marriage.

www.ingramcontent.com/pod-product-compliance
Lightning Source LLC
LaVergne TN
LVHW100522110826
845146LV00002B/737

9798994109311